FORSAKEN

THE MYSTICAL VEIL
BOOK 3

Shelley Dorey

DEDICATION

To the Indigos.
I know you're out there.

Contents

One

A chuckle bubbled in my throat and I had to turn away. Roy, with the steady, intense focus of a surgeon, had arranged his ghost busting equipment on the table like a kid at a Science Fair. Before I could laugh out loud, Gwen nudged me with her shoulder, her eyes shooting a warning for me to shut up.

Roy held up the first object, a gadget that looked like some kind of fancy TV remote. "This is an EVP, it records electronic voice phenomena, which the human ear can't discern. If a ghost is around and wants to communicate, we'll catch it with this!"

My eyes closed slowly and I shook my head. "I hate to burst your bubble, Roy, but Gwen and I don't need that to be able to communicate with them. And from what we've heard about the Ayers estate, your gadget will probably run out of recording space." Under my breath, "...even if that thing *does* work."

Gwen flashed a warm smile at Roy, "I think it's great you've done all this. Your first actual case, working with us and you've got the scientific angle covered." She darted another glance my way, "Having this as back-up, won't hurt." There was no room for argument from the set of her jaw.

Hard as it was to keep my mouth shut as Roy picked up another instrument and started explaining how it worked, I managed to hold my tongue still—quite a feat if I do say so myself. There was a time and place for fun but not right then, not with Roy. And actually, I had to give him credit for jumping in feet first. He had done all the research, found suppliers and did the purchasing entirely on his own. Okay, I *did* pay for it all, but that's all I had to do. He even lugged it around.

I also knew I had to keep my wisecracks to myself for Gwen's sake. The soft look in her grey eyes gazing down at him spoke volumes. It was cute in a 'Lady and the Tramp' kind of way. Gwen, with the smooth long lines of a Jaguar, towered over him by a good four inches, while Roy was compact and sturdy. But they'd hit it off right from the start. She even found his corny jokes funny. He was a great pilot and had proved his worth when we were in a jam, but, comedy was definitely not his forte.

His eyebrows arched high over sparkling eyes. "This is the pièce de resistance! An EMF sensor. Apparently ghosts can alter electromagnetic fields and when that happens— Bingo! This little baby will catch it and we'll know they're there even if they choose to stay silent."

Nope. I bit my cheeks, holding my mouth closed. There was no way I was going to deflate him, telling him that the hair on the back of my neck told me exactly what that machine could. Not to mention the fact that, I not only sensed spirits but I could *see* them as well. The times where Gwen and I joined forces our hands locked together, turbo charged my own psychic energy. Roy would see that tomorrow, when we visited the estate.

"What about these other things, Roy?" Gwen folded her lanky body into a chair at the table lifting another small, plastic box.

Roy's chest puffed out, rocking back and forth from his toes to his heels. "Motion detectors that will automatically trigger the camera. Which, by the way is full spectrum with night vision, of course."

I rolled my eyes. "Of course. How silly of us not to know that."

Roy huffed a sharp sigh. "Keira...you might thank me for bringing this tomorrow."

"Why? We're not here to make a *movie*, Roy. Our job is to find the ghosts who've been bugging the workmen and holding up the renovations. Once we make contact, we convince them to leave. Cut and dried, case solved, roll credits with time left over for sight-seeing. I've never been to Australia, although you probably have, right?" As a pilot, he'd probably visited lots of places.

He wandered over to Gwen and his hand rested on her shoulder. The love in his eyes gazing at her might have made me upchuck if it had been anyone but her...and actually him too, if I was going to be honest with myself. Things had gotten pretty serious between them over the past few months. And she deserved a decent guy like Roy.

"I've been here a few times. I took an extended layover and explored around Sydney and Queensland. But to be here now, with Gwen. Well..."

"And me! Remember *me*? Keira? The name ring a bell?" I laughed, shaking my head at them. If not for me, they never would have met.

He pulled a face, looking at me with puzzled eyes. "Vaguely." He nodded. "Yes, the same Keira who signs my pay check. That would be you, right?"

"Smart ass!" I grabbed a pillow from the bed and tossed it at his head. "Look, it was a long flight and I'm bushed. I'm going back to my room to hit the hay." I paused in the doorway and grinned looking back at them. "And the camera is for ghosts only. I don't want to see any naughty flicks of you two."

"That's sick, Keira!"

I dodged the pillow that Gwen threw at me. "See you in the morning. But not before eleven, okay?" It was going to be another long day. We'd probably end up staying the entire night at the creepy estate, if what I've heard was true. Ghosts and poltergeists for sure, were there. My chest fell and I blew a soft sigh. The real threat was the presence of demons. Some of the stuff that had happened there, more than suggested it as a likely cause.

I'd dealt with them before and it hadn't been pretty.

Two

It was almost three in the afternoon by the time we found the Ayers property. After leaving the port city and the pristine blue of the ocean, it had seemed like miles and miles of road cutting through scrubby flat land. Our destination was in the foothills of the distant mountains, hulking under a cloud scattered sky.

When we turned from the main highway onto the dirt road leading to the estate, my body sank lower into the car seat. It became harder and harder for me to breathe as we drew closer. There were many spirits there, a build-up of energy that was dark, powerful enough that it permeated even the land leading to the main house.

I looked at Gwen sitting in the front passenger seat of the Jeep four by four. The muscle in her jaw clenched and her eyes were narrow, staring ahead. She felt it too. Even Roy had become quiet, no longer cracking jokes in a mangled Australian accent.

The two story monstrosity of a house came into view when we rounded the bend in the drive. It was an architect's dream or nightmare. Curved turrets flowed out to two wings overlooking opposite sides of the property, all poised above a humongous wrap-around veranda. The dark windows were *everywhere* along the various angled sides, multiple lenses like an insect's eye, always watching.

"There they are." Roy leaned forward, peering through the front windshield while he turned the key, killing the engine.

His voice broke through the spell that the ominous structure of the building had cast. It was the first that I'd noticed the two cars parked at the side of the house. A middle aged woman appeared when the front door opened, followed by a blonde, younger woman and a barrel-chested, man, whose white teeth flashed in his tanned face.

Gwen muttered under her breath, "This is it, then." She opened the door and I let out a long, slow sigh, before flipping the handle of the car door to join her.

"Hello! How was your trip in? Any trouble finding it?" The silver haired woman, wearing a friendly smile below cat-like green eyes, stepped down the few steps. "I'm Eve Parsons. I head the committee for this project."

Since Roy was the first one to stride over, he extended his hand to her. "I'm Roy Harrison. This is Gwen Jones and of course, Keira Swanson, who you've been in contact with."

I let Gwen go ahead, while I sneaked a peak up at the window above the veranda. Had it been a flash of sunlight on the window or had there been someone there for just an instant? My gut was telling me that it hadn't been a trick of the light. But I didn't sense malice. If anything, I caught a sense of curiosity in the spirit which had shown itself for a moment.

When I took Eve's hand in mine, murmuring a 'pleased to meet you' her thoughts cascaded through me. Worry, that the project would cease, after pouring a boatload of money into renovations—money the foundation could scarcely afford to lose. The home for run-away boys was in serious jeopardy.

Her smile faltered for a moment, replaced by a blank

look as she looked at me silently. Hmm...she had sensed me picking up on her thoughts. She recovered and then with a sweep of her arm, invited the other two people forward. "This is Jane Boniface, our co-chair and Sam Brown, Director, at our most successful facility."

Jane reached forward and her hand taking mine was a limp noodle. My impressions of her were fleeting. She was more concerned with getting back to the city and shopping for an evening out with a new boyfriend. As far as she was concerned Ayres Home was a nuisance, a lost cause, and that wouldn't change with us being there.

But Sam was a different kettle of fish. His dark eyes were piercing above a warm smile. He really *did* care and had even invested much of his own savings into this project. He wasn't convinced that the problems with Ayres house were supernatural though. A private contractor, working for a for-profit firm wanted nothing more than for this charity to fail. They might have something to do with all the problems. For sure, it wasn't anything that couldn't be explained logically.

"I'll show you around the place and stay with you." Sam's dark eyes took in the three of us in one fell swoop, before turning a flinty look at Jane. "I know you're anxious to get back to town. Eve, I'll call you later."

With that, Eve and Jane strode over to the red SUV parked there. After a short wave, the vehicle was soon kicking up dust in its wake, going down the dirt driveway.

"So, the work has stopped temporarily? There's only us here now?" Roy took a few steps closer to the house, his hands in the back pockets of his jeans staring up at the windows and turrets. "It's quite a place. Lots of history here, I bet."

Sam looked down at the ground for a moment. "Look, I'll be honest with you. I'm not sure the problems here have anything to do with ghosts. There have been some pretty strange accidents that have happened to guys working here but, the place is also a bit of a legend. It's a self fulfilling prophesy. Expect creepy things and that's what you're bound to find."

He was trying to be nice but everything about him screamed frustration. The facility he managed was busting at the seams. The need for a bigger institution was so great and this ghost cleansing thing was a stumble down a blind alley as far as he was concerned.

I stepped closer to him, "Sam? I'd love for you to be right about that, the self fulfilling prophesy thing, but I *know* you're not. There's strong energy on this property...old and powerful spirits. I felt it when we turned into the drive." It was time to dispel another of his concerns. "We've got experience in confronting the paranormal. Believe me, I'd like to clear this place as much as you want it up and running. It's a good cause on so many levels. This is pro bono, by the way."

His mouth fell open for a moment and then he nodded, smiling. "That's mighty nice of you! The foundation will sure appreciate that. God knows, we could use a break."

Roy smiled and his hand rose to clap lightly on Sam's shoulder. "How about you tell us about the house?"

He meant well but it wasn't the way we normally did things. He still had some things to learn.

"No. Actually, I'd rather do a walk through." I stepped by Gwen, noticing the smile twitching the corners of her lips when she glanced at Roy.

Her voice trailed behind me. "After Keira and I go through it, *we'll* tell you about the house. How's that sound?"

Gazing up at the entrance, a shudder rolled through my shoulders. I took a deep breath and clasped the tourmaline stone that hung from a silver chain around my neck. Part of my Nana's legacy to me had been this protection stone. I had the feeling I'd need it.

Three

Be careful there! Not all of the original boards have been replaced yet." Sam was at the bottom step, following Gwen and Roy.

Crossing the veranda, the creak of wide wooden planks protested my every step. The house had to be well over a hundred years old. The paint was chalky gray from years and years of weather beating down on it. When I reached for the door handle to open it, my body shivered from a cold dread in my bones. Skittering voices whispered in my head, *'Go away. Not welcome here'*. The house was home to legions of spirits, people who had lived and died there over the years.

I took a deep breath, grounding myself as Nana had taught me. There was no way I wasn't going in there. I stepped inside and looked around. The smell of fresh pine mingled with the stale odour of decay, while dust motes flitted in the light from the stained glass transom window. It was cold, far colder that the day outside. The air was thick, forcing me to focus on pulling oxygen into my lungs.

"This looks like a formal foyer, from the original plan of

the house." Gwen's voice behind me was low. "Damn, it's cold in here."

My eyes flashed wide at the creak of the multi paned French door opening before me. I had been about to turn the handle but it had opened on its own. But rather than dread, the feeling rushing through me was welcoming. Whatever entity had done that was curious and anxious for us to enter. Not all spirits in the house were dark. Some were just confused.

When I stepped inside, piles of new lumber as well as stacks of sheets of drywall and unopened paint cans sat near the wall to my right. The area around me was like the hub of a wheel, where rooms ran off to the sides like spokes from a hub. In front of me was a sitting room of sorts, empty of furniture but with a curved bay of windows overlooking the back yard.

Gwen stepped up beside me and led the way. "Let's start in here, Keira. We'll work our way around."

I glanced back at Roy and Sam. Roy was watching us closely while Sam was nonchalant, a small, almost scornful smile playing on his lips. Well, he would soon see.

I squared my shoulders following Gwen into an oval room, lined from floor to ceiling with shelves. The air in this room was lighter, more peaceful than the foyer. The light filtering in from the large bay windows brought a cheeriness that I'd hardly expected to find anywhere in that house. Images of a young woman in a long, white dress reading, while perched in the window seat, brought a smile to my lips. An essence of her peaceful moments was in there still, her favourite room.

"You're picking up on this too." A peek at Gwen confirmed what I'd sensed in her mind. Her gaze was wistful as she looked at the window seat.

Roy followed us in, his head craning as he examined the space. "Wow. I love the curved lines in this room. There's not a right angle to be found. What workmanship," his voice barely above a whisper. His fingers trailed over the window seat, as he gazed around with awe.

Whatever it was about the house, we were all doing it. Speaking in low whispers, like we'd dropped into a church or something. The shards of red and green reflections from the top panes of the stained glass windows were reminiscent of a church's interior.

Gwen led the way out of the room and into a small alcove. There was an archway at the end of it that led to another long room, again with a magnificent display of windows, showcasing the side yard. The backdrop of mountains could be seen, hulking behind the dark green of a wooded area.

When I moved closer to the window, a cold wall of pulsating energy pushed at me. *'GET OUT!'* echoed in my head, while a sharp pain pierced low in my stomach.

I gasped and my hand closed around the stone of my necklace. Immediately the pain subsided. The effect of the stone calmed me enough that I took a deep breath to clear and center myself again. Whatever that cold energy was, it was masculine and powerful, with a heavy presence. And old. Was this the founder of the home, the man who'd built it, and raised his family there?

Gwen's hand lifted to rest on my arm, and the image became clearer. A dark haired man with a full beard and moustache, his eyes narrow, and menacing formed in the dank air. He towered over me and his body was a barrel, with muscular arms and legs. My hand covered Gwen's and I stepped back towards the doorway, pulling her along with me. He didn't want us in there? Fine. For now.

"What's wrong?" Roy said, alarm in his voice as he peered first at Gwen and then at me.

Gwen reached out and tugged at Roy's sleeve. "There's an entity here that is not friendly."

"What?"

"It's an old man. Come with us."

He looked around, examining everything, his normally jovial face a tight mask. After a couple moments, he gave us a sharp nod. "I'll be right back." He strode out of the room and the front door banged shut behind him.

I sighed. Roy was set on helping with this initial tour, even though Gwen and I would be better at sizing it up.

We continued on, passing through a good sized area with cabinets and shelving that led to a kitchen. I wasn't surprised to find that the energy dominating this room was gentler...feminine and much more welcoming than in the last room. An image of three women shimmered before me. The closest was buxom and elderly with grey hair while the other two were younger, laughing and impish. Their dresses were from an earlier time period, Victorian maybe.

"I like this room." Gwen wandered across the wide space and when she turned her smile was serene. "It *feels* good. I can just about smell freshly baked bread."

Sam's voice intruded in the still air "We haven't done much in here yet. It's going to take new plumbing and wiring to bring it up to code." He lingered in the doorway and there was a spark of hope in his eyes, gazing around the room. Even though he didn't realize it, the atmosphere had affected him as well.

Roy brushed by him, holding two copper rods, the bent handles loosely clasped in his palms. The rods which had been perpendicular, crossed when he stepped farther into the room.

"It works! I read about this and thought I'd give it a go. They're dowsing rods." He grinned and his gaze flickered over to us before focusing on the metal sticks crossed in an 'X' before his chest. "These rods have been used to detect water but nowadays, ghost hunters use them to pick up energy fields, as in *ghosts*!"

I couldn't resist. "Yeah, I know, Roy. Careful. There're three female spirits watching you, shaking their heads and smiling."

His eyes opened wider looking around the room. "Where? Show me!"

"Not right now; we need to continue our walk through."

I grinned at Gwen and walked through the door to a brighter room that ran halfway across the width of the house. Again, large windows dominated all the exterior walls. Whoever had built this house had created an airy feel to it with the vista of the outdoors shining in. Despite the brightness, the golden oak floors and wall sconces perched on the archways between the windows casting an amber light, the atmosphere in the space was blank. There was no energy to be felt at all in this room—it was totally neutral.

BANG! My heart leapt high in my chest. "That came from the other side of the house!" My eyes were as wide as Gwen's before I raced through the door at the far side of the room. It was the sitting room that I'd seen at the back of the house, when I entered the foyer.

A ladder was on its side, crossing the middle of the floor. I jerked back when an old man formed in the air above it, hovering like a hawk. Even though his form was grey and wispy, waves of dark rage emanated from his fiery eyes. Gwen's hand gripped my wrist, her fingers shooting a surge of energy through me.

Murder. This was an angry, evil man who had lived here. Not the owner but some sort of workman or servant.

"What the hell?" Roy paused in the doorway. The dowsing rods hung limply at his side while his eyes were huge marbles staring at the ladder.

Sam stepped into the room. "The ladder could have shifted when we walked into the house." He shook his head from side to side, scowling. "See, this is the kind of thing that the contractor was talking about. But one guy was on the ladder when it fell before. The poor bloke's arm was broken and then they all fled like rats from a sinking ship."

I stared hard at the ancient spirit hovering in the air. His mouth morphed into a grin, while his eyes were flinty watching Sam. That bastard had caused the injury and was now gloating! My jaw clenched and I stepped closer to the thing. "You don't belong here anymore. You have to leave this house."

A whoosh of energy hit me like a wall, knocking me flat on my ass on the dusty floor. His words filled my head. *'Bugger off. Who are you, to tell me what to do?'* echoed in my mind.

"What the ..." Roy whispered as he and Gwen rushed to my side, pulling me to my feet. "Are you okay, Keira? What the hell was that?"

But Gwen knew. "It's the real bad ass who's been causing so much trouble. I got a quick impression of his name...Amos or Alfred. Something with an 'A'."

I turned and looked at Sam. His mouth gaped open and the dark tan of his face looked painted on. He was becoming paler by the second. "I don't know...what...just...happened." He shook his head, eyes focused on the ladder on the floor.

There was no use getting into it right then. There was much to be done and 'Doubting Thomas' that he was, he'd just have to see for himself.

My fingers closed around the stone and I took a deep breath, facing the evil spirit once more. "What do you want? Why are you still here?"

The spirit pulled back, and the image faded. But the energy still tingled through my fingers and up my arms. He may have vanished from sight, but he was still there, with no intention of leaving. This one would give me trouble.

Four

C'mon. Let's finish the downstairs." Gwen's fingers clutched my arm, tugging me along after her. The sudden push with me banging to the floor had shaken her up as well. But underlying the fear in her gut, anger roiled.

As we walked through the door leading to the far side of the house, it struck me. This was like the night we'd encountered the demon in my grandmother's room! It had been scary as hell when the entity attacked all of us physically. If that guy in the sitting room, wasn't a demon, he was sure close.

I took a deep breath and opened a door on the right. It was a bathroom, yet the far wall was stripped to the wood studs, like a skeleton.

Sam's voice drifted from behind, "We're expanding this room. With twenty six boys living here, we need additional toilets and sinks. At least that was the plan..." He couldn't disguise the tremor in his voice, still reeling from what had happened in the other room.

"God this place is so remote. If I was a teenage boy, I'd be bored to death, living out here." Roy's eyebrows bobbed high when he turned to Sam. "You sure about this?" But it was the spookiness rather than the location that was getting to Roy.

"These kids need a break from the city, all the temptations and stress."

Roy snorted. "Not sure they'll find this relaxing. Not unless we can convince these ghosts to leave."

I continued on wandering through a series of rooms on the south side of the house, leaving Roy and Sam in their conversation. He was right. If we didn't clear this place of all the spirits still residing there, the Boy's Residence would be shot.

When I stepped into the first room and then the series of other small rooms, the energy field was again blank, but this time it felt like it was being blocked. But not entirely. I caught fragments of energy wavering in that part of the house. I swear it was like there was a dozen souls there, still tied to the property. I turned to Gwen, "Why do you think they stay here? I don't get it. I know you sense them too."

She nodded, her eyes taking in the room from top to bottom. "I think it has a lot to do with that thing in the sitting room."

"Yeah. It's blocking me from any contact with the spirits here. I feel their desire to communicate but there's also fear. But, before we do anything about him, I want to see the rest of the house...see what other surprises are in store for us. This place is infested."

"I noticed a set of stairs near the dining room and..." She jerked her head up, indicating ahead of her, "...this is a second set. I guess, considering the size of the place, that makes sense."

I followed her down the hall, noticing the stairs that were off to the right. "Probably the ones at the back of the house were for servants at one time." My gut clenched tight looking at the wooden stairs. A tattered wool rug snaked up the center of the steps. Even so, every step I made, produced an eerie creak slicing my last nerve like a cheese grater.

I almost ran into Gwen, when she suddenly stopped, staring up to the top of the stairs. My heart skittered high in my throat seeing the whitish apparition floating there. It was a woman, her dress ending at her ankles. She leaned forward and her finger crossed her lips before pointing to the area behind her.

Oh God. It was difficult to breathe again. A shiver tingled the hair on my neck and I reached for Gwen's arm. "We need to stick together. Take my hand and don't let go." I wasn't sure if I was saying this for her benefit or mine.

Immediately her thoughts pulsed in my mind. *'That woman gave us a warning. The REAL bad one is up here.'* My eyes met Gwen's and I nodded. We were definitely on the same page.

When Roy's voice sounded at the bottom step, I held my hand up like a traffic cop and waved him back. It would be better for Gwen and I to scout this area on our own, without any distractions from Roy and Sam.

As I was about to continue, my foot stepping to the next stair a series of thuds shook the very wood under my feet.

"What the hell was that?" Roy darted up the stairs right to my back, so close I could feel his breath warm on my neck.

My legs shook but I managed to climb the stairs, with Gwen tugging me along. If there was any other way of doing this, I'd jump at the chance. Something was up there and it didn't want us to come any closer. Hell, I didn't want to either!

"Oh my God!" Gwen turned around facing me and Roy. "Every door in the upstairs must have slammed shut. *That* was the noise!" She turned back, peering above the top stair and down the hall.

"Maybe we should go back. At least get some sage or holy water or something to protect us! I don't like this." At

Roy's shaky voice I turned to look at him. His complexion, fair under the mop of blonde curls was even paler. While behind him, Sam's eyes were as round as golf balls.

"Stay here! Gwen and I have protection. If we need you, we'll call." My voice was a harsh whisper, as if I was afraid whatever was up there would hear me. Good luck with that. It knew we were here and it was doing its best to scare us off.

"No way! I'm coming with you." Roy stepped up and edged in the narrow stairwell, beside me.

His jaw jutted out and I couldn't resist the quip bouncing from my tongue. "Okay, but it's your funeral."

"Shut up, Keira! Don't say things like that in here, especially to Roy." Gwen yanked my hand, pulling me along with her.

There was a long hallway, with a series of heavy, wooden doors shut tight. At the ear piercing squeal of a rusty hinge, my gaze flickered to the door at the end. Inch by inch it opened, the darkness revealed like a mouth gaping wide in a shuddering creak.

Shivers skittered up my spine, watching the door open on its own. *It* was in there. Whatever energy had slammed all the other doors shut, was waiting in there for us. I took a few deep breaths, one sweaty hand clutching Gwen's, the other grasping my tourmaline stone. At the surge of calm energy that flowed suddenly between her and me, I looked over, meeting her steady gaze. "This one's gonna be tough."

After the quick roll of her eyes, she whispered. "Enough already. Let's do this."

My head swirled with whispers, emanating from behind the closed doors that I walked by, but still, I kept on. Unlike the other rooms where the natural light flowed through the windows, this one was dark. A smell of rotting meat wafted in the dank air.

A beam of light flashed and I jerked, only to see Roy standing next to Gwen, a flashlight in his hand.

I stepped through the beam and into the room, taking

shallow breaths through my nose. "Who are you? What is your name?" The room was empty of furniture and the window on the outside wall had been boarded up. Spears of light peeked through the spaces between the boards. My fingers were sweaty on the stone hanging from my neck. The energy in that space was heavy with malice. In the corner of the room a dark shape moved. I gasped, my hand squeezing Gwen's, hard.

"GET OUT! THIS IS MY HOUSE!"

It was a roar, shaking the walls and reverberating through every cell in my body. Immediately a wind rose, buffeting us with dust and dirt! The smell of rotting flesh was putrid!

My jaw clenched tight and I stepped into the maelstrom. "I command you to stop! By all that is good, I command you! Leave this place!"

"DIE!" The thing grew bigger, waves of black expanding, hovering over half the room!

A board nailed to the window frame wrenched loose and flew through the air. Gwen's hand shot forward, knocking it down just before it smashed into my face. She yelped and blood rose from a gash across her knuckles.

I hissed a breath through gritted teeth. "STOP THIS! You have no power over me! In the name of light, by the power of goodness, I COMMAND you to leave!"

The surge of power between Gwen and me exploded, filling the room with a shimmering energy. We strode forward, together, the wall of light around us, expanding even as the thing in the corner shrank back. In a moment it had dwindled from a massive entity down to a dark, hulking mass on the floor the size of a garbage can. We towered over over it as it continued to wither down. My hand left the tourmaline and swept through the air above the foul entity. "Leave this realm and never return."

I stared hard at it, willing it with every fibre of my being. Slowly, it faded. Moments passed like hours, until it finally vanished, leaving only the foul stink. I let out a long sigh, my knees watery. It was only with Gwen's support beside me, her hand in mine that I managed to stay standing.

"Let's take a minute, Keira. That was hard on us both. I can't face any more spirits until I sit down for a moment or two." She led me from the room, leaving Roy there, a look of blank wonder in his eyes.

We sunk down onto the dirty old floor, with the window beside us. It was only then, when I glanced down the hall, that I noticed that all the doors had opened.

Sam stood at the top of the stairs, his mouth was an open cavern. He shrugged his shoulders, gazing at the doors. "I didn't do it. They all just opened on their own. What the hell is going on here?"

Five

I didn't have the energy to answer Sam. It was like I'd just completed a marathon; I was gasping for breath, willing my heart to slow. Gwen was in the same condition. Her hand was clasped with mine and she closed her eyes for a few moments, taking long measured breaths.

"I guess you believe now, huh?" Roy brushed by Sam poking his head in the first room. "This room looks clear but maybe I should get my EMF and the other equipment to test it. You two will be all right here for a few minutes, right?"

"I'll go with you and help carry the stuff. I still can't believe what I just saw." Sam shook his head and followed Roy down the stairs.

When they were gone, and the front door banged shut behind them, whispers started, soft at first, becoming louder with each second that passed. I gazed down the hallway and an image of a young boy peeking out from the second room down shimmered softly. It was soon joined by a second child and then a young woman, all drifting from the open doors into the hallway. Gwen gasped and her hand squeezed mine tighter.

'Help us.' Over and over, the whispers sounded in my head, becoming louder.

At their pleas, my heart ached and sunk deeper to my gut. Their fear, the isolation they'd felt all these many years being trapped in this house wafted into my soul. That thing! The thing we'd encountered in the room had held them here. They were brothers and the woman was actually their aunt, who'd died years before they were born. She had stayed in this realm to protect them as best she could. The boys had died when they'd gotten lost hiking in the outback.

Gwen jerked my hand. "There's more spirits here. I feel them." Her eyes were wide staring at me and she shifted, about to stand up.

"Wait. Just another moment. They've waited all these years...another few moments won't matter." Whether it was knowing what waited on the floor below or the ebb in my energy, I just wasn't ready yet. Gwen sank down again and looked down the hall, but as talented as she was, I knew she couldn't see what I saw.

Roy's voice echoed from the downstairs. "Everything okay, up there?"

"Can you bring us something to drink when you're coming? Water? Anything." In no time at all he appeared at the top of the stair. In his hand were two bottles of water, while his equipment bag was slung low on his shoulder.

"Sam's setting up the motion detectors in that sitting room. I think we've made a believer out of him." Roy strode forward, going right through the vapour entities that hovered in the hallway without seeing them. His shoulder gave a shudder and he handed the water bottles to Gwen and I. "It's chilly in here, isn't it?"

"Could have something to do with the ghosts you just walked through, Roy." I uncapped the bottle and took a long swig, gulping down half the bottle.

"What? Holy shit!" He scrambled to get the EMF

recorder from the bag, and then began waving it in the space he'd just left. "This is a tri-meter so I'm bound to get something."

His meter was almost at the chin of the female spirit, who backed away from him immediately. "I've got something! Look the needle's off the charts! There's a ghost right here, Gwen!"

The two boys, edged closer to him, trying to see what he had. It would have been funny if I'd had any more energy or patience. Boys and their toys.

A piercing blare sounded from the floor below. Roy's eyes became wider still. "That's an alarm for one of the motion sensors! I've got to go!"

When he disappeared down the stairs, I turned to Gwen. "Shall we? I think it's time these spirits moved on." I got to my feet and reached for her hand once more. The short break had done us both some good. The energy was once more flowing between us with a steady pulse.

"Let's do this!" She smiled and we walked close to the two boys. From the corner of my eyes I noticed the young woman, edge closer too.

The first name—Timothy—sounded in my head. "Timothy, your time here is over. You are free to go to the higher realm where the rest of your family is." He looked up at me with heartbreaking hope as The Veil took shape beside us. He approached it, and an expression of pure happiness washed over him. He leapt into the golden glow without looking back and was gone.

I didn't even need to say anything to the second ghost. He watched his brother go and then stepped into the wall of light right behind him.

There was just the young woman now. Jennifer. It came to me, even as she turned to smile shyly at Gwen and I. "Jennifer. You're free now. Go." I felt her gentle thank you before she stepped into the sparkling glimmer.

Tears stung the back of my eyes and I glanced over at Gwen. Her eyes were red rimmed and a river of tears rolled down her cheek. It had always been like this when we helped spirits transition on to the next realm. We stood silent for a few moments, our hands clasped while our emotions ran their course. I'm not religious, but it was a sacred moment, full of grace and awe.

But it wasn't to last long.

"Gwen! Keira! Come down here! You won't believe this!"

I looked over at Gwen. No Roy. I'd believe anything in *this* house.

Six

You go down. I'm going to make the circuit around to the other set of stairs. I want to make sure we've got them all."

"You know I can't do that, Keira." Gwen clapped her hand on my shoulder. "Where you go, I go. That's the rules of this gig, right?"

"Right. My Guardian." I grasped the sleeve of her jacket before she started away, heading round to the other half of the upstairs. "Gwen. I'm glad that we're doing this together again. After all that happened with my grandfather—"

"Don't call him that. He was a sperm donor for Pamela. David Holmes has no more right to be called grandfather than..." She slapped the wall with her hand. "....than this has to be called grandfather. He's an evil, horrible man. Too bad he hadn't died that night."

My sentiment exactly. I probably shouldn't have even mentioned Holmes's name. There was no love lost between Gwen and Holmes, not after he'd kidnapped her and Roy— not to mention her brother Sean taking a bullet rescuing us.

The fact that Holmes had gotten away, still gave me nightmares. He was still out there, plots and schemes bubbling to the surface in his lunatic mind.

I took a deep breath walking by a window in the hallway. The sun had dipped lower on the horizon, the few outbuildings casting long shadows across the lawn in the back yard. We needed to get this done soon. I had no wish to be there after nightfall knowing there might still be malevolent spirits hanging around.

The tour through the other bedrooms and the bathroom was quiet. "I think this area is clear, Gwen. We'd better get downstairs and see what Inspector Gadget is up to."

"Keira! I swear if you keep this up, I'm going to deck you." Gwen shot me a warning with her eyes. "Why'd you hire Roy if you don't think he's up to this?"

"He gives great Omelette? He's a seriously good 'Guy Friday' not to mention a decent cook." The truth was I liked him, but she didn't have to know that. Seeing Gwen get all huffy when I teased Roy was half the fun.

She darted over to the back stairs and turned, shooting me an evil grin. "You better let me go first. If I'm behind you, I might be tempted to push you down the stairs, you bitch."

"That's the Gwen I know and love!" I nudged her shoulder with my hand. "Maybe I'll push you first! How'd you like that?"

She glared at me before moving quickly down the stairs, her feet thudding on the wood. "Sometimes I think Sean was right about you. You *are* seriously immature!"

"Ha! What would he know about it?" But an image of Sean formed in my brain and I felt butterflies take flight in my stomach. What the hell was that all about? True, he was gorgeous but he was always belittling me like the Asshat he essentially was. There'd been a few times when we were searching for Gwen that his shell had broken and he'd actually been decent. But once we were home safe and sound, Asshat returned. Hard to believe he was Gwen's brother.

When I passed through the dining room and stepped into the sitting room, all thoughts of Sean fell like a stone from my mind. Roy stood in the centre of the room, holding the EMF gadget, while Sam was standing behind the camera, bent over, gazing through the lens at the corner of the room. But what got my attention was the old man, his image a dark cloud wavering ominously close to Roy.

"Roy! Step back!"

I strode across the dusty floor, stepping over the ladder that still lay there. This time, I was ready for it. I fingered the tourmaline and my gaze locked with the angry entity. "Alfred. That's your name, isn't it? Alfred Grimes." Even though my mouth had gone dry and my heart pounded fast, I wasn't giving an inch. When Gwen's hand closed over my other hand, the power that jolted from us was a bright flash skewering the ghost.

Its eyes blazed red for a moment before turning to settle on Roy. The EMF gadget fell to the floor and Roy yowled, holding his hand in the other. "It burnt me! What the hell? The EMF...it got so hot, I've got third degree burns!"

The camera flew across the room and bounced off the wall! The ladder on the floor began vibrating, rattling and then pounding down against the hard surface! All hell was breaking loose in a cacophony of bone jarring thuds.

"Stop it!" I bounded closer to the entity. Immediately my hand went numb from the icy cold enveloping it. My stomach rolled. I took a deep breath, struggling to keep my lunch down.

"GET OUT!" Its roar blasted through the room.

I felt Gwen pull back a little. "Keira!"

"KILL YOU ALL!"

It had grown in the energy lapse when Gwen faltered. I grasped her hand in an iron grip. "NO! In the name of God and all that's good, I command you! GO!"

Red sparks of rage seethed in its eyes. His lips pulled back, revealing yellowed fangs, a line of crimson blood rolling down his chin, into the white beard. All the while the ladder rattled and bounced, the sound of its clatters filling the air.

"Keira!"

At Roy's shriek, I risked a glance behind me. He was rising in the air, his feet and arms flailing like a marionette. Higher and higher, until the top of his head brushed the ceiling!

There was a flash of Sam racing from the room, followed by the front door banging shut. It was just the three of us now, facing the entity.

"Oh God, Keira! We've got to help Roy!" Gwen pulled back but still I hung onto her hand.

"No! Gwen! We have to stay together. It wants to separate us!" I caught the glint of the crucifix hanging around her neck, just barely visible through the open collar of her shirt. "Your cross! Hold it in your hand!"

She gripped it tightly and then nodded, stepping close to me again. "Put him down!" She spat the words at the thing. "NOW!"

For just a second, the sneer dropped from its mouth and its eyes dulled. The energy sparking between Gwen and I became turbo charged, a white hot glow sizzling, sparking in the air around us. It was like my chest would explode with the power claiming it.

"Alfred Grimes, you must go." The words were gentle and kind, leaving my mouth of their own volition. It was like some other spirit or entity had claimed my vocal chords. I gave my head a shake. What the hell was that? In an instant Alfred's life filled my mind. Oh the poor man. I quickly got my bearings back. "You were murdered here. Burnt alive in the stable. But there's nothing more here for you."

I felt the sense of a woman's spirit, her emotions rushed through me. A cascade of sympathy, sadness and regret filled my heart, and spread out to him. And then, in a final surge was love; an abiding love that had endured for years and years.

It was working! The entity shrank and the banging ladder ceased its thudding. At the thump behind me, I glanced back. Roy was once more on the floor, laying on his side and holding his ankle.

The energy emanating from Gwen and I formed a glittering wall beside Alfred. It was The Veil! Thank God! A hand reached through it, the fingers long and delicate, beckoning to Alfred. The name Emma flitted through my head. That was who had entered me briefly. She called to him; a sweet voice of longing and love.

"Alfred, Emma wants you to join her. Leave this house that caused you such pain. Go through The Veil and be with her." Tears rolled freely down my cheeks. My throat was tight and I willed him with every cell in my body to go to her, his wife.

"She loves you, Alfred." Gwen had picked up on the energy as well.

Alfred had changed. A moment earlier he was a dire, savage entity consumed with rage. He looked broken now, every bit the tired old soul that he was. He staggered with halting steps to The Veil, and expression of wonder and fear lining his face. His hand rose and his fingers curled around Emma's. He fell into the shimmering light. The last I saw was his eyes closing slowly.

I took a deep breath, trying my best to stay upright. I wanted to sleep for a week. It had taken every last bit of energy in my soul to do that transition and it wasn't over yet. There were so many still left. I breathed in deeply.

"Okay, let's move on," I said. "There's a lot more still here."

Gwen's hand squeezed mine. "I don't think so. Look." I looked to where she nodded. It was a whirlwind of vapour, mingling yet showing separate spirits, hurtling towards The Veil of light that still shimmered. The spirits who had been trapped, held hostage were now free to leave, now that Alfred had gone. Even the ancient one in the far side of the house—the one I suspected was the man who'd built the house—rushed through.

They left, sliding easily through The Veil and onto a higher realm. And then it too twinkled, winked and was gone.

Gwen looked at me and I nodded. She swooped from my side to see to Roy. The last vestiges of the day cast a golden light through the window.

It was done.

Seven

When I walked out the front door, Sam was propped up against his car, talking on his cell phone. He clicked off and hurried over to my side.

"It's over?" His eyes darted to the door and he crossed his arms over his chest. "If I didn't see all that with my own eyes, I wouldn't believe it."

"I don't blame you in the slightest, Sam." I waved my hand back at the house. "This kind of thing is..." I groped for words; man, was I beat.

"Unbelievable?" he said with a smile.

I nodded. "The house is clear now, but I want to check the outbuildings as well." I slumped down onto the step. I smiled up at him. "You wouldn't happen to have any key lime pie, would you?" It was Nana's favourite way to celebrate a successful transition, although he wouldn't get my weak attempt at humour.

He took a seat next to me. "I'll buy you all the lime pie you want, if this works." He looked away for a moment and swallowed hard. "You know, there was a handyman who died here, burned in a fire. Was that the thing in the sitting room?"

I nodded and took a deep breath. "That fire was set deliberately. Alfred Grimes was murdered. That's why he stayed behind, tied to this place with his rage. Even the original owner, Mr. Ayres was held hostage here by Alfred. There was a lot of anger and fear in that house."

"Shit! I was so stunned by everything I forgot to ask. How is Roy?" He glanced over at the door and the answer to his question appeared, hobbling behind Gwen.

"That thing wrecked my equipment! Not to mention scaring the crap out of me and twisting my ankle." Roy gripped the post next to him, his face a tight grimace of pain.

"I'll buy you more, Roy." I made a weak attempt at humor. "You really take this flying seriously, don't you? Hell, you don't even need a plane anymore."

"Keira! He could have been seriously hurt you know! Admit it. That shook you up as well. We're lucky that other spirit showed up, that woman. I'm not sure Alfred would have left if she hadn't." Gwen put her arm around Roy's waist and pulled him closer.

I couldn't argue with her. There were times when I wondered if Nana was looking out for me on the other side. This was one of them. After confronting the entity upstairs, and then to face the real bad ass in the parlour! That ghost, *Alfred*, had been full of rage, bordering on demonic. If not for the love that Emma had showed him, we'd probably be still in there, battling him.

I was curious and a little scared though. Emma had definitely entered me somehow to help with that task. I've never felt a spirit...*inside* of me before. Is that what a possession is like?

I pushed myself up from the step, feeling like I was sixty four, not the twenty-four that showed on my birth certificate. I was so drained my legs and arms quivered.

"Anyone want some Gator-aide? I could use one."

Sam rose, "Let me. You brought a cooler right? I think we could all use a round. Actually, if you had some gin that would come in handy."

I smiled. "A man after my own heart. Would you mind getting the rest of the gear as well? We brought sleeping bags."

He paused as he was about to step off the veranda. "You're really serious about spending the night? After all that?"

"It's the only way, we'll know for sure." I gazed at the expanse of property, the mountains hulking dark in the distance. The light had faded and going into the outbuildings would require flashlights. With any luck, they would be free of any spiritual entities.

***

Gwen led the way to the larger of the two buildings. It was a combination workshop and barn, and the smell of grease and metal mingled with the faint odour of manure. The beam of light showed old wooden stalls, a rafter where still some decayed hay clung, and a long work bench where rusty tools sat.

I took a deep breath, centering and opening myself to spirits, looking around the building. But it was clean energy. The only nasty bits in that building were insects and mice, something a good fumigator could take care of.

"Whew! Nothing to see here, folks." I backed out of the building, just barely catching myself from stumbling on the raised doorframe. Thank God it was almost over. I was a walking zombie. Transitions always wore me out, yeah; but that soul to soul contact with Emma had left me a wreck.

Roy's hand clasped under my elbow. "Here. My eyes are better than yours. Besides which, you're not getting any pity points. I claim all rights after my solo flight in that parlour."

"Your ankle's better now though. You aren't limping as much." I smiled up at him and then turned to where Gwen's light shone.

"Probably had more to do with the shock of it. Shit, that was scary. Lifted like I was a rag doll." His voice was barely above a whisper.

I totally got what he was saying. It had happened the night the demon had fought Nana. I'd been thrown high, bouncing against a wall. A shudder went through my shoulders. That kind of thing never gets old.

Gwen opened the door to the small shed and pointed her flashlight inside. "Yikes!" She lurched to the side and a blur of dark energy shot by her.

"Get away with you!" Sam stepped forward, his feet pounding, kicking up dirt at the object. "It's a dingo! They're wild dogs. Probably found a way in there."

"Oh my God! A dingo!" Gwen's light swivelled and the eerie glow of white eyes reflecting the light back, shone in the dark night.

"I got this," I said and stepped inside. I put the flashlight on another one at the back. "Nice doggy! Do you like me?" It turned its head, looking straight at me and snarled, before scampering off into the night.

"I see you've still got your charm when it comes to dogs. Even wild ones are scared of you." Gwen chuckled, but before she took a step inside, Sam was right next to her.

"You'd better let me. There might be more in there, and I've dealt with these little buggers before." He took the light and disappeared inside.

"Something tells me, this building is clear as well. I mean aside from the dog." Gwen stepped in after Sam.

I didn't have to go inside to know she was right. All the ghostly energy had been in the house and we'd taken care of that.

Eight

Three days later, I slathered sunscreen on and settled myself on the beach. It was a rare day for that time of year in Australia, when the temperature hit almost eighty degrees and I was taking full advantage of it.

Roy and Gwen could tear up the miles sightseeing but I was still recharging after the experience in Ayres House. Besides which, when they were together, I had to focus on keeping my telepathic skill in check. There was no way I wanted to read their thoughts, most of which were kind of sappy and lovey-dovey. Even Gwen had commented on how restrained I'd become. Considering that she'd quit working with me when my ability to read thoughts had amped up a few notches and ...Okay, okay. I'd been showing off a bit back then. Could I help it? I was like a kid with a new toy. Sue me.

I had just got myself prone on my stomach, the music from my phone low, the sun's rays hot on my back when the phone rang.

I frowned seeing 'Unknown Caller' flash on the screen.

Even before I clicked it to answer, my gut tightened into a knot. It was deja vu, if nothing else. Holmes. Every cell in my body screamed the hard truth. I took a deep breath, "Hello?"

"Keira."

At just the sound of his voice made my stomach churn, and I had to swallow the bile rising in the back of my throat. "What do you want? I know it isn't to turn yourself in to Inspector Kreely." I sat up, gripping the phone so hard my fingers hurt.

"I need to see you. We never finished our little talk the last time." As always his voice was slippery and equally repugnant as an eel sliding across my flesh. My eyes narrowed. Talk! That was a laugh! If you call abducting my friends, threatening our lives a talk, I'd hate to have an argument with him!

"I've got nothing to say to you Holmes, except turn yourself in. Get some psychiatric help, Looney-Tunes." Sean was right. Sometimes I could be childish.

"You're going to need to hear what I've got to say. Have you spoken with your mother in the past few days?" The menace in his oily voice was clear.

"Don't you *touch* my mother!" I had to warn Dad about this. He'd know what to do to protect her.

"Yes, poor innocent Susan. Such a shame she never inherited your grandmother's or my abilities. Skipped a generation. But she does enjoy running her restaurant. I had lunch there yesterday. It's a bit shoddy and the wine was watered down. I would have expected better. Must be Richard's influence."

Oh God. My heart raced in my chest and I breathed fast. He was in New York! The threat against Mom just ramped up to the stratosphere. I had to buy time to get in touch with Mom and Dad...and Inspector Kreely. "I will meet with you but you have to leave my parents out of this. Where are you now?"

"Well, I'm not on a beach tempting skin cancer. Really

Keira. The sun ages you as well."

I pulled my sunglasses down, peering around at the beach and the land bordering it. I was completely alone. It was a weekday and Australia's winter. Who else would be on the beach? Yet, he knew I was here. Someone was watching me.

My stomach sank as a new thought popped into my head. He'd kidnapped Roy and Gwen once before. For all I knew, he could have got them again.

"I'll be in touch again, Kiera. This time, no tricks and no one gets hurt, got it?" The line went dead.

I hit the link on my phone to dial my parents. It would be around eleven pm their time, but maybe Dad was still up, especially if there was a hockey game on. It rang a few times before he answered.

"Keira? What's wrong?"

Just the sound of his voice, made my throat tighten and I had to fight the onslaught of tears. "Daddy? David Holmes just contacted me. He made a threat against Mom."

"What? Oh my God. What the hell is wrong with that man!" His voice was so loud, I held the phone out from my ear.

"Simple—he's crazy." But it wasn't simple at all. This would never stop until he was locked up. The police had the evidence; they just didn't know where he was. Again the image of an eel flitted through my head.

"It's a trick, Keira. He just wants to get to you. You can't agree to anything he asks. Stay away from him!" Concern for my safety had made his voice even louder, blaring in my ear.

"Don't worry, I don't even know where he is." I kept the fact that Holmes was having me watched to myself. Dad was already upset enough. And it was also skirting the fine line of truthfulness. I'd meet with Holmes. It was the only way to ever stop him.

"When are you coming home? I'll take Susan to Kingston. That way I can keep an eye on both my girls. He's never found it...not that I know of."

"I wanted to stay another week but now I'm not sure. I'll talk to Gwen and Roy and let you know our flight plans." This time my chin quivered and the words were hard, barely a whisper. "I love you Daddy. I'll see you soon."

I started to ring Gwen but the feeling of someone watching my every move was too strong. I threw my cover-up over my shoulders and gathered my things, scurrying from the beach. I'd call her from the hotel room.

***

"Gwen?"

"Yeah." There was a slight pause. "Is something wrong, Keira?"

My head fell back and I flopped down onto the bed. Thank God, she was all right. "No. I just wondered when you'd be back. It'd be nice to have dinner together." I tried to keep my voice as casual as I could but the silence before she replied told me she wasn't buying it.

"Actually, we were going to stay the night here but we can come back and meet you for dinner. There's something wrong, isn't there? Is it—"

"Yes. Holmes called me a little while ago. This time he threatened *Mom*. Dad is taking Mom to Kingston as soon as they can."

"Oh my God! Why can't the police *find* that bastard!" The muffled sound of her voice followed, relaying what I'd said to Roy. "Stay in the hotel room, Keira and lock the door. We'll be there as soon as we can. I'm going to call Sean. He should know this as well."

Shit. This was spiralling fast. But Gwen was right. Sean had every right to know, seeing as how he'd been shot in the skirmish with Holmes that night. If he hadn't rushed in when he had, things might have turned out differently. Maybe Holmes wanted *revenge* on him, as well as getting me to work with him.

"I'll be careful. I'll book the first flight out of here tomorrow morning for us. You guys be careful too.

Remember he has a network of thugs working for him."

"You're preaching to the choir, Keira. See you in a few hours."

"Later." I clicked off and then scanned the phone to find the number for my next call.

It was probably very early morning in Isle of Wight but I had to talk to him. Not even my parents would know what I was about to suggest to Inspector Kreely. He was the only one who might go along with it, the only one I could trust not to give it away. I needed him on my side.

"Hello?"

I sighed hearing the hoarse, sleepy growl of Dan Kreely's voice. "It's Keira Swanson. I heard from David Holmes just now. Sorry for the early call but—"

"That's okay." At the mention of David Holmes, his voice became crisp. "What did he say? Where is he?"

"I don't know where he is. He wants me to meet with him. I'm in Australia and he's having me watched! He knew I was on the beach." My heart beat faster, even though it was good to be able to unload the whole story.

"*Where* in Australia? I'll make some calls and get some police protection for you. With any luck, we might even be able to trace the call."

"Port Augusta, at the Helio Hotel. He made threats against my mother. She's in New York but she and Dad are flying in to Kingston tomorrow." Again, my throat grew tight, fighting the tears at the thought of Holmes doing anything to Mom.

"Good Christ! What's her address? We've got to get protection for her as well."

"33 Bethune, Manhattan." I pictured the brownstone townhouse I'd grown up in and said a silent prayer. It was late there and they'd be all locked in tight for the night, thankfully.

"I'll call you right back." There was a click and the line went dead.

There was nothing to do but wait.

***

Fifteen minutes later, there was a tap at the door. My heart leapt to my throat and I scrambled from the chair to rush over. "Who is it?"

"It's the police, Miss."

I pulled the door open a few inches, keeping the lock bar in place. Outside were two policemen, in dark uniforms. The older of the two men, flipped open a leather wallet to reveal his badge and name—Officer Brendan Wall, Australian Federal Police.

"Everything all right, here, Miss?" His blue eyes were focused on the room behind me.

"Yes. Just a minute." I closed the door and unhooked the security bar. When I opened it, I stepped back, a long sigh of relief skittering from my chest. "Come in."

"We received a call from an Inspector Kreely in England to check in on you." His words drifted over his shoulder as he stepped by me, taking in the entire room.

The younger of the two, flashed a small smile as he strode by. "No need to worry, Miss. We'll check the room and keep an eye out." He pulled a folded sheet of paper from his shirt pocket and spread it for me to see. "This is the   guy,   right?   David   Holmes?"

"Yeah." My jaw tightened and I pulled back staring at the sketch. It was a composite sketch, drawn by a police artist in Isle of Wight. David Holmes was an enigma, flying so far under the radar that there were no photos available of him.

My cell phone rang and I rushed to pick it up. 'Inspector Kreely' showed on the screen. "Hi."

"The Australian Fed Police are on their way and New York has been secured as well."

"Actually, the police just arrived. Thanks." I watched the two men check the bathroom, balcony and even the closets, their hands on holsters, ready for anything.

"They'll stay with you and see you to the airport. You

said you're leaving right?"

I looked down at the hardwood floor. "Yes. First flight out of here is at nine seventeen. We'll be on it. But what about after, when I'm back home in Kingston?"

"Don't worry. We'll have a lookout there as well."

"I need this to stop, Dan. I'm going to meet with him when he calls again. It's the only way we can get him." I sunk down into the chair and watched the two officers head for the door. "Hang on." I called to them. "Are you leaving?" Again, my heart skipped a beat.

"No. We'll be outside. Just thought you wanted some privacy for the call." The younger one, smiled shyly at me.

"Stay. Please. It's Inspector Kreely. He might want to talk to you as well." I slumped back into the chair. "My parents can't know that I'm going to meet him. This is just between you and me, Dan. Even Gwen and Roy can't know. I can't risk endangering their lives anymore."

"What about Sean Jones? You're not going into this alone are you? I'll be there along with other police but I'd feel better if he were with you when you meet up with Holmes. The guy's got guts and a fair share of smarts."

"No. Absolutely not. Holmes wants me. He said no tricks. He might kill Sean this time. It's got to be just me." My plan had to work. I'd never have any peace in my life if it didn't. And not only that...if Holmes got what he wanted, it might be the end of the world as I knew it.

Nine

Almost twenty-four hours later, Roy drove the car down the long driveway to my house in Kingston. Well, mansion was a more accurate term.

"What the heck?" Roy leaned forward peering out the windshield.

"Your parents throwing a party?" Gwen turned to look at me, question marks in her eyes.

I stretched higher and saw what they were talking about. Of course there was Mom and Dad's rental car but also three other vehicles, one of which was Sean's. I'd recognize the ice blue four by four anywhere. At the sound of a vehicle behind, I turned to see. A grey police car was close on our tail. Of course. Inspector Kreely had said he's have a police guard watching us.

I huffed a quick chuckle. Parking was going to be tight and I *owned* the joint.

When the front door opened, my father stood there for a moment before bounding down the stairs and coming over to where we parked. The steady resolve I'd worn like a shell since the phone call from Holmes, melted, when I stepped out and nestled into his arms. "Daddy." Once more I was his little girl, secure for even a brief time in his hug.

"Keira. I'm so sorry about all this. But don't worry, the police are bound to catch him before too much longer." His hand stroked my head before I pulled back looking up at him.

"How's Mom?" But I needn't have asked. She raced down the stairs and joined us. I turned and we hugged, each of us fighting tears.

"Hi Mr. Swanson." Gwen pulled back from her short hug with my Mom and gestured for Roy to step closer. "I'm not sure you've ever met Roy. He's working with us now. Roy, this is Keira's dad, Richard Swanson."

"Pleased to finally meet you." He shook Dad's hand and then turned to Mom. "Nice to see you, Mrs. Swanson." Of course, he'd met her at the airport when I'd first came to Kingston. God, that seemed like a lifetime ago, even though it was less than a year.

"It's Susan. Nice to see you again, Roy." She patted his arm and then turned to me once more. "We've got a full house inside, Keira."

Gwen raced up the stairs, rushing to give her brother, Sean, a hug. His eyes met mine for a moment, and I had to look away. He wouldn't be there, along with my parents if not for Holmes's crazy obsession about getting me to work with him. Again, I'd upset Sean's life, but at least this time, Gwen was safe.

When Devon appeared in the doorway, his hands gripping his walker I glanced at Mom. She wasn't kidding. Even Gwen's dad was there?

When I stepped up the granite stairs, I paused clearing my mind and smiling at Sean. "Hi. We have to stop meeting like this." For once, he didn't block me in reading his thoughts. He was actually *relieved* to see me?

Immediately, his next mental comment knocked the legs out from under me. *'Dilettante?' 'What the hell is that supposed to mean?'*

His next thought was like the crack of a whip. *'Grab a dictionary.'* My eyes narrowed for a moment glaring up at him. Damn. He was good, almost as good as I was at reading minds.

'*Better.*' He smiled and his chin rose high.

I pushed past him to greet Devon. "Devon! It's good to see you! How are you doing?"

Before he had a chance to answer, Sean jumped in, "I think we all need to talk about what we do next about Holmes."

It was only then that I noticed another guy in jeans and a ball cap standing in the foyer. From the way his dark eyes flickered over each of us, assessing the situation, he was another cop that Inspector Kreely had arranged. He stepped forward and extended his hand, "I'm Brian Fowler with the RCMP."

"Hi. I'm Keira Swanson." Behind the slight smile, he was stifling a chuckle, thinking how he'd been given a cream puff assignment, guarding a girl who was not only rich, but hot as hell. Lucky him!

I felt the muscles in my neck tighten to steel cables. "You *do* know that Holmes kidnapped my assistant and shot her brother, don't you, Brian?" The sharp pull back of his head and smile falling from his mouth, told me I'd scored a point. This wouldn't be a walk in the park for him. And besides...he was a Mountie. Where was the flaming hot red uniform? I'd been ripped off getting this loser in the ball cap.

"Yes...yes, of course." His tone now carried respect even if '*bitch*' flashed in his mind.

Whatever. I turned when Dad herded everyone inside and closed the door. "Let's all go into the dining room. There're sandwiches and drinks laid out, in case anyone's hungry."

I glanced around. There were seven of us, more people than had been in that house in a long time. And of course, Mom and Dad were the perfect hosts, even having food ready.

Sean stepped over, and as he was about to touch my

arm, he pulled his hand back. '*Chicken!*' I flashed it at him and smiled, remembering the surge of energy that had sparked when we joined hands so long ago in Ireland.

'*That was then.*' His head was high, his blue eyes narrow, looking down a straight, perfect nose. "When we're done in there, we need to talk."

It was superfluous, his spoken words. I knew what he wanted. It was about the money. "Can't understand how I did it, can you? You hate taking money from me. Tough. Deal with it." I stalked away, following Devon into the dining room. If nothing else, I had one up on that Asshat Sean.

Money. Yeah, I'm totally loaded. When my Nana took me into her life almost a year ago to teach me about the paranormal she was incredibly wealthy. Her psychic abilities gave her one hell of an edge in playing the stock market, and when she passed away I was her major heir. I had been paying Asshat a ton of money that he didn't want, for him to quit his job in the big city and live here in Kingston to look after Devon, his father. More importantly, Devon is Gwen's father, and I really need her to help me in my work transitioning spirits to the other side through The Veil.

And Asshat Sean has been too proud to take my money. He kept sending it back until I paid a couple of hackers from the nearby University to ensure that the money would get into his bank account and stay there. His only way of getting rid of it now would be to withdraw it in cash and burn it.

Nobody... I mean *nobody* has it in them to set fire to hundreds of thousands of dollars. Not even Asshat Sean.

Do I feel smug? You betcha'. I gave him a cheese grin and followed the crowd to the dining room.

When we were all seated, Dad stood at the head of the table and cleared his throat. "We're all together...at least anyone who might be threatened by David Holmes. We've got Brian here to watch the inside of the house, while there's an unmarked car in the driveway and officers covering the perimeter. I suggest that we stay together until the police get Holmes. There's plenty of room here. What do you say?"

Devon's smile lit the room, even though of all of us, he was in the worst shape with his MS and all. "For years I've lived down the road from this place. Finally, when I get a look inside, you don't want me to leave." He chuckled. "But I've seen what damage this Holmes guy caused the last time. I'd like to know that my kids and Keira are safe. If being here—"

"Dad! I'm not sure that's necessary. We're not that far away." Sean shook his head and for a moment his eyes met mine. It wasn't that he didn't want to stay...he was *afraid* to stay. Oh my God! Afraid of being near me, twenty-four, seven.

My mouth fell open. Had he meant for me to know that or was it a chink in the wall he normally used to shield his thoughts from me?

'Stay.' I shot the message across the table to him. *'Think of Gwen and your dad. I can protect them here.'* If he was opening himself to me, then it was my turn to reciprocate.

"It would make our job easier, if all of you were together." Brian stood up and wandered to the sideboard to grab a sandwich.

Gwen went over to her father, standing behind him with her hand on his shoulder. Looking up at her brother she said, "Sean, I think you and Dad should stay. The house is *huge.*"

"Fine. But just for a few days. Hopefully in that time, the police might have a better handle on Holmes this time." Sean's eyes darted over to me before turning to his sister.

A long slow breath eased from my chest. It was only then that I became aware that I'd been holding it in, waiting for Sean's answer. Relief and...

NO! I wasn't interested in Sean. He might be an Adonis but he was also an Asshat, always belittling me. Still...

Ten

An hour later, sitting with my mother in the sunroom, having a cup of tea together, she leaned over the table and her voice dropped. "So what is up with you and Sean?"

I jerked back and felt my cheeks grow warm. "What do you mean? He's Gwen's brother. That's all."

"Come on, Keira. I saw the way you two look at each other. There was some kind of silent communication sparking between you." She lifted her cup and her eyes were sly gazing over the rim at me, "He's gorgeous. Don't tell me that fact escaped your notice."

Sometimes, reading people's minds could be a curse. My Mom's thoughts were X rated right then. Eeew. "Stop! He treats me like a jerk. How could I be attracted to anyone like that?"

'How indeed?' That last thought was definitely a shade of Nana. I could certainly tell that Mom was her daughter. Or was Nana hovering above the plants in her favourite room with her favourite girls? I wouldn't put it past her.

Dad popped his head into the doorway. "They're back with Devon's things. Sean asked if you could meet him in the living room, Keira. Gwen and Roy are helping Devon get settled in your Nana's old room."

"You'd better go talk to him, Keira. Be nice." Mom chuckled and winked at me.

"Stop. Just stop, okay?" But my cheeks were flaring red when I got to my feet and walked out the door.

"What was that all about?" Dad's words drifted in the air as he joined my mother.

Argh! It wasn't all bad enough that my mother had to add matchmaking to the mix? The smell of meat roasting in the oven filled my nose as I walked by the kitchen. Of course. My parents would be in their glory, cooking a feast for everyone, even that cop guy. My quiet retreat had turned into *their* restaurant.

I took a deep breath before striding into the living room. Sean was standing at the sideboard, pouring a drink. "If that's a gin gimlet, make it two, will you?" I glanced at the grandfather clock perched in the corner. Yes, six o'clock. That had always been my Nana and my cocktail hour. Why was I feeling her presence so sharply today?

"Of course. I remember what you drink." He turned, walking slowly over with two frosted highball glasses in his hands. But this time, the wall in his mind was securely in place.

"Oh. So we're back to that are we?" I took the drink from him and patted the spot next to me on the sofa. Even from where I sat, I could sense the angry red aura wrapping his body. When he sat at the far end of the sofa, I knew he was trying to keep everything in check with no chance of my power getting to him.

"The money, Keira. I've tried spending like a drunken sailor...even changed banks, but still my account never drops below a hundred grand." His eyes narrowed, looking over at me. "How did you do it?"

"I have my ways. Take it. You earned every penny. At least you have the freedom now to do whatever you want. I still think your talents are wasted working in the corporate world." It was hard to hide the frustration, knowing that with his seriously strong, psychic abilities, he could use that power for good. Hell, Nana had seen his strength and tried to recruit him to work with her to protect The Veil.

"For your information, I quit my job." He smiled for the first time and it was like the sun coming out from behind a dark cloud, lighting up the day.

The butterflies in my stomach noticed the boyish dimple, the iridescent blue of his eyes framed with dark lashes. My voice was a hoarse croak. "What?"

"Since you insist on giving me money, the least I can do is earn it. Besides, when I went back to work, I was bored sick working with Customs agents." He cupped the drink in both hands, huddled forward on the sofa. "I felt alive when we were in the United Kingdom, working together against Holmes."

I blinked a couple of times staring at him. *CLOUDS, Keira! Guard your thoughts.* He can't know about the plan I'd outlined to Inspector Kreely. It was too dangerous and there was no way I'd ever let anything more happen to Sean. He'd been through enough.

He looked over at me and the smile dropped from his lips. "What? I thought you wanted me to do this. Work with you and Gwen. You hired Roy, for God's sake and he has zero talent in this."

I had to keep this light. "But he's got all the gadgets and he's really keen. He's showing some promise. And let's face it, he and Gwen are a team, like peas and carrots." It was a bad Forest Gump impression but it brought a smile to his face.

His hand reached over and rested on my shoulder. For a minute my eyes closed, my body basking in the power surge between us. If anything, it had gotten stronger since our time in Ireland. Acceptance, even real care and affection—it was coming through loud and clear. He wasn't even attempting to block the communication flowing from him to me. When I opened my eyes, I fell into his gaze.

It was like I was in a trance, every cell in my body alive and firing, the energy flow between us growing stronger with each breath.

"Keira?" Gwen's voice broke the spell. She appeared in the archway of the living room, "I figured I'd find you in here. Mind if we join you? I see you're keeping to your grandmother's tradition, cocktails at six."

If there was a time that I fervently wished that Gwen had psychic ability, it was then. Hell, even some social skills would have been nice. I was still trembling, from the energy release between Sean and I. He had pulled back to his side of the sofa. "Yeah. Except I didn't dress for dinner." Even to my own ears, my voice quivered.

"C'mon, Dad."

It was then that I noticed Devon behind her. He looked from Sean to me and then cleared his throat. "This sure is a nice place, Keira."

"I'll pop into the kitchen and grab a couple of beers, Dad. I want to check up on Roy anyway, make sure he's not in Richard or Susan's way." With that, Gwen headed off to the kitchen.

I squared my shoulders sitting straighter when I looked over at Devon. "Thanks. Are you all settled in, now?"

He nodded and then took a seat across from me. "I hate being away from the house but I suppose it's for the best. At least for a little while."

"Hey, it might even be fun! We can play cards, watch the Yankees beat the Jays..." I tried to sound upbeat but I knew what he would really miss in his house was his wife, Mary. Her spirit was still tied to the place and I had no desire to convince her to move to the next plane—not as long as Devon needed her.

"Dad." Sean leaned forward and set his drink on the coffee table. "I'm not going back to Toronto. I'm going to stay with you and maybe help Keira and Gwen when I can."

"What's this?" Gwen came through the door and handed a beer to her father.

Mom and Dad were right on her heels. Mom looked over at me and shrugged. "Roy kicked us out. He's looking after the rest of the dinner."

Gwen took a seat between us on the sofa. "You're giving up your job in the Big Smoke? About time, I'd say." She glanced over at me and there was an impish grin on her lips. "Won't this be cozy? Me and Roy and you and Sean?"

"I'll say." Mom threw the words over her shoulder as she walked over to the sidebar to help Dad with their drinks.

My neck felt like a bed of hot coals, while my cheeks were flames. What was with Gwen and Mom, so obviously matchmaking? It was embarrassing!

"Well, I hope you're not taking on any new assignments...not until this thing with Holmes is done." Dad glanced over at me, the muscle in his jaw working below steely eyes.

"I'm not taking on anything new. That stint in Australia was hard. I think Gwen and I both need to rest for a bit." Anything to change the topic of conversation from any budding romance between Sean and I. He liked me. Cared about me. That was as good as it was likely to ever get.

Right?

I hoped not!

While Mom and Dad sat close to Devon, making light conversation, Gwen rose to her feet, "I'm going to see if Roy needs any help."

Then it was just Sean and I again huddled at each end of the sofa. I threw a thought his way. *'We can try it. If it doesn't work, we'll go our separate ways. No harm, no foul.'*

'You are talking about the job, right?' There was a rakish smirk on his face and he winked.

Damn! He was as expert as Mom and Gwen in making me blush.

And... to tell the truth...I kinda liked it.

Eleven

Later that night, I climbed into bed and stared at the ceiling reliving dinner. Everything had changed between Sean and I. Ever since that episode in the living room when his feelings for me had hit me like a wall. He'd even been fun at dinner, cracking jokes, teasing Gwen and offering to clean up. Or was it me that had changed in how I treated him? There was no sting in any of the banter I threw his way. Hell, it bordered on being flirty.

At the light tap on my door, my heart leapt into my mouth. I didn't even need to answer to know it was Sean. His energy was an aura that cut through walls and doors. I ran my fingers through my hair and rushed to answer it, tugging the shoulder of my nightgown higher.

He stood there in a pair of pyjama pants, holding a toothbrush and toothpaste in his fist. But it was the sculpted pecs and the washboard abs that I could hardly keep my eyes from feasting on.

"Do you mind if I use your bathroom? I think your Mom's in the other one and I didn't want to disturb Dad or

Gwen to use theirs." He smiled sheepishly, stepping softly into the room when I opened the door wider. It was a ruse. He'd purposely waited until the bathroom was occupied to come knocking at my door. He wasn't even trying to block me entering his mind.

Oh God. I'd also dropped my guard. Again, my face flared hotly when I saw the twinkle in his eyes after reading my X rated thoughts.

CLOUDS! Keira, think CLOUDS.

He shook his head. "Clouds, Keira? Seriously?" He stepped closer, so close I could feel his body heat.

My hand rose to shield my neck and the top of my chest. "Jody. She taught me to use them to block my mind from other people."

"And how well did that work out for you? She was also working for Holmes." His hand rose and he tucked a lock of my hair behind my ear. A sweet gesture that made my body tingle with the shot of energy sparking from the tips of his fingers. "You need to think solid. Brick, granite, steel...but not anything as vacuous as clouds."

I drew back. "You can read me through my wall of clouds?" Oh God. This was *so* not good.

"It's a little fuzzy but I get the general gist. You're planning on meeting with Holmes. That came through. I can't let you do that. Not without me there. This is bigger than what Gwen is capable of handling." Again, he stepped into my space, his breath warm on my skin.

My hands rose and I covered my face, trying to blot the image of him out. It was hard to breathe, let alone think with him standing so close to me, especially with the bare, smooth muscles...so touchable. "No! You're wrong! I'm waiting for the police to catch him. Inspector Kreely has a line on where he is."

His hand cupped my cheek and he leaned so close, our noses almost touched. The hot warm energy was making me dizzy. "Don't lie to me, Keira. You gave me the slip in Ireland going off to fight Holmes on your own. I forgive once, but not the next time. It's too dangerous. Do you hear me?"

And just like that, he walked over to the bathroom door. I stood, a molten puddle of goo listening to the water run and the sounds of him brushing his teeth. I took a few breaths, grounding and centering myself. God, it had been too long since I'd been with a guy. He was really getting to me.

When he came out, I squared my shoulders. "I can't allow you to put yourself in danger. You did it once and that was enough. I won't lie to you, Sean. When Holmes calls, I'm going to meet him. It's the only way I can finish this. Those are my terms. If you don't like them, leave now."

"We go together, Keira. Don't you think I want this guy stopped as much as you do? He's psychotic. You can't do it alone." His jaw was set tight, his eyes hard staring down at me.

It was hard to resist his offer. But the scar in his abdomen where he'd been shot was a keen reminder of how close to dying he'd been, fighting Holmes. "I won't be alone. As soon as I find Holmes, Inspector Kreely and the police will be there to arrest him."

"And Kreely is okay with you on your own, walking into what is probably a trap?" His lean, muscled arms crossed over his chest, and there was a small smirk on his face. "Really, Keira? I doubt that very much."

Oh God. My head fell back and I sighed at the ceiling. It was no use. He was too good at this mind reading thing. "No. He wanted you to come with me."

"Aha! See? If you won't listen to me, at least listen to a professional." His hands gripped my shoulders, giving me a small shake. "This is his job, Keira. And it's my job to protect you. Where would you have ended up if I hadn't shown up the last time?"

It was something I shuddered to think about. But it wasn't this cut and dry...not this time. "Holmes will only deal with me. He's threatening my mother this time. If he catches sight of you with me...that could be catastrophic."

"He won't. He didn't know until it was too late, the last time. He won't this time either. As for your mother, she'll be safe here. There're police stationed here." He folded me into his arms and stroked my hair. "Keira, we need to do this together. Promise me, you won't slip away on your own to meet him."

I let myself fall into the warm energy that pulsed through us. It was easy to believe that with our combined power, we could defeat Holmes. It also felt nice to feel safe and cared for. I pulled back and looked up into his eyes. "I'll think about it."

"Good." He gave me a quick kiss on the forehead and released me. "We'll talk more about this tomorrow. Just us."

"Why not now?" The sense of loss, his stepping away was like a kick in the stomach. My fingertips and toes still tingled from the touch of his body next to mine. I took a step closer, reaching for his arm but he stepped back again, strong-arming me with his hand held high.

"We need to rest. And if I stay here any longer, that's not going to happen, is it?" His eyes twinkled and a smile flashed on his face. "You won't be able to control yourself."

I couldn't help rolling my eyes even though there was more than just a kernel of truth to what he said.

"See? You know I'm right." He turned and his step was jaunty walking back to the door.

"You're so stuck on yourself!" I grabbed a pillow from the bed and threw it at him.

"No more than you are!" He dodged the pillow and slipped out of the room.

For not the first time, I wondered what it would be like, if he'd stayed the night with me. All that energy flowing between us!

Twelve

It was almost two am by the time I finally dropped off to sleep. I couldn't help second guessing myself about allowing Sean to help me. And then there were my parents. If Mom and Dad knew what I was planning, meeting with Holmes, they'd have a fit. Gwen would be hurt of course. Or maybe, she'd be relieved. She'd had a harrowing time at Holmes's hands. But I still wasn't sure about putting Sean at risk.

"Keira?"

"Uh huh?" On one level, I knew it was a dream, on another, it felt so real. Nana's voice, the wavy image of her frail form standing at the foot of the bed, her blue eyes sad and solemn, was before me

"Nana?" I could feel the cool air when I sat up and tossed the comforter back.

She floated closer...so close, the scent of roses had instantly filled the room, while her frail hands clasped mine. Even though her hands felt as thin and delicate as ever, a sense of comfort... no, *certitude* enveloped me at her touch.

"Keira. He's going to contact you in two days. Remember what I told you about fear. Holmes fears you and rightfully so. But he isn't alone. He's desperate to use you. You must not allow this."

The enormity of the task, meeting my evil grandfather was paralyzing. "How do I stop him? The police...they'll be there to arrest him. He's even threatening Mom, Nana."

She sniffed and her chin rose high, looking away for a moment. It was so characteristic that it brought tears to my eyes. She'd left waaaay too soon after I'd just met her.

"I know. But you will stop him before that." Her eyes closed for a moment and suddenly we were no longer in my bedroom. The cool, damp air sent a shudder through my shoulders and I looked around. Velvet floral patterns covered the Victorian furniture, the fire in the stone hearth sending a golden glow over the wide planked floor. The room was massive with extremely high ceilings and arched narrow windows.

Nana tugged my hand to get my attention again, "There are people who want to help you. Let them. You will need their help. Give him the tourmaline stone, Keira. He thinks that's where your power lies, but he's wrong. When the time is right, you will subdue him."

"*Subdue him?* I want to kill him! That man is evil, Nana!" Even though I would tell the Inspector about Holmes, I knew this was the way it had to end. He was too powerful and too far gone to lock up. I didn't think for a second that any prison could hold him against his will.

"Love will be your weapon. You must *not* kill him. Fear and rage are Holmes's currency. He knows nothing else. Don't fall into his trap. Love will conquer." Her eyes were sad looking at me.

I leaned forward, squeezing her hand. "I can't, Nana. He needs to die."

"No child. He needs love to finish this. You'll see. Just remember, I'm with you, always." Her words trailed off and her image began to fade.

"No Nana! Don't go!"

"All ways."

And then I was once more in my bed, the tears freely rolling down my cheeks. She was gone. Again.

***

At the soft tap on my door, I rolled over and pulled the pillow over my head. I had just fallen asleep and now, it was morning *already*.

The door creaked opened, "Keira? I brought you a coffee."

When I sat up, Gwen was walking slowly over to the bed, a steaming mug of coffee in her hand. A peek through the window, showed a blue, cloudless sky and the sun radiant in full glory. "Thanks. What time is it?"

"A little before ten. Everyone else is up and had breakfast, but we let you sleep in." She handed the mug to me and then sat next to me on the side of the bed. "How are you feeling?"

"Tired. What little sleep I got was filled with dreams.

"You don't look like they were good dreams."

"No... not really. I dreamed of Nana..."

"Well that's good, isn't it?"

"No, not really. Holmes... well, he was part of the dream too." I took a long sip, watching her over the rim of the mug.

"Oh. Well thank goodness it was only a dream, right?" She stepped to the window and pulled the sheers apart. "It's a beautiful morning and all is well with the world." Unlike me, Gwen was a morning person, her eyes bright above the spray of freckles on her pert nose. There ought to be a law against being so chipper before noon.

"I can't believe that Sean quit his job and is going to work with us." She smiled and picked at a cuticle, trying to sound casual but leaving her comment dangling in the air, waiting for me to take the bait.

But it was an opening for me as well. "Would you mind

if we take him on the next assignment? Or maybe even you and Roy could take a break, maybe go somewhere nice for a romantic holiday. Your time together in Australia kind of got shot with the Holmes thing."

Her eyebrows drew together and she examined me with her eyes. "But you're not taking any assignments...not until we hear from Inspector Kreely, are you?"

I huffed a sharp sigh. "We can't wait forever. Who knows how long it's going to take and I for one, refuse to sit still with Holmes dictating my schedule." This time it was me trying to sound casual. "I might let Mr. Thompson know, I'm available after I've rested a couple more days."

The truth was, after the dream last night, and the leaden lump in my gut telling me I'd be hearing from Holmes, I had to set the stage. But when I left I would be alone. The decision settled, surprising me in its certitude. I cared too much for Gwen and Sean to risk their lives.

"I don't like this. Why the rush? It's not like you need the money and a few weeks isn't going to make that big a difference to any wayward spirit." Her eyes were narrow slits. She wasn't buying this.

It was time to try a new tack to throw her off. "Maybe I want to get away with Sean. See if we can work together or if it was just a one-time thing in Ireland."

Romance. It flashed in her mind and she smiled. "As long as you let Kreely know where you'll be. He can have police watch over you in case Holmes shows up unannounced."

The thought of her brother and I getting together was the deciding factor in her agreement. I was surrounded by matchmakers!

At the second tap on my door, her accomplice stepped into the room—Mom! "Keira? Your father and I were just making a grocery list. Is there anything in particular you'd like me to add?"

It was on the tip of my tongue to come back with a smart ass comment to their meddling—oysters, chocolate, Spanish fly—but I refrained. "Marshmallows, cantaloupe and check the key-lime pie supply. Other than that, gin. Lots of gin."

"Got it. Are you getting up sometime in this century? There's a houseful of people, not to mention armed guards staking out the driveway. Sean—"

"That's what this is all about! You and Gwen plotting and scheming to get Sean and I together!" I threw the covers back and nudged Gwen so that I could get up. "Well Mom, as I was just telling Gwen...You'll be happy to note, I'm thinking of asking Sean on the next assignment."

Mom's eyes darted to Gwen and her mouth fell open. "What about David Holmes? Shouldn't you—"

"No." I pulled my robe from the chair and shoved my arms into it. "I'll be careful and let the police know where I am. Hell, I could even hire bodyguards when I go to amp up the security, but I refuse to put my life on hold."

"You need to talk to your father first. I don't think this is one of your better ideas." It was the 'mater familias' role she played so well, getting all huffy.

"I will but it won't change anything. Actually, Sean's eager to work with me as well." With head high, I walked over to my bathroom and closed the door. Let them chew on that!

Thirteen

When I finished in the shower and walked back into the bedroom to get dressed, I hesitated for a few moments, staring at the oak dresser where my jean shorts and T shirts were tucked. It was a gorgeous day outside, perfect for the orange sundress I'd picked up in Florida. I'd been schlepping around in jeans and yoga pants for too long and it was time to get a little girly. Even if only for a little while before I was summoned by Holmes. Make hay while the sun shines and all that... It had nothing at all to do with Sean being downstairs. Not a thing.

I held the dress up in front of my body, smiling at my reflection in the mirror. It was a good colour for me, making my blue eyes stand out, highlighting the golden tan and blonde hair, a fact that Sean was sure to notice. My cheeks flushed a little when I set the dress aside and reached for my underwear. I was as bad as Mom and Gwen. Still, I took a little longer than normal, blow drying and styling my hair and applying make-up.

When I was completely satisfied with the look, I walked

out of the room and down the stairs. The cop, Brian, looked up from the cell phone in his hand, his net surfing completely forgotten. "Good morning! Are you planning on going out? I'm not sure—"

"No. Just hanging out here, don't worry." I smiled at him and then paused, my heart doing a somersault when I heard Devon and Sean in the living room. I could just go in there and say hi. It was my house after all, but still I hesitated.

My mother stepped into the foyer from the kitchen. "That's a lovely dress, Keira. Did you get that in New York?" Her eyes, as self satisfied as the cat who'd swallowed the canary, darted to the archway of the living room.

Busted. My cheeks became warm and I stammered, "No. Florida. Remember that trip...Gwen and I clearing the Nursing Home?"

"Keira? You're finally..." Sean's mouth fell open and his words trailed off when he stepped into the doorway and saw me. His eyebrows rose high and he smiled. "Wow."

Despite the fact that my cheeks were roasting, I grinned, "Apparently, I don't wear a dress often enough, judging by everyone's reaction. It just felt like a dress kind of day." The 'wow' was a serious understatement to what was really going on in Sean's mind. And the fact that he allowed me in to sense it, was a positive sign.

And if he was smoked by me, I wasn't immune to him either. He was like a tall Greek god, with a shock of dark hair falling over his forehead, his ice blue eyes melting my insides with the intensity of his gaze. The white golf shirt and jeans only accentuated his totally ripped body. He nodded and the slight smirk on his lips told me he was reading me loud and clear as well.

"After you have breakfast, I'd like to get together...and talk." Among other things, flashed in his mind but never left his lips.

"Roy and Gwen are cleaning up in the kitchen but there's a plate set aside for you, Keira. If you and Sean want to go to the sunroom, I'll bring you fresh coffee and your breakfast." Mom stepped between Sean and I, putting her hands on our shoulders and herding us to the sunroom.

We walked side by side, purposely keeping a safe distance so that we didn't touch. I don't think either of us could have stood it, if we had. Behind me, Mom checked in on Devon, playing the perfect hostess before heading to the kitchen.

"Your Mom's nice. Actually, I like both your parents." He smiled down at me and then paused, letting me step into the sunroom ahead of him.

"I think the feeling is mutual. They like Gwen, but I think they're happy to see a man at my side, especially now with that lunatic Holmes, still out there." I plucked a wilted leaf from one of the plants on my way by and took a seat. God. I was getting more and more like my Nana, looking after the greenery.

"Your grandmother's favourite room. I remember having coffee in here with her. In some ways, I regret turning her down. But, maybe I needed her granddaughter to convince me that this is what I should be doing." He took a seat next to me, his leg just barely touching my knee, but sending warm waves of energy through me.

I took a deep breath. "I had a dream about Nana last night. It was so real, that I swear I could smell her perfume." When I looked at him, surprise radiated from his eyes.

"She came to me as well. Funny. I'd swear she was haunting the place if I didn't know better."

My eyebrows creased in thought. Nana didn't move on? I looked around the room trying to sense her presence, but felt nothing. I figured if Nana's spirit was here I'd feel her blaring like a foghorn. After all, just in Australia I felt all those spirits well before I got to the house. I looked at Sean. "You don't think she's here."

"No. I don't feel her at all." He shrugged. "I don't see my mother's spirit back at home, but I do feel her presence as soon as I walk through the door." Sean's mother passed away years ago, and the home he grew up in is just down the country road from the house we were in. When I first met his sister Gwen, I saw his mother's spirit lingering there. Neither Sean nor Gwen are able to see her like I am. Their dad can though.

Even though my mission in life is to help spirits cross over to the next realm to protect the balance of the Universe, I don't have the heart to try to convince her to cross over. I don't have the power to force spirits; just communicate with them and convince them. But Sean and Gwen's mom isn't ready to leave, and neither is her husband Devon ready to fully let go.

Sometimes you gotta make exceptions, right?

"Hey," he nudged me. "You're lost in thought."

"I'm trying to figure out Nana. I think she came to both of us somehow. Is she able to cross back and forth? I've never met any other spirit that was able to."

He snorted. "If anyone could, it would be Pamela." He glanced up when my mother appeared in the doorway carrying a tray of food.

"Here you go! If you want anything else, I'm afraid you'll have to fend for yourselves. Your father and I are going to take the boat out and Devon's beating Gwen and Roy in a game of rummy." She set the tray down and her gaze drifted between Sean and I, her smile so obvious that once more my cheeks flared hotly.

"Thanks Susan. Enjoy your boat ride." Sean beamed up at her and reached for his mug of coffee.

She winked at me and then was gone. I grinned and then quipped to diffuse the clear attempt at her matchmaking. "You realize she's picturing grandchildren, don't you? I'm sorry about that." I sneaked a peek at him before reaching for the omelette and plate of toast. But he was laughing, so he totally understood.

"She'd make an awesome grandmother, spoiling and coddling your kids."

In a flash, I threw up a brick wall around my mind and shielded my thoughts. What the hell? 'Your kids?' He'd shut me down in no uncertain terms, saying that. There was no 'our kids'. It might be a silly comment and crazy for me to react like this but still it stung. He should have just said, 'she'd make an awesome grandmother' and leave it at that.

Maybe I was getting ahead of myself like Mom and Gwen, but I didn't care. It *hurt*. I sat straighter, shifting my leg away from his, catching the puzzled look on his face from the corner of my eyes.

Sean could probably have any girl he wanted. This was just shits and giggles for him, a mild flirtation. It should be for me as well. My stomach fell. If only the crack about grandchildren had never left my mouth.

It was time to get back on track here. "I told Gwen and Mom that I'm taking you on my next assignment—kind of a trial run to see if we can work together, although I'm still not convinced it could work." I stabbed some egg and popped it into my mouth. The way his head pulled back a bit at my words gave me a little satisfaction. Yeah, I know. Sometimes I can be childish, wanting to hit back.

"You're not sure?"

I chewed and slowly swallowed, relishing the disbelief in his eyes. "That's right."

He scoffed. "I kinda think I was a fair bit of help the last time I stepped in you know." His neck was getting red and I was enjoying every bit of it.

I shrugged and speared another forkful. "Maybe. Maybe not. After all, it was you who wound up in the hospital, right?"

"Taking a bullet for you." His voice was dead level. Good. Now we both were stung. Fair is fair.

I put down my fork. "If you say so."

"I do say so."

I made a short wave with my hand. "Whatever. At any rate, I'm pretty sure I'll be hearing from Holmes again."

"Well...if Holmes contacts you, I'm going with you." The

wall in his mind was firmly in place as well, shutting me out.

"Maybe. Maybe the Inspector has caught him and we won't need to worry anymore." I took a sip of coffee watching him over the rim. I was still smarting from the rebuke about the grandchildren. "I also told them I could hire private security as well for the next assignment. You wouldn't mind that, would you? I could have some buff bodyguard tucking me in at night. That would be fine with me." I smiled sweetly and pushed the plate away, my appetite now gone.

"Sure. Suit yourself." He pushed back his chair and rose. "Let me know when you get the call from Holmes or even a new assignment. I'm going to join Gwen and Dad for a while." The brick wall fell away for a moment. *'Bitch'*. Was his parting thought.

Fine!

Fourteen

The next forty-eight hours were entirely miserable for everyone staying in my house. The chill between Sean and I had Gwen and Mom walking on eggshells, wondering what had happened. Dad and Devon managed to stay above the fray, exchanging silent glances above the chessboard when either me or Sean happened to drop into the living room.

Roy spent the time rifling through the recipe book, trying new things but mostly avoiding being anywhere near Sean or I. Even Brian kept to himself, stationed at the door or going outside to chat with his fellow cops. Dinners were a sullen and hurried affair.

I still hadn't heard from Holmes. That, plus Sean's cold shoulder, his nose surgically inserted in a book ignoring me, were playing on my last nerve.

Finally, I'd had enough. It was just the two of us in the living room, killing time until we could justify going to bed. I strode past him, purposely knocking his feet off the ottoman on my way by. "Hey! Would you like a drink? I'm getting one...or maybe one dozen is more like it."

"What the hell is wrong with you?" He rose to his feet, glowering down at me. I didn't need to read his thoughts to know how pissed off he was. His fingers curled and uncurled into tight fists. If I was a man I'm sure he would have belted me.

"Nothing." I poured the gin into the shaker, purposely letting my guard slip to the side for a few moments. *You hurt my feelings, Asshat!*' It was a blaring scream that I projected at him before the wall once more wrapped tight around me.

He nudged me aside and took the shaker from me, adding lime juice and sugar. *'Having a hard time finding any hot security guys to keep your bed warm?'* The bitter force of his thought made me falter for a moment.

When he turned to hand the drink to me, my hand flew up to slap his face. How dare he say that! But his fingers caught my hand in a steel grip.

"You were the one who said it, not me." His face was so close, I could smell his aftershave, while his eyes stabbed me to the core. "Grow up, Keira!" He flicked his wrist, flinging my hand away before taking a long haul of the gimlet.

"You're *such* a jerk." I took my glass and walked over to the sofa, flicking a piece of fluff from the surface before sliding into the soft cushions.

"Again with the name calling. I don't know what bee crawled up your ass but I've had it with your snarky moods. For two cents, I'd leave you to deal with Holmes on your own." He flopped down on the sofa, keeping his distance at the other end of it.

"Good. Who asked you to? You'd probably slow me down anyway." I sniffed and downed half the glass. I needed another drink if I had to sit here and listen to him anymore. I focussed on the shaker, picturing it on the table in front of me. It rose from the sideboard and drifted slowly across the room, coming to a soft landing on the coffee table. For once, my levitation skills were spot on. Usually I missed the mark and considering who was sitting watching, that would have been hugely embarrassing.

When I leaned forward to refill my glass, the shaker slid away, perched perilously close to the edge of the table. My gaze shot to Sean, who had a satisfied grin plastered on his mug. He'd done that! I hadn't known he was capable of telekinesis!

I focused once more. I smiled when the silver canister slid back to my hand. But before my fingers could make contact, it moved away again.

"Stop that!" I leaned over about to grab it when it lifted high in the air above me.

I glared at him and then popped up higher, my hand swiping for the shaker. Again, it moved just out of range of my fingers.

"Say you're sorry and I'll let you have it." He smiled at me but his eyes were still hard steel.

"I'll let *you* have it if you don't give me that bloody shaker!" This time I leapt up and grabbed it. But it was too fast and it tipped, spilling gin gimlet all over my arm and chest.

He burst out laughing, glancing over at me and trying to stop. That was it! I took what was left in my glass, ice cubes and all and dumped it on his lap.

The grin on his face faded, "Okay? Are we done now? Can we be adults again and talk?" He plucked the ice cubes off and popped them back into my glass. "You were hurt, I get it. It was the 'your kids' comment, wasn't it?"

"Yes." It came out small and petulant. I pulled the soaking wet shirt away from my body, looking down at the soggy mess of my clothes.

"Sorry. I'm just not sure I'll ever have kids. That's way down the road, if ever." He got to his feet and held his hand out, helping me to my feet. "Do you want to go get changed? I know I do. If anyone comes in here, they'll think..." He rolled his eyes, censoring what he was about to say, "...that I'm incontinent or something."

I grinned and then my fingers closed around his, as he helped me to my feet. Damn! It hit before either of us could take a breath—that old power exchange running full tilt between us. I saw his eyes spark as he felt it too. We held hands walking from the room and up the stairs. There were no barriers between us, only relief that we'd got past the tiff without killing one another.

He held my bedroom door for me and I stepped inside. When it snicked closed behind me, I could feel his presence, knew where this was leading...oh God, I couldn't wait. His fingers cupped my cheek and he bent lower to kiss me. If the touch of our hands sparked a surge of energy that tingled in every cell, his kiss would be a flame thrower.

Our mouths met— oh boy...

I pulled him closer, my hands gripping the back of his neck, my tongue dancing a tango with his...falling into the surge, hungry for more. His thoughts, desires filled my head, amplifying my own. We pulsed against each other, our hands drifting softly, pulling into each other. The wet shirt and pants were forgotten; there was only the kiss... and what a kiss. It took kiss to a level I had never thought existed.

If a kiss was this awesome, what would...?

Sean was on the same page. His hand slithered between us and fingers flicked the top two buttons of my shirt open. I panted into his skin, my tongue tasting the sweet saltiness of his neck.

Tap. Tap. Tap.

We both pulled back but not before my father's head popped in, next to the edge of the door.

He cleared his throat and looked down for a moment. "Uh...sorry. But Sean, your Dad needs you to go to the house. Your neighbors have returned his dog. Apparently he howled the last couple of nights and they've had enough."

I could feel Sean's panting breath, and saw the look of embarrassment in his eyes facing my father. I buttoned my shirt and caught Dad's gaze dropping to the wet spot in Sean's crotch. My face and neck were a furnace knowing how this looked. "I spilled a drink, Dad. I was going to get changed and—"

"Sure. No problem." He backed out and the door closed softly.

Sean shook his head from side to side, blowing out a fast gush of air. "You know how this looks right? It's not bad enough that he caught us in your room, kissing but..." He tugged at the front of his pants. "THIS? I look like a teenage boy, for God's sake!"

This time it was me who had to hide the grin and laughter. "Just go! Get the stupid dog. I think the moment is over anyway."

"Just for now." He leaned over and kissed my forehead. "Another time and definitely another place." He popped out the door and his footsteps clumped down the stairs.

Fifteen

I was still smiling reliving the scene, when I peeled off the blouse and tossed it into the hamper. Should I tell Mom what had just happened? Or *Gwen*? It was a choice that made me giggle.

At the ringing of my cell phone, I stopped and looked over at the dresser where it sat. I didn't even need to pick it up to know who it was. The fun was over. The man's timing was abysmal or perfect, depending on who looked at it.

I picked it up, my jaw tightening when I saw 'Unknown Caller' on the screen. "Yes? What do you want?"

"Is that any way to greet your grandfather, Keira? You can be so cold—must be your father's influence. How are he and Susan? You've got quite a household right now, don't you? Hail, hail, the gang's all here." It was meant to be light and amusing but as usual it came off greasy slick.

"Where are you?" Just because he knew about the guests staying with me, didn't mean *he* was anywhere close by. He had his minions everywhere.

"I'm in my old haunt, the UK. I love it here...so much

history. Why don't you join me? There are quite a few homes and castles that I own here."

"Ireland? Again? Really Holmes, that's getting old. Why not somewhere warm on a beach? Surely you own some beachfront in the south of France. Never been there and I'd love to see it." There was no way I was going to make this easy for him. He wanted me to team up with him? Well, he'd better start dancing to my tune.

Nana had said he was actually frightened by my power. But his slick, sweet tone didn't show anything like that.

"Catch the one ten flight to Dublin at Toronto Airport. Air Canada, the tickets are booked. All you need to do is bring your passport and come alone. No Gwen, her brother or anyone. Got that, girl?"

"Got it, *old man*. You just leave my parents and friends out of this. I swear if you make any more threats against them, I'll finish you." Nana's words from my dream played in my mind—the tourmaline stone, his mistaken thought that it was the source of my power. It was time to dangle a carrot.

"Even if I agree to work with you, I'm not sure what exactly you hope to accomplish."

"Oh, you will work with me, once you know what we can achieve. You can't even imagine the possibilities. Eternal life, even. I'll be in touch when you land."

The phone went dead in my hand. He was truly psychotic. Eternal life...yeah, right. With the tips of my fingers, I set the phone down. Even talking to him made my skin want to crawl off my body. How could this man be related to me? What had Nana ever seen in him?

A shudder rippled in my shoulders and I crossed the room to take a shower. I'd have to let Inspector Kreely know about this. And there was no way I would see Sean when he got back with Devon's dog. It wasn't worth the chance that Sean would know somehow that Holmes had made contact. But the bigger challenge would be keeping him in the dark that I was going, on my own.

Shit! I'd have to be out of the house before eight to make it to Toronto for the flight, especially an international flight. I also needed to get out of the house while everyone was sleeping, even if I had to sit around waiting longer at the airport. That meant I had a few hours to pack, call Inspector Kreely and try to catch an hour or so of sleep before the drive.

As I was about to slip out of my wet clothes and take a shower, there was a light tap at my door. Oh no. It had to be Sean. I took a deep breath envisioning a brick wall, hiding my thoughts and plans. When I opened the door, Sean's face lit up and he smiled, causing a few bricks to wedge free. For just a moment I was caught off guard. Did he have to be so damned cute with that lock of hair that flipped onto his forehead, his face glowing from racing up the stairs?

"Hey! You want to pick up where we left off? I'm game." The smile fell from his lips and his eyes pierced through me. "What's up?"

Damn, he was good. "Nothing. I'm just tired. The dog problem's resolved?"

"Yeah. He's in Dad's room. That's okay, right?" He stepped forward, cupping my cheek with his warm hand. "Keira? What's up? You have a funny look in your eyes."

For a moment I was tempted to tell him, agree to his help in the confrontation with Holmes. His look of concern and affection was a laser melting the core of my body and resolve. The decision I had just made faltered and wobbled. I chewed my bottom lip as we gazed at each other.

The expression of delighted anticipation fell from his face and he took a deep breath. "Okay. You don't want to talk...I get it. Just when we seem to be connecting, you shut me down." He stepped back from the door and turned. Looking back over his shoulder, his smile was weak, "Get some sleep. Maybe, you're right. The timing isn't the best...with this Holmes thing and your parents just down the hall."

I nodded and closed the door gently, feeling the weight of the world cascade onto my shoulders. Tears stung the back of my eyes and I could only stand there silently. It was so unfair! Holmes had put another wedge between Sean and me. If not for my horrible grandfather, I'd be with Sean right now. The first guy I seriously liked in a long, long time, for sure. Who am I kidding? I have never been this smitten. And he was attracted to me as well! Hell! He even wanted to be at my side in this battle, despite the fact the last time he'd almost died! Damn that David Holmes!

My hands rose to swipe at the tears but more flowed from the corners of my eyes. Mom and Dad...even Gwen. I had to leave all of them in order to save them from that evil old man. Leave my home and possibly never see any of them again. The sadness in Sean's eyes when he turned away haunted me as much as any spirit I ever dealt with during a transition through The Veil.

I walked over to the dresser and grabbed a tissue, blowing my nose and trying to get a grip. There was no other way. I had to do this alone. I held the tissue between knotted fingers. No. Not alone. Nana had said there were people ready to help me and that I should let them. God, did she mean Sean? I shook my head. Not Sean. In this I was adamant, even if Nana had meant him to assist me in the upcoming battle. My eyes narrowed. Again, it all came round to Holmes. I had to *destroy* him if I was ever to live my life.

Her words of fighting that beast with love echoed in my head. Love! Ha! There was no way I could do as she wanted and show even a morsel of compassion. I took a deep breath and turned, striding towards the closet to get my suitcase. First things first. I threw the suitcase on the bed and grabbed my phone. It would be very early morning in England but I didn't think Inspector Kreely would mind. He'd said to call him anytime, day or night when I heard from Holmes.

After about six rings, his hoarse voice filled the small cell phone, "Hello?"

"It's Keira, Dan. Sorry to wake you but I heard from...Holmes." His name on my tongue made me almost gag.

"What? Where is he?" His voice was sharper now and I could picture him sitting forward, all thoughts of sleep gone. "Finally a line on *that bastard*". I could almost hear his teeth gritting.

"He's booked a ticket for me to fly to Dublin tomorrow afternoon at around one." Whether it was the anger in his voice or just that my pity fest had cried itself out, I felt stronger, ready to do this. "Can you contact the security force in Kingston and tell them I'm meeting up with you? I'm leaving for Toronto in a couple of hours and I don't know how I'll get past them without waking the whole house up."

"You're coming alone? Where's Sean? Isn't he going to be with you?"

My heart lurched low in my gut and I sighed. "No. I need to do this on my own, Dan."

"I don't think that's a good idea but you can count on me to be there. I'll be at the airport waiting and watching. You won't be alone. I'll make the call to Kingston. Be careful, Keira."

With that, the phone went dead. Time to pack and get ready to face my enemy.

Sixteen

It was just after midnight, Dublin time when I finished going through Customs. The airport was bustling with people arriving or waiting to catch a flight. I trekked the long corridor to the front of the airport, pulling my luggage behind me. I hadn't seen any sign of Inspector Kreely or police watching me, but my intuition screamed that they weren't far away, probably following my every move.

I paused next to a low upholstered bench and flopped down. I unzipped my suitcase and found the burner phone. Kreely and I had agreed that I would get one and we'd use that phone to communicate. Holmes had my other phone number, and with his resources who knew if he was able to listen in? We weren't going to take a chance. I turned it on and stuffed it into my purse and fished out my regular cell phone.

I turned it on and my stomach lurched seeing the number of times Sean had tried to call as well as Gwen and my parents. They would all be worried sick about me. Before I had a chance to dial in for messages, the phone rang, startling me back to the situation at hand.

It was Holmes. He sure didn't waste any time. My jaw tightened. "What? I'm here."

"Welcome to the Emerald Isle, Keira! I trust your flight was good."

When there was no response to his easy banter, his tone changed and became more officious. "Go to Terminal One, Gate C8. A black Rolls will pull up there in ten minutes. It will take you to your next destination."

My eyes narrowed, "Where would that be? I'm sick of your cat and mouse games, Holmes. Either tell me, or I'm on the next plane outta here."

"I won't do that. You've tried tricking me before, girl. Sorry, but my game, my rules. You know the penalty for cheating. How *is* your mother, by the way?"

I peered around the airport hoping for any sight of Inspector Kreely. If they were watching, and I was pretty sure they were, they had to know that Holmes had made contact. "You're such an asshole! My mother, *your* daughter, is fine...under armed protection, I might add."

"Brian Fowler? He works for me, Keira. Amazing how little it takes to buy people, isn't it?"

The wind went out of my sails. I had to let Kreely know this. But it made me wonder even about him even. What if Holmes had found *his* price?

"Fine! But if you touch one hair on her head, you'll pay with your life! I'm on my way." I clicked off and then continued, looking for the lady's bathroom. I had to call or text Dan Kreely and let him know this. I had no idea how many of Holmes' people were watching me, but surely a bathroom break wouldn't be too suspicious.

I had barely closed the door to the stall when the burner phone beeped. I got it out of my purse and saw the message.

WHERE TO NOW? KREELY.

I sunk down onto the toilet seat, while my fingers flew over the keyboard.

TERMINAL ONE, GATE C8, BLACK
ROLLS PICKING ME UP, TEN
MINUTES. BRIAN FOWLER WORKS
FOR HOLMES. I'LL BE IN TOUCH.

I flushed the toilet in case there was someone outside the stall watching me. When the phone was secure in the secret compartment of my purse, I left the stall. But if Holmes was watching, the bathroom was empty now.

As soon as I found the gate number and stepped outside, the Rolls pulled up and stopped. A husky, black man in a suit got out from behind the wheel, rounding the car to take my bag.

Out of nowhere a van came to a screeching halt behind the Rolls. Two women, dressed in black shirts and pants like Ninja jumped out of the passenger doors! The first one, a muscular black woman rushed the Rolls driver and he crumpled like a rag doll, onto the sidewalk.

The second woman almost yanked my arm out of its socket, dragging me to the gaping side door of the van. "Quick! Get in!" Her accent was French or Swiss; it was hard to tell, but judging by the white blonde pony tail flipping over her shoulder, I'd guess Scandinavian.

"Who are you? Are you with Holmes?" I stood my ground, holding the sides of the van to avoid getting trapped inside with them.

The driver turned, revealing dark flashing eyes above high swarthy cheekbones. A mane of dark wavy hair framed her pretty, middle aged face. "No. Just get in. We're friends. Hurry! We've got to get out of here."

"Who sent you? Sean? My parents?"

"No. No they didn't." She had a funny look on her face—almost amused at the situation.

The second woman shoved me again. "Okay? Satisfied? We have to GO!" She shoved again and I lurched forward, barely managing from falling flat on my face. The door banged shut and she pressed into me, pushing me to the seat.

I pushed back, shrugging her hand off me. "Hold on! I don't know you. I'm supposed to be in that Rolls!"

"Trust us. You don't want that." The driver's eyes met mine in the rear view mirror for a moment before the van wheeled out and sped down the roadway in front of the airport gates. I managed to slide into the seat and grab my seatbelt.

My jaw tightened. "You don't understand. My mother will be hurt or even killed, if I don't show up in that car."

But it was the black woman sitting next to me who answered, "Susan is fine. Everyone you left behind in Kingston is fine. We made sure of that. We've been following your progress for some time now."

"Who are you?" They knew my mother...where I live, were watching me?

The blonde in the front passenger seat turned to face me. She was close to my own age with a clear almost translucent quality to her pale face. Her dark blue eyes softened a little watching me.

It was only then that I realized that I hadn't picked up any thoughts or emotions on my psychic radar. Whoever they were, they were gifted and powerful.

"We're Illuminata. I'm Astrid." She nodded to the driver, "She's Zara and—"

"I'm Shaniqua." For the first time a slight smile played on her full scarlet lips, the only sign of make-up on a face that sure didn't need embellishment with the wide flashing eyes and high smooth forehead. "And of course you're Keira Swanson, Pamela's granddaughter."

My gaze flitted between Shaniqua and Astrid. "I thought Illuminati were some secret society of men. Kind of an old boy network." I shook my head. "Waitaminnit. You knew my grandmother?" Surely they couldn't be all bad if they were watching over my parents and knew Nana.

This time it was Zara, glancing into the rear view mirror to meet my eyes, "We met Pamela only a few times but we have followed her work for years. She was trying to achieve the same things we are—harmony and order. She focused on The Veil, the afterlife while we work primarily in this realm."

"There *is* a society of males, the Illuminati who are all about power, money and greed. The Illuminata are women. Earth mothers and daughters seeking peace and survival of all life. We know about David Holmes and his plans. You cannot join with him. We can't allow that." Shaniqua reached over and squeezed my hand, softening her words with a warm smile.

"I wasn't *going* to help him. I want to stop him for good this time. We agree on that at least." But their methods..." You're as bad as Holmes kidnapping me like this, endangering my mother!"

"Anyone in this van put a gun to your head?" Astrid sneered back at me.

She had a point there. "Okay. Where are we going?"

"We own an Abby on the outskirts of the city. You'll stay with us until we come up with a plan to take care of Holmes." Zara's small nose and profile were highlighted in the headlights from oncoming cars, as I watched her. She was the leader of this troupe. It showed in her age and confident tone.

Still, their methods left me cold. "Look, I *had* a plan and I wasn't alone. You may have sealed my parents' fate by interfering like this." I glanced over at Shaniqua and sighed.

"We know about the Inspector. So does Holmes, by the way."

"Oh damn..." I couldn't help but worry about everyone back in Kingston.

Zara caught my eye. "Your family is safe. Our people intercepted a few of his men, on their way to your house a couple hours ago, and I don't believe there are any more with that task. Holmes is powerful yes, but he's also stretched thin you know." Before I could say anything about the cop at the house Holmes bribed, she continued. "As for Brian Fowler, he's one of ours, even though he's also on

Holmes's payroll."

"What? Like a double agent?"

Shaniqua chuckled. "More like a triple agent or something, but yes, he's on our side." She tilted her head at me. "Which means *your* side."

Zara turned once more, "Your grandmother visited me in a dream. She asked us to help you fight Holmes."

Just like in my dream the other night where she'd told me when Holmes would contact me. She'd also said there were people who would help me. This had to be them—the Illuminata. I was definitely not alone in this.

Oh God! Inspector Kreely! I fished the burner cell phone from my purse. I was about to dial his number but Shaniqua's hand covered mine. The thought blared in my mind. *'No. Not your phone. You can make any calls once we're safe at the Abby.'*

And like clockwork, Astrid turned to gaze at me as well as Zara eyeing me in the mirror. I nodded and silently pulsed the thought, *'Okay.'* It was weird doing this with almost total strangers. But I had the feeling they were about to become powerful allies.

Seventeen

We had left the glare of the city and were now in the countryside. "How much farther?" I stifled a yawn. I'd been up for more than 24 hours and I was worn out. I tried to sleep on the plane, but I wasn't able to. "And just what is this Abby?"

"Five minutes. The Abby is a private place for girls with special abilities." Zara's forehead met mine from the rear view mirror. "Indigo children. Have you heard the term before?"

I shook my head.

"They were first identified in the nineties as children possessing an indigo aura. They usually are diagnosed at a young age as having learning disabilities." She gave a sharp shake of her head in disgust. "In reality, it's because they are gifted with paranormal or sensitive abilities. They have trouble fitting into conventional schools. We give them something they never had before in a school setting, Keira."

"Kind of like Hogwarts? These kids are learning to be wizards or something?" I couldn't help the snigger that erupted from my chest.

Zara eyed me in the mirror; her mouth twitched in disappointment. "No, not like that. We give them a place where they're accepted." Her eyes flitted from the road to mine. "Many children who are gifted have a hard time fitting in with other kids, don't you agree?" She watched me closely.

Oh God. It came back to me in a rush. First grade. 'Krazy Keira'. I dropped my head, staring down at my fingers. Almost twenty years later and it still hurt like hell. Mom and Dad put me in another school, yeah; but I always was the odd man out. I didn't read minds or anything like that—kids just sensed that I was 'weird' in some way. And were cruel. I spent that time of my life keeping as low a profile as I could and it worked. I never got...not one...invitation to a sleep over.

Zara's voice was gentle, just loud enough to be heard. "These children's gifts manifested very strongly at a young age, Keira. They are powerful, and frightened those around them with their gifts...gifts they themselves are still trying to understand." I looked up at her. "The difficulties you may have had when you were small were a hundred times greater for these children."

I turned to Shaniqua. "I want you to be honest with me."

Shaniqua huffed a sigh that hit me in the face. "What do you think I've been doing here?"

"What was it like for you in the fourth grade?" I tried to make my expression with as stony an expression as I could manage, but my left eye still twitched from remembering the pain.

"Fourth grade?" Shaniqua's head snapped like I'd just slapped her. Her lips were a firm line. She looked me dead in the eye. "They made fun of me..."

"Why"

"Because I was weird."

"Too sensitive, too odd -ball?"

She made a sad smile that I recognized instantly; I had

made the same one a million times as a kid. "Yes...I knew when there would be surprise quizzes, I knew what boy liked what girl..."

"And what girl wanted what boy to like her." When she nodded, I added, "And you thought everyone knew that, right?"

"Yes. So when I talked about it, I couldn't understand why they were so shocked." She leaned over and tapped my thigh. "They thought I was weird, just like what happened to you."

From behind the wheel Zara snorted, "Yeah. And that was only the warm-up for puberty." We all laughed.

"Still sounds like Hogwarts to me, then. All the 'gifted' children gathered in one place, right?"

"No it's more of a sanctuary than school, although we have a curriculum of academic study. They're special and need to be sheltered."

"Sheltered?"

Zara nodded. "Think of these children like refugees, not in a special prep school, Keira."

"What do you mean?"

Beside me, Shaniqua huffed a long sigh, "Ever read about Anne Frank? The Abby is more like the house Anne hid in than Hogwarts or *Miss Peregrine's School for Gifted Children*, believe me. There are governments and powerful businesses that would use these girls for their own gain." Her eyes narrowed and her breath became more cold and steady. "Imagine the power the CIA would have if its spies could read minds. Who could control the CIA then?"

Astrid piped up. "Or businesses using them for industrial espionage."

"Or like my grandfather."

Zara nodded. "We believe your grandfather is a greater threat than any government or business organization. Others want profit or power, he wants to destroy the nature of things."

And he needs me to accomplish it. When I was with

Gwen, my own powers were magnified. When I was with Sean *everything* became a lot more intense. How much would Holme's own gifts be enhanced with my willing assistance?

Shaniqua nudged me. "You need the sanctuary of the Abby too, Keira."

Not me. I need to handle Holmes on my own. I kept my silence and kept my mind walled off. "I don't know about that," I replied. I looked out the side window, watching the dark shapes of trees and fields as the car slowed. Indigo children. So there were other people, aside from the three women in the car who were gifted like me. Children who had difficulty fitting into society or even school because of their psychic gifts. Kids who would be used and moulded for the benefit a select group...kind of like Holmes wanted with me.

Zara flipped the turn signal on even though we hadn't passed another car in the last few miles. We were in the middle of nowhere.

The van turned down a long rough driveway and came to a stop outside a stone, three story building. Only a single light shone from a stained glass transom above the door. Zara turned and smiled, "We're here." She got out of the van and then unlocked the massive oak door, holding it wide for me to step inside.

I looked around, feeling the strongest sense of deja vu that I'd ever experienced. I'd been there before! The wide gleaning plank floor, the velvet floral upholstery, the high ceilings...And then it hit me! It was the place in my dream the other night! This was the house Nana and I had been in!

Shaniqua's hand lifted to rest on my shoulder, "If you're hungry, I can fix you something to eat."

When I turned, I looked straight in her eyes. We were the same height but she was heavier, and her arms and shoulders were well defined with muscle, like a panther. Before I could reply the beep of the cell phone in my purse, caused me to jump. I looked over at Zara, holding my phone out. "It's Holmes. What should I tell him?" By now he would know I wasn't in the Rolls on my way to see him.

She tugged the dark hoodie from her body and hung it by the door. When she turned her fingers threaded through her hair pulling her dark locks away from her face, "Tell him you found another ride. It's time to push back. He doesn't know about us and it's got to stay that way for the Indigos. Actually, don't answer. Who knows if he can somehow trace you here. He can wait."

My fingers trembled a little as I watched the cell phone, saw the 'Unknown Caller' message. But it was time to take control. I let it go to voice mail.

I smiled, feeling some of the weight drift from my shoulders. It felt good to be in a position of strength, with friends to help. Even through the cell phone, I had felt the white rage in Holmes's mind. His granddaughter was no longer dancing to his plans and machinations.

Astrid picked my suitcase up from the floor. "I'll take this up for you. I want to check on the girls anyway. We don't go out that often and..." The rest of her words were lost as she hurried from the room.

Zara shrugged and smiled over at me. "Astrid is our resident worrier. She was abused as a child and came to us when she was only seven. She's been here ever since. We're her family now and she's pretty protective." She pulled herself to her feet and stretched her arms over her head, before wandering across the room to the sideboard. "Care for a glass of port? It will help you sleep. This old place creaks and bangs all night long."

"Make it a double in that case." I gazed around the room, recognizing the furniture even to the dark wainscot and floral sofa. "I got the strangest feeling when I came in here. I've been here before."

She smiled as she handed me a glass of ruby liquid. "You have. You were here with your grandmother a few nights ago. It's the farthest you've ever been in your astral travels." She flopped down onto the sofa arranging her feet under her ample hip, before patting the spot next to her.

"I thought it was a dream."

"No, it wasn't."

Astral travelling. I'd heard of it of course. It had come up in a conversation with Nana. I took the seat next to Zara, still gazing round the room in wonderment. "You know a lot about me...things *I* don't even know."

"We've been interested in you since you were a little girl. Pamela told us you would carry on the line. Although for a while it looked like it might even be a young man who would do that. She was quite excited about him."

Nana wasn't the only one 'excited' about Sean. "Yeah... well..."

"No matter. It's come to you and Holmes." Her fingers threaded through her hair, lifting and tucking it behind her head. A few silver hairs at her temple glinted in the light when she turned to smile at me, her teeth brilliant in her Indonesian features. "I'm glad it was you, though. Especially now with David Holmes acting up."

She made him sound like an errant schoolboy instead of the psychotic maniac I knew him to be. And she had to be referring to Sean when she mentioned the young man. I rolled my eyes and sighed. Sean. If not for that damned Holmes. I turned to her, "Nana told me to subdue him but not to kill him. Love. That's the weapon she said to use."

She nodded. "I know that's hard to hear. He almost killed two of your friends. But your grandmother was..." a chuckle tickled her lips, '...or rather her energy still *is*, sharp as a tack. Hopefully, that option will be open to us. Holmes is his own worst enemy." She reached in her pocket and pulled a small cell phone out, extending it to me. "I don't like you using your cell phone anymore than you have to. Here. Use this. You'd better call your police friend."

I dug out my burner phone. "I can use this one."

She shook her head. "No. Use this one, it's safer, believe me. Now call your police friend. He's probably worried Holmes got to you."

Inspector Kreely wasn't the only one. My shoulders

slumped thinking of the people I'd left at home. I took the phone from her and then grabbed my own from my purse to get the number. After a couple rings, Inspector Kreely's 'hello' was puzzled, if not downright defensive.

"Hi Dan. It's Keira. I'm okay. I'm with friends of my grandmother's. They picked me up at the airport before Holmes had a chance. I'm staying here for a few days."

"Where exactly is *that*, Keira?"

I glanced over at Zara and she nodded. Even if she didn't read minds, Dan's voice blared through the phone. His frustration and worry for me came through loud and clear. It was just one more twist in the quest to find Holmes and arrest him. "It's an old hide-away in the country. Miles from Dublin. Ah..." I watched Zara shake her head from side to side. "I can't tell you where. I'll let you know when I hear from Holmes again."

"And if you do, what are your intentions?" He sighed. "As if I didn't know."

"I intend to put a stop to him," I replied, my voice even. "I'll let you know when I'm leaving."

"I don't like this." There was a pause before he continued, "We got the guy who was driving the Rolls. He couldn't tell us much, just that some agency hired him. He was still groggy from whatever drug your friends hit him with."

Zara leaned closer and grinned, speaking close to the phone. "We didn't drug him, actually. Just a persuasive word and the right touch."

"Who was that?" This was followed by another exasperated sigh. It had been a long day for Dan. "Never mind. You probably can't say anyway." He paused. "Keira, Sean contacted me."

My heart leap-frogged into my throat. Of course Sean would contact the Inspector. He knew that I was bound to be working with him. "What did you tell him?"

There was a fast huff. "Just that you were on your way to Dublin. He said he was catching the first flight he could and that he'd contact me when he arrives. He was pretty upset."

That was an understatement. Him, my parents, Gwen. All the messages on my phone were testament to that sad fact. I'd listen to them when I went up to my room later, when I could be alone with my emotions.

"I don't want Sean involved with this Dan. This is my problem and I'll deal with it."

"*We'll* deal with it you mean. I'm not sure how I can stop Sean but I'll try. Just call me when you hear from Holmes again and for heaven's sake, *be careful.*"

There was a click and the line went dead. I handed the phone back to her and sighed. On one hand I couldn't deny the glimmer of happiness that Sean cared enough to insist on being there but...what if this time he didn't survive. All because of me. I could never live with myself if something really bad happened to him.

"He's on his way, isn't he?" Zara's eyebrows arched and she smiled. "Try not to worry about that. Things will work out with Sean."

If she knew him, she wouldn't say that. This was probably the last straw for him. I'd lied to him, made him think I'd bring him with me to help in my confrontation with Holmes. They say that the road to hell is paved with good intentions, and they're right. I felt like hell for what I was putting the people I cared about through.

Astrid entered the room and walked over to the table to get a glass of wine. Her face that had seemed so flawless in the dim light of the car, now showed furrows between her pale eyebrows. There were few laugh lines bordering her mouth.

"I'd say we deserve this after tonight." She turned and carried the glass to take a seat across from us. "All's quiet upstairs, Zara. Lilli was still awake watching a movie. She'll see you in the morning, Keira."

Zara nudged me with her hand. "Lilli's a doll. She cooks and generally runs the day to day maintenance of the house. You'll have to be careful of her pastries. They're addictive,

I'm afraid."

"Speaking of which!" Shaniqua appeared with a tray of cheese and what looked like French croissants. She set the tray on the coffee table and then took a seat next to me. It was a regular girls' party, except for the fact that it was a diabolical grandfather who'd brought us together.

She turned to me. "No more than one drink for you. Zara and I talked. We think you need to learn control and how to better use astral travelling. Sometimes, the time around dawn is best, when you're relaxed and barely awake. I'll be in at five thirty."

The time of day was ridiculously early, yet I nodded. I'd done it, yet I hadn't even been aware of it.

Astrid leaned forward skewering Zara with her eyes. "Do you think that's wise, Zara? I mean we're taking a big enough chance as it is. We've got the girls to think of. In the astral plane, Shaniqua can't control everything. "She glanced at me, arching her eyebrow, "...especially when she's dealing with a *neophyte*."

A neophyte? She might have spent most of her life at the Abby, being immersed in this psychic crap but I was Pamela York's *granddaughter*. I sat straighter, shooting a dark look at her. If she could read my thoughts (if she was even *capable* of that kind of power!), she wouldn't like my smartass comeback.

Before I could say a word, Shaniqua spoke up. "I believe I'm the one most qualified on questions of astral travel, dear." Her voice was firm.

"Ladies! It's been a long day for all of us. We'll finish our wine and then get a good night's sleep." Zara had the final word and Astrid's pale cheeks flushed a lovely pink.

Eighteen

I was dreading it but it had to be done. Nestled in between crisp cotton sheets, and plush down duvet, I clicked my phone to listen to my messages.

Sean — *"Keira! You had to do it, didn't you! Go off on your own, taking your life in your hands! You really have no clue what you're up against. Where are you? Call me!"*

I sighed and clicked for the next one.

Mom — *"Keira. I'm worried about you. Forget this or at least wait until your father or Gwen or Sean or ANYBODY is there to help you. Better yet...get on the next plane home! Call me."*

Gwen — *"Hey! We're supposed to be partners, right? Why the hell did you go off on your own, sneaking off like a thief in the night! Don't do anything stupid. Wherever you are, wait! We'll be over there on the first flight to help you. Call me."*

Sean again — *"I'm at the airport. Thank God Kreely let me know where you are. At least ONE person knows what he's doing! Your Mom and Dad are worried sick, if you care. I had the devil's own time making Gwen and Roy stay put. They wanted to come with me to save your sorry ass. I'll be in Dublin at ten tomorrow morning*

Ireland time. I'll expect to hear from you with your location." (followed by low cursing before a hard click ending the message)

I took a deep breath letting it out slowly. So tempting to call him and tell him not to come. Just to hear his voice, but it would only make me angry when he yelled at me. Besides which, he wouldn't listen anyways. Damn Inspector Kreely for giving me up. NO! Damn Holmes for being such a sick bastard!

I set the phone on the bedside table and settled in deeper under the covers. Hopefully Zara was right and things would all work out. It was hard to convince my heart of that. After a few tears, I closed my eyes, trying to put it out of my mind. Five thirty would come pretty fast.

***

My eyes creaked open at the soft nudge to my shoulder. Shaniqua held me in her gaze as she pulled a chair close to the bed and sat. The room was still heavily shadowed with only a golden ribbon of light peeking through the folds of the curtained window.

"Close your eyes." Her voice was a gentle whisper. "You've done astral traveling before, Keira, even if you weren't conscious of it. It's time to learn control, to use it wilfully. Let's start with focusing on your breathing...slow, steady breaths."

It was *always* the breathing. Anytime I needed to learn a new skill, it started with breathing exercises. I inhaled to a count of three and then exhaled to the same count. Clearing my mind to do this was second nature after my sessions with Nana.

"You are in a good place. You are safe. This is an entirely natural experience you will go through."

Her voice was light and confident, totally at ease. After a few moments of breathing, being still in my body, physical sensations began to fade.

"Picture your left foot. Really see and feel it in your

mind. Experience the warm heaviness in your foot. Now, picture it rising above you. We start with one small part and slowly expand."

It was the oddest experience, all my attention focused on my foot. I could feel it rising...floating above...see it in my mind's eye.

"Let go of everything. You will feel a trembling at first. It will become a vibration that extends to your whole body. This is natural. It is the state where your very being is shaking its bond to the physical."

Darkness infused with many small lights dancing across my closed eyes. I let the lights go, thinking of the deepest darkness and felt myself drift to a state verging on sleep. In the next heartbeat, an energy buzzed and sizzled in my mind and chest, vibrating quickly through me right to my toes. I was an electrical generator, whirring faster and faster until ...it popped!

Immediately quiet and peace filled me.

My head lifted and there was a slight resistance in my chest before I could sit up. And then I lifted higher, weightless as a feather, the ceiling of the room almost touching my face!

My next thought became reality when I looked down at my body lying still on the bed! Shaniqua sat quietly next to it. A spiraling gossamer rope of energy connected my ethereal self to the physical one below. I was totally aware of everything around me, even though my body was in a resting state. And seeing my connection to it—knowing I couldn't float off into space without a life-line, was freaking amazing! It was the ultimate freedom floating up there!

Sean. No sooner had the thought skipped through my awareness when I was there with him. The airplane. He sat next to the window, his hands clasped over his stomach as he gazed out into the night sky. From the twitch of his jaw muscle, he was still steaming about being left behind. But that wasn't all. Worry—his foot tapping restlessly on the floor. He jerked and his eyes flashed up to where I was. And then he shook his head, turning back to the window.

Had he sensed me? He was still so angry. The elation (of astral travel) that had claimed me earlier deflated like a balloon spiraling through the air. And then I was back in my room at the Abby, laying in the bed. My eyes opened, to see Shaniqua watching me, a smile on her lips.

"You're back. How was it?"

"Amazing!" Every cell in my body was energized, tingling with the thrill of it all. Now that I was back, the bulk of my body struck me after being so free and weightless. "How long was I gone?"

"Maybe two or three minutes?" She shrugged and sat back. "And yes. I could see your spirit lift from your physical body." She'd anticipated my next question. Her head tilted looking at me closely, "What do you recall?"

The floating sensation was still sharp in my mind. I'd seen Sean. It was a bit fuzzy and I closed my eyes trying to relive it. His image was vague but the emotion I'd detected left a strong imprint. "I was with Sean. The memory is wooly, but I know I was there."

Shaniqua leaned over and patted my hand, her eyes soft and smiling. "That's the tricky part with out of body experiences. *Recall.* You felt déjà vu when you arrived here. This time you actually remember more, that you were with Sean. It takes practice, Keira. Rome wasn't built in a day."

"But I don't *have* the luxury of time. I've got the feeling that I need to get really good at this, really fast." I sat up, feeling the lumbering weight of my body, every muscle now leaden compared to the airy lightness of being I had just experienced. "What about Sean? Would he have known I was nearby? He's got some serious psychic talent."

"Maybe. According to Zara, he *is* very special." The smile dropped from her face and her eyes became hard. "Are you ready to find Holmes? You know that's why I'm here, helping you with this. He's able to cloak himself from people like me. But you're his flesh and blood. He can't hide from you, although I'm sure he'll try."

If my body had felt heavy the moment before, it was nothing to the sinking dread filling my chest. "Give me a few minutes, please. I'll try but—"

"Absolutely! You need to get back to that state of relaxation where your essence drifts from your physical body. Especially when you are learning. There will come a time, when you can do this at will. For now though, close your eyes and breathe."

It took longer this time. The room was getting lighter from the dawning morning, and my mind couldn't or more likely, *wouldn't*, let go. I went through the same process, even picturing my left foot again. Finally, the vibration came, filling my body and then the strange electrical pop in my head. I was free. But I wasn't alone. Shaniqua's essence hovered over her body, which was slumped in the hard chair. She reached for my hand and it was like grasping the thread of a spider web. It was there but so faint, it was gossamer.

She nodded. Holmes. Immediately we were in my grandfather's bedroom, looking down at him. His mouth gaped open, while his snores vibrated the air near his face. He was peaceful in sleep, splayed on his back with the comforter tucked under his flabby chin. The room looked lived in, with clothes crammed into the closet and a mess of coins and papers strewn over the dresser. It was one of his homes, not a hotel room.

Then we were outside, looking up at a two storey brick building, the gravel drive long and bordered by trees. I'd been there before! It was his place in Isle of Wight. The nerve of him going back there! It was the one he'd taken Gwen to, where Sean had been shot rescuing her. Just to be sure, I checked inside again, saw the dining room and the front foyer. It was definitely the place.

In the flash of a thought, we were back in my room at the Abby. Shaniqua's hand slipped from mine and I watched her essence join with her body. My eyes popped open and my hand lifted to flex my fingers. I sat up and looked at her.

Shaniqua rolled her shoulders and stretched her neck to the side. "Do you remember much?"

"It was his house in the Isle of Wight. I remember that foyer and the outside of it. We have to let Inspector Kreely know this. Holmes is in his place at the Isle of Wight now, but something tells me it won't be for long." I threw the covers back and shoved my feet into my slippers.

Shaniqua's head shook slowly from side to side. In a voice filled with wonder she said, "I don't remember a damned thing. You *are* powerful..." She glanced at her watch. "It's just after six. The girls will be getting up soon anyway. I'll meet you downstairs." She rose to her feet and left the room.

I wasted no time in throwing my robe over the nightgown and following her. I heard some low murmurs from the rooms that I passed as I walked down the hallway. Still, my steps were quiet going down the stairs and into the living room. Shaniqua stood next to Zara, who was holding her phone in hand, extending it to me.

She had already clicked the number captured from the last call I'd made to him. The police man's voice was hoarse with sleep when he answered. It seemed like I was always getting the poor guy out of bed. "Hi Dan. I know where Holmes is. He's back at Priory Bay."

"How do you know...Oh, never mind. It's just the way things are with you...and that blasted island. I'll call you right back." The phone clicked off. A weight lifted up from my shoulders. With a bit of luck, Holmes would be arrested and I'd never have to see or hear from him again.

Yeah. Fat chance.

Nineteen

Coming out of the shower, I emerged into a giggling flock of girls lined up in the hallway armed with toothbrushes and toiletry bags. There were seven of them in pink bathrobes and slippers, staring at me.

"Who're you?" A girl with black, bobbed hair, braces flashing, stepped forward. "You look too young to be a teacher and too old to be an Indigo."

I smiled looking down at her. "You'd be right about that. I'm Keira. I'm just visiting for a few days."

A girl about eight years old, with flashing dark eyes, reached for my arm, squeezing it as she bounced excitedly. "You're American!"

Another girl sidled closer, looking up with wide blue eyes, a red jumble of curls falling over her shoulders, "What are you doing here?" Her voice was low and serious.

"I...I..." I stammered, not sure how much to actually tell them.

A girl with blonde hair in pig tails pushed through from the edge of the group. "Come on! Leave her alone. She's not one of us." Even though she was only fourteen or so, she had a disdainful air, tilting her chin high and dismissing me.

Before I had a chance to say anything more, Shaniqua called as she raced up the stairs. "Girls! Mind your manners." She smiled at me and then turned to the girls waiting for the bathroom. "Breakfast is in twenty minutes. You'd better get a move on or Lilli will have a fit."

I stepped away from the girls to join her. "Is this all of them?"

"It's enough, I'd say." She laughed. "Looks like you beat the rush for the bathroom. Take your time getting dressed, you've got half an hour. I only threaten twenty minutes to the girls so they'll shake a leg." She turned and her footsteps thudded quickly on the stairs going back down.

***

I took my cue from Shaniqua, picking jeans and a light cotton sweater to wear that day. I wasn't sure what to expect next after my session that morning with her. When I entered the dining room, following the sounds of girls chattering and the smell of breakfast, all eyes were on me, including Astrid's who was in the process of pouring glasses of milk from a pitcher.

Zara sat at the head of the table, her wavy dark hair pulled into a messy bun with tendrils drifting carelessly over her green blouse. She flashed a warm smile. "Keira, meet my entourage. Girls, please welcome Keira. You may start, Sophia." Her hand tapped the dark haired, pretty girl with an olive complexion, sitting on her right.

Her braces glittered when she smiled. "Pleased to meet you, Keira. I'm Sophia. I'm ten years old and from—"

"Genoa, Italy." I'd read her thought and decided to jump in, if only to counteract the crack that had been made earlier about me 'not being one of them'. I glanced to the blonde girl sitting across from Sophia and smiled seeing her sit back with narrow eyes. Turning back to Sophia, I continued, "You have two older brothers and a little dog, Tino, who you miss a lot."

Sophia's mouth fell open and she grinned. "You can read minds?" She glanced at Zara, "I mean do telepathy?" Her eyes sparkled when she looked back at me.

"Of course." My spine straightened and I held my head high, even though I'd only learned how to do it in the last year.

The girl next to her, the one with reddish hair framing a face sprinkled with a generous helping of freckles spoke next. "I'm Kristen. That's kind of like your name, Keira. Can you teach me to do that? I mean read minds? I'm pretty close to doing it but maybe you could teach me a trick to getting it."

"As if." The blonde haired girl, easily a few years older than Kristen, thrummed her fingers on the table, glancing up at me from under tight eyebrows.

"Esther! That's not how we speak to the other children or guests." Astrid's voice was low but firm. She glanced at me and her eyebrows rose before giving her head a little shake.

"But it's true! Keira just learned how to read minds. She wasn't born with the gift...not like me or even you, Astrid. And you're one to talk. You don't like the fact that she's even here!" Esther sat back and folded her arms over her chest, doing a practiced pout with the lower lip.

The little witch! I held my tongue. She was only a child after all. Well, not really—she looked like she was about 14; a smart assed teenager if ever there was one.

A girl with glasses and mousy brown hair sitting next to Esther, leaned forward glaring at her like an angry owl. "Must you *always* be so mean, Esther? And if we're discussing telepathy or telekinesis or actually anything paranormal, you are far from the most gifted!" She turned to me, "Sorry for her rudeness." Her accent lilted; sort of like an English accent, but not quite.

This time it was Zara who brokered peace. "Enough of this sniping, Esther. Rita is right; that was rude. It doesn't matter that Keira just came into her skills. What matters is accepting her and being kind to other people." She leaned forward. "*Especially* to people who are like *us*."

The door from the kitchen opened wide and a middle aged woman, huffed her way into the room. Two bright spots flared on her round cheeks while her eyes took in the room in one fell swoop, settling briefly on Esther, before flashing a smile my way. "So you're our guest this morning, Keira. Welcome! I'm Lilli. I hope you like waffles because I've got a batch on the griddle."

It had all happened so fast that I didn't know what to think. Zara certainly had her hands full looking after these girls, especially Esther. And there wasn't any love lost between Rita and Esther from the way Rita had pounced, taking my side.

But the tone in the room had changed with Lilli's arrival. Her Slavic accent and stern eye kept these girls in line more than Zara's soft approach.

"Pleased to meet you Lilli. I *love* waffles. But I was warned you'd spoil me with your cooking." I smiled when I saw her wink and then turn to go back into the kitchen. She knew who the trouble maker was and she was having none of it.

There were only a few girls left to introduce themselves - Rita was from Wales. That explained the accent which I wasn't familiar with.

Irina with dark braids and gold rimmed eyeglasses, from Russia, Noor a dusky skinned girl from Pakistan and lastly Mary-Jane, a very young girl who was so shy she could hardly speak.

I took the empty chair next to Mary-Jane. She was a waif with tangled light brown hair and the biggest brown eyes I'd ever seen.

Shaniqua entered carrying a platter of waffles and a pitcher of blueberry syrup. She set it in the center of the table and then grabbed the coffee pot from the sideboard to top up Zara and me. As she poured, she glanced over at me.

"You did well this morning. Pretty good for your first time."

When I nodded I could feel seven sets of eyes flash over to watch me, and a barrage of different appraisals and questions flooded my mind. *'Where is she from?' 'What can she do?' 'I hope she's nice'* came through in a little girl's voice and I saw Mary-Jane looking at me with a hopeful smile. *'She's probably going to mess everything up!'* I looked over at Esther who had a look of contempt on her face. What the hell was her problem?

Esther was curious, but seriously guarded. She knew she was special, all of the girls there knew they had gifts others didn't. But there was also fear. Fear that I was going to bring trouble and mess everything in her life up, just when it was going well. And that fear made her angry. We had a bit of a stare-down and the message *'She's a neophyte and doesn't know what she's doing!'* came through loud and clear.

I couldn't help but chuckle. Was she somehow related to Sean? When Esther saw me snickering, the look of daggers made it all worthwhile.

Zara cleared her throat and we looked away to her. She kept her voice light when she said, "The girls have academic lessons with Astrid after breakfast. They'll be busy with that until lunchtime, after which they've an hour of free time. Shaniqua keeps them busy in the afternoon with sports and exercise before another free period where they can pursue whatever interest, or hobby they choose."

It sounded like what I would take to be a normal boarding school with a regimen of academic and athletic endeavors. But surely that wasn't all of it? I mean these girls were special with psychic abilities. I sipped my coffee and looked around at them.

Sophia, the little Italian girl who'd been impressed by my telepathy broke the silence. "Keira?"

"Yes?" Uh oh. I knew where this was going and I didn't need to be telepathic.

"Would you like to join us at free time after lunch? I'd like to learn telepathy." Her cheeks flushed pink and she cast a furtive glance at Zara, "I mean, you've spoken about it but I don't seem to be able to get it. Maybe another teacher would help me. Just different words or something."

"Yes! Me too! I'd like to learn." Kirsten joined in, looking eagerly at me with a wide grin.

I glanced at Esther, only to find her eyes narrow and a small smile curl her lips. "Yes. I'd like to see that as well."

Rita sat back rolling her eyes and sighing loudly.

Oh God. But what could I say? Zara hadn't laid out any plans for me. Besides which, maybe I could help them, seeing as how I had only recently learned it. If Esther wanted to be a jerk, that was her problem. The other girls were pretty sweet.

"Sure. I can try to help you, as long as that's okay with Zara." I took a sip finishing my coffee, watching Zara and Esther over the rim.

"It's *your* free time. If you'd like to spend it with Keira, it's fine with me." She smiled and then rose to her feet. "If you're through Keira, I'd like to spend the morning with you in the library. There are things that I think you should know."

I placed the napkin beside my plate and then stood up, fluttering my fingers at the girls and then throwing a wink of my eye at Mary-Jane. The poor little tyke was probably only five years old, growing up away from her parents and family. Did anyone read her bedtime stories or kiss her goodnight? She was so shy and absolutely adorable. She grinned and her cheeks flushed looking down at the table.

The library was at the back of the house with an expanse of windows overlooking the garden area. A complete playground area with swings, a climbing fortress and slides was bordered by hedges and flower beds. I gazed around the room, at the other three walls with shelves and shelves of books.

Zara eased down onto a plush leather sofa and with a sweep of her hand invited me to take the matching chair across from her. "I'm glad you did so well with Shaniqua trying the out of body travelling this morning. It was easy for you to visit Holmes because of the blood tie you have. But—"

"Oh God. He's able to do the same with me, of course." It hit me as she was talking. I flopped down into the chair and my shoulders slumped. I knew there had to be a catch. "Is there any way I can prevent that? Surely you don't want him visiting here! Not with the Indigo kids. That would be a gold mine for him to exploit."

Her eyes closed and she sighed. "It's part of the reason Astrid was reluctant for you to try the astral projection here. If he doesn't have this ability, no problem. But I'm pretty sure he does, and going down that path is tricky. Think of it like a door that was closed, opening a crack to invite you, or in this case, *him*, in."

"That's the last thing I'd ever want to do—somehow bring him here, to the Abby. Maybe Astrid was right. Maybe I should leave now." Oh my God. Then what?

She leaned forward and folded her hands together on her knees. "The tourmaline stone your grandmother gave you gives you some protection—at least from the *entity* that controls your grandfather. You know of course that Holmes is possessed. At one time your grandfather was a decent man. Not the pillar of the community, but decent enough. Why else would Pamela have fallen for him?"

"You know him? Have you ever met him?" Maybe if I knew more about him, that knowledge could help me somehow. A seed of hope and curiosity grew in my mind.

"No. I was strictly forbidden to go anywhere near him. My mother had much more *experience* with him. After he and Pamela parted ways of course." Her face looked sad as she became lost in her memories—memories she didn't try to conceal from my probing mind.

Oh my God! Zara's mother had an affair with David Holmes! I could see a vision of her in my head. A petite, Indonesian woman, with long lustrous hair, her cherry lips always laughing, dark eyes dancing. She'd been to New York

City to visit relatives during a sweltering summer, before returning home to start her career as a teacher. She'd returned home, but she was carrying his child.

I sat looking at that child.

I gulped and strained forward to the edge of my seat. "You're my...my *aunt*, or kind of my aunt?" I looked at her closely. I could see that her skin was lighter than any other Indonesian I'd ever met. And her eyes, while dark and slightly upturned in the outer corners held a hint of Caucasian. In looks she was the polar opposite of my mother but still, her kindness was like Mom's.

"How about half-aunt?" She laughed and then sat back again, settling deeper into the sofa. "My mother, Dahlia, was smart like your grandmother. She hid me away. I was raised by an uncle. He was a poor fisherman in Manado, in the north east. When I was older, I attended a boarding school in England." Her delicate hand swept the air, indicating the Abby. "The rest is history."

I was gobsmacked by the fact that we were related. Too bad Holmes was the connection though. "But my mother...she never inherited any psychic ability. I thought it skipped a generation or something. Your mother...she had some talents? And you, too?"

"My grandmother did! I was bound to inherit some of her *talent*, as you call it. Maybe that was why my mother was attracted to David Holmes. She told me that her attraction to him, despite him being white felt natural, familiar. It didn't hurt that he was rich and really charming. Although I'm sure the charm was feigned. Sociopaths can do that. And from what I know of him, he is definitely a sociopath."

"And he *never* knew about you? Did he never try to contact your mother again?"

"It was a fling for him. A rebound affair after Pamela broke it off. My mother realized too late his true nature, how evil he was. My grandmother knew and it was she who insisted that I be kept an absolute secret from Holmes. It's also why I never do out of body travel. I don't want to open that door. I only agreed to you being instructed because things have advanced to this degree. You need to defeat him for good this time."

My chest tightened as I looked at her. She was Holmes's daughter. She had inherited psychic power from both Holmes and her grandmother. Why did it have to be ME who had to defeat Holmes? She'd escaped his clutches and now had a pretty easy life here at the Abby.

She sighed, "Life isn't fair at the best of times, Keira." Damn, she picked up on my thoughts! Before I could say anything, she held up a hand and continued. "Your grandmother knew that. She knew that Holmes would come after you but she also had a great deal of faith in your ability to overcome. You are more powerful than I could ever be. What you do, protecting The Veil is important, but so is what *I* do. These children here need protection from the world." She paused and looked me in the eye. "Holmes is just one of many, many threats to these girls."

Like it or not, I was stuck with this job and I'd chosen to go it alone.

Oh no! Sean! I pulled my cell phone from my pocket to check the time. Ten minutes after ten. He would have landed in Dublin by now! He'd be expecting my call! And there were all the other calls to make, to let Mom and Dad know I was fine, and Gwen as well.

"I need to make some calls. Just to let my folks know I'm fine. Can I use your phone again?" I stood up when she handed it to me. "Give me an hour and I'll be right back."

"Please don't reveal anything about me or the Abby. Who knows what resources Holmes has?"

"No problem!" I hurried out of the room and walked out the front door. After all I'd heard, I needed to clear my head in the fresh air. Zara was my aunt? Wow.

Twenty

Sean

He hurried from the Customs desk and then stopped to flip his cell phone from Airplane Mode. The flight had battled some head winds and actually landed fifteen minutes later than scheduled. Just as he was about to hit the button speed dialing Keira, his phone rang. His eyes narrowed seeing the unknown number. "Hello?"

"Sean, it's Keira. I'm sorry—"

"What the hell were you thinking of, Keira? You lied to me! You heard from that bastard and then sneaked off in the middle of the night!" His knuckles were pale gripping the phone so hard. It was a good thing it was the phone and not her throat.

"I had to! This is MY problem not—"

"NO! It's OUR problem! You know what he wants to do! This is bigger than you and me!" People stared at him as they wandered by, on their way to meet people from overseas flights. He didn't care, let 'em. "Where the hell are you?"

"I'm not telling you." Her voice was low and icy cold.

"What?"

"I mean I can't..."

"Shit Keira! I need to be with you when you face Holmes. You have no idea—"

"Again! You keep treating me like I'm an idiot. I KNOW what I'm doing!" This time he had to hold the phone away from his ear, her voice was so loud.

"You know nothing! Nothing about how bad, bad can be." His breath huffed through flared nostrils, picturing the last time he'd seen Holmes, when he'd been shot. He'd seen the demon that lurked inside the old man, a demon as old and powerful as time.

"Oh yeah? Well I know he's on the Isle of Wight, Asshat! At least he was last night."

"How do you know that? Were you there? Did you meet with him?" Oh God. It was worse than he'd imagined. And where the hell was Inspector Kreely?

"In a manner of speaking, I was there. I also was with you on the plane coming over here." She was being coy, trying to be clever and it wasn't working.

"What are you talking about?" But as soon as the question was out of his mouth, the answer was in his head. She'd done astral travelling! It was something he'd never dared to try, not with his record. This was getting really out of hand! She was the *last* person who should be spying on Holmes while in another level of being.

She had to understand that. He had to try a new tactic to break through her thick skull.

"I need to see you, Keira. Please don't shut me out."

"Oh, did you miss me?" the sarcasm dripping in her voice.

He drew in his breath so sharply his teeth hurt. No way was he going down that road. "I'm trying to keep you from being more stupid than you already are! Keira, you don't know, you idiot, how bad it can get with this guy!"

There was silence for a few moments. "Keira?"

"I'm here. I can't have you with me, Sean. Go home." The line went dead.

All the names he'd ever called her flashed through his head—Einstein, naive debutante, neophyte. He sighed. Her last words had been halting, like she was on the verge of tears. He stared at the blank screen, "Awesome job, Asshat," he said aloud to himself. He took another deep breath and then sighed.

He clicked a button on the phone to get Inspector Kreely, and waited while it rang a couple times, never pausing for the pleasantries of even a hello. "I'm at the airport in Dublin. Where are you?"

"About twenty minutes away from there. I heard from Keira early this morning and—"

"I know! You're having Holmes's place on the Isle of Wight checked, right?" He strode quickly, making his way across the airport to the exit.

"My guys checked it. Holmes wasn't there. I see you've been talking to her as well. Did she tell you where she is?" Dan Kreely sounded like he was exhausted, even more tired than Sean after the seven hour flight.

"No. So I guess that means you don't have a clue either." He pushed the door open, and stepped outside, his nose wrinkling at the smell of exhaust from taxis and airport shuttle busses.

"Stay at the airport, gate D. I'll be there shortly to pick you up."

***

Before long, a black car pulled up to the curb beside him. Kreely leaned over from the driver's seat peering out the passenger window, beckoning him to get in. Sean threw his bag in the backseat and got in beside the Inspector. "Hi."

The Inspector looked him up and down. "You hungry? You look almost as tired as I feel." He pulled away from the curb.

"Thanks, I probably am that tired. I've been up for a while. No, I ate something on the plane." He slipped the seat belt on and then looked over at Kreely, "That phone she's using...you couldn't get any sort of a trace on it?"

He shook his head. "No. I tried but it's some kind of disposable. She said she's safe staying with friends of her grandmother's. There's not much we can do but wait to hear from her, I'm afraid. Holmes is one slippery guy." He slapped the steering wheel. "He's always one step ahead of us."

"Well if he isn't on the Isle of Wight, there's a good chance he's back here somewhere. He knows Keira landed and is here. He's got to find her as well." Sean looked over at the Inspector. "We've just got to beat him to the punch." Like THAT was going to be easy. Ha!

Twenty One

When I went back into the Abby, I headed to the library again. Shaniqua's dusky arm was draped over Zara's shoulder as they sat on the sofa, speaking softly. They both paused and looked over at me when I entered, pulling apart slightly. It hit me between the eyes. There was more to their relationship than co-workers. Even though Zara had to be almost fifteen years her senior, Shaniqua was in love with her. It was kind of sweet, the affectionate look they exchanged before Shaniqua stood up.

"I spoke with my parents. They're worried of course and want me to catch the next flight home. Sean is fit to be tied and Gwen's not my biggest fan at the moment either. Oh yeah, and Holmes is not on the Isle of Wight anymore. Kreely let me know." I blew out a long breath through pursed lips.

Shaniqua squeezed my shoulder on her way by. "You're doing the best you can, girl. In time they'll see that." She smiled, "I've got to help Lilli with lunch. See you then."

I flopped down on the sofa next to Zara, my aunt. I still

couldn't get over that fact! It was certainly a family of secrets and intrigue. First I meet a grandmother, I never knew existed and then find out she's some kind of ghost whisperer and then find out my father is a Guardian, keeping watch over my mother! Not to mention my demented, possessed grandfather! And now...an aunt?

She smiled and it was like the sun coming out from behind a cloud. "Never a dull moment, huh? I bet you wish that you were back in New York applying yourself to that acting class."

I sat still and looked down, thinking back to that time in my life. It seemed like another person in that world. It wasn't who I was. "Y'know? As bad as it is right now, and don't kid yourself, it's bad, I wouldn't change all that's happened in the past year. Well, except for Nana's death and Lawrence's. If I could change that I would in a New York minute. But—"

"Keira? Have you given any thought to the rest of your life? Or even the next five years? Where do you see yourself?" Her hand slipped over my arm as she gazed at me.

My eyes opened wider but my mind was a total blank. "Continuing my grandmother's work? Which brings up the question of what's happening now with The Veil. I'm sidetracked with this Holmes business and unable to do any good in the world. It's important to do the transitioning of spirits...for The Veil, right?"

She laughed and gave my arm a small shake. "Well you're right of course, but it's not all on *you*. There are others doing this work. Your grandmother was elderly and she slowed down in her later years. You're still needed but the need to eliminate Holmes takes precedence. But getting back to my question, what kind of future do you see for yourself? Will you marry, have children?"

I smirked, "You sound like my parents. Are you related to my mother?" I made a short wave with my hand. "Oops! You are!"

"Very funny." She shook her head. "You know, when you just did that, I saw so much of Pamela in you. Funny, but with an edge to it. You're quite like her, you know." She shook her head but the grin never left her face.

"That must have been weird. Meeting her when you're the daughter of another of Holmes's women. She knew that?" I could barely imagine the look on Nana's face meeting this woman. Of course she'd be pissed off at first— who wants to know their ex had moved on? That alone would have been priceless, picturing my grandmother's face meeting this woman. I could hardly keep from bursting out laughing at the thought.

"It was awkward for the first ten minutes or so. But she understood. If she hadn't ditched Holmes maybe I wouldn't be here. She didn't hold it against me or my mother. They're probably together, two old souls watching down at this crazy situation, rooting for both of us."

"Well I for one wouldn't mind their help. I don't have any sort of plan for dealing with my grandfather. I was going to try to trick him, make him think I was on his side and then somehow destroy him. Do you think he'll buy it, Zara?"

"He's devious and cunning. And he has help. You will have to be careful keeping your thoughts hidden. And never show fear. You give power to the thing that controls him if you do. That's why we felt it was important for you to come here, to throw him off balance. It doesn't hurt that you're increasing your own power just by being here."

"You're right. I was able to Astral Travel without a hitch."

She nodded. "Yes. What you did that first time took years for Shaniqua to be able to accomplish."

"I think I understand. I've been working at Telekenisis since I met Nana. That was hard to get a handle on." I glanced at the glass on the table and with a thought I lifted it, having it rest in my hand.

Zara laughed. "It was less than a year ago you met

Pamela! What you just did now, I *still* can't do and I've been working on that for years and years!"

I lifted Zara's glass and held it in front of her. I then lifted the wine bottle and topped both of us off. "Hey, I could take this on the road as the 'World's Greatest Juggler'!"

Zara held up a hand. "We've got more important things to worry about right now, Keira. Her face tightened. "I wish we knew where he is right now."

Shaniqua appeared in the doorway, "Lunch is ready. The girls are in the dining room waiting for you."

I got to my feet, hoping that lunch would go better than breakfast, especially with that little snit, Esther. Only fourteen years old and an expert beeeyotch.

***

After lunch, Sophia led me to a classroom near the back of the building. There were desks with laptops sitting open, artwork plastering the walls and of course a blackboard where math equations were scrawled. As I looked around it occurred to me that it must be pretty challenging teaching them considering the range of ages, from five to fourteen. Astrid had to be pretty flexible and intuitive to achieve that balancing act. It was a one room schoolhouse like I'd read about in history books.

Kristen was excited to learn whatever I could teach her regarding telepathy. She raced ahead of us, her red hair flying from her shoulders, taking her seat in the classroom. So far it was just the two girls who wanted my help with this.

"So, Miss Keira," Sophia said, her Italian accent dancing over her words. "How do we do this telepathy?"

When I pulled up a chair between them, Esther sidled into the room. She smiled and stepped forward, holding her hands clasped behind her back, her chin high.

Ignoring her I smiled at Sophia, "When I learned to read people, I started by holding—"

"You really don't know what you're doing, do you?" Esther stood behind the other girls, her eyes narrow and a smug look on her face.

I stared at her, trying to read her thoughts. Why did she hate me so much when I'd done nothing to her? But her mind was hidden to me now; at breakfast I was able to get a sense of her feelings, but here she was as firmly vaulted as Sean had ever done with me.

"See? This is just like how you've always been isn't it? You try something and never end up completing anything. Even in school when you were my age, you never had any real friends did you?" She came even closer, daring me to argue.

My eyes flew open wide. Her mind was closed to me, but she was able to leaf through my memories like it was a copy of The National Enquirer! My mind slipped back to that time, going to Trinity Manhattan, grade six, standing on the outskirts of a group of 'cool girls', watching them giggle and whisper, casting glances my way. I'd never fit in even though my parents were as wealthy as theirs and I dressed as nice as them. They had always excluded me from their games, not outright mean to me, just leaving me out. The same hurt from years ago flitted through my body.

"Esther..." Sophia scolded.

Her pig tails flounced over her shoulders as she turned on Sophia. "It's true! She never had friends, was too scared to talk to the boy she had a secret crush on, Bobby Murano! He ignored you too, didn't he Keira? Even your so-called friends in high school used you and never really liked you. You suspected it and it was true!"

How was she doing this? She was reaching down to my deepest memories and wrenching my heart right out of my chest! I'd only ever been able to sense events and emotions in others that were current, things going on in their lives that occupied their thoughts. I pictured a brick wall surrounding my head and body. *'GET THE HELL OUT!'* was a mantra in my mind, focused on Esther.

She giggled and it sliced through me like a hot knife through butter. "No. Your wall doesn't work with me."

I got to my feet and glared down at her. "Why are you doing this?"

"Because I *can*. It just shows that you don't belong here. You aren't nearly as special as even that chair." She met my gaze, never wavering.

"KEIRA!" The high pitched shriek from the back of the classroom ended the staring contest. It was Mary-Jane, the littlest of all of them, standing there with terror in her eyes. "Hurry! He's almost here! You've got to get away!" The little girl stumbled and her eyes rolled back as she slumped to the floor.

I rushed over, lifting her head, giving her a little shake to bring her around. Oh my God! Only five years old and fainting with fright! What the hell was going on?

Her eyelids fluttered as soft as a butterfly's wings and tears welled. "Your grandfather! He's at the door! Run!"

Twenty Two

My heart pounded fast against my ribcage. I eased the child's head back onto the floor and leapt to my feet. I pointed at Sophia. "Here! Look after Mary-Jane! Lock the door when I go out. Don't open it under any circumstances! Stay in this room until Zara or your teachers say it's okay!"

I rushed from the room, shutting the door behind me. My last sight was Esther squatting down next to Mary-Jane, holding her hand.

As I was about to pass the kitchen, Astrid barged out of the door, her face a mask of fury. Raised voices, Zara's and Shaniqua's arguing with a man, blasted from the front foyer!

I turned to her, "It's Holmes! He's found me. Get the rest of the girls and take them to the classroom. Mary-Jane, Esther, Sophia and Kirsten are already locked in there. If there's another way out of there, a backdoor, take them and run!"

Her pale blue eyes were wide with fear. Irina and Noor were in the library reading, but where was Rita? The thought flashed in her frantic mind before she darted away. Oh God, let Rita be there too!

I took a deep breath and my hand rose to grip the tourmaline stone.

Twenty Three

When I stepped into the open space of the front foyer, my jaw tightened. Holmes and his goon dominated the space. How the hell had he found us?

"She's here we know it!" It was that same guy Keith, the one who had been with Holmes in the Isle of Wight. The bastard who snatched Gwen. The bastard who shot Sean. He was playing 'Igor' to Holmes' 'Dr. Frankenstein'.

"Stop it!" At my shout, Holmes looked over at me and a slow smile spread under the walrus moustache. "You found me, so let's go!" I marched to the front door. Isle of Wight or Bantree; it made no difference to me as long as I could get him out of here before he got his hands on the children.

"Not so fast." He rocked back and forth on his heels, gazing around at the set of stairs and the entry to the living room. "I rather like this place. It's got a good feel to it, you know. I like the vibe here." He started humming the old Beach Boys tune *'Good Vibrations'* watching us with a look of amusement. I felt like a mouse caught by a cat.

"You aren't welcome here." Zara stepped forward, shielding Shaniqua behind her. "I'm the owner of this Abby and if you don't leave now, I'll call the police. You're trespassing." She glanced over at me, "You don't have to go with him, Keira."

The goon who stood next to Holmes, snorted, "We'll leave when we damn well please, lady." He pulled a gun from the inside of his jacket, pointing it casually at Shaniqua.

Holmes glanced over at the guy, "Check the other rooms, Keith. I know there're more people here. Get them and bring them to me, so we can keep an eye on them."

My gut clenched and I stepped in front of Keith, blocking him from going down the hallway where the girls were barricaded...at least I hoped that they were all together now. "Hold on!" I turned to Holmes, "This isn't part of the deal. Either we leave now or I'll never work with you. These women are nothing to do with what's between you and me; I forbid you to hurt them in any way."

Keith shoved me aside. "Forbid us? You're forgetting who's holding the gun, now aren't you?"

I had to stop him! He went a few steps, and was almost at the entrance to the dining room when I turned, my thoughts a burning rage focused on his gun.

"Shit!" The gun clattered to the floor, while Keith held his hand up, the palms of it a bright red. Still holding his hand he spun around, a killing storm in his eyes.

"That'll be enough." Holmes's words were low and menacing, gazing at Keith. "Get the gun and continue searching the house. It's fine now."

Keith stopped but his look was murderous, glaring at me. "I'll deal with you later." His voice was barely above a hissed whisper before he turned and got the gun again.

"Don't try that trick again, Keira. Two can play that game and I'm better at it." No sooner were the words out of Holmes's mouth when Shaniqua let out a blood chilling howl of pain, her hands beating at the flames that licked and curled around her ankle.

"No!" Zara beat me there, her hands flying at the flames claiming Shaniqua's jeans. The two women fell to the floor, Zara's hands flew over Shaniqua's lower leg, smothering the flames. The smell of burnt fabric wafted in the room.

"I did *that* with just a thought, Keira." Holmes looked over to me with a satisfied smile. "Would you care to see more?"

"Stop it!" I held up my hands. "You win."

"Look what *I* found!" Keith chortled as he frog marched Lilli down the hall, before him. The older woman's face was scarlet, her blonde hair hanging in limp strings around her face. In an instant I knew what had played out in the kitchen. She had tried to throw a pot of boiling water at him but he'd caught her hand; instead, some of it splashed on her.

He pushed her towards me and I took a deep breath willing coolness onto her fiery flesh. Whether it worked or whether the concern for Shaniqua and Zara won out, she scrambled over to kneel next to Shaniqua.

"Are you all going to behave now, or do we have to continue this game?" Holmes glanced down at the women on the floor before turning his steely eyes to me.

For the first time I really looked at him, meeting his glare. The aura that exuded from him, swirled in a sickly green haze but under it, like a serpent coiled in his mind was the demon.

My jaw dropped. I'd seen that demon before! I'd faced it when it had attacked Nana and Lawrence. I'd only beaten it back when Gwen had joined the fray. It was then that it sunk in—I had made a serious mistake. I needed Sean's help, or even Gwen's, to destroy that...that *thing* for good.

I had to buy time to come up with some kind of plan...at least keep the Indigos safe. I forced a smile at my grandfather, "Alright already. I still don't know why you need me when you're obviously more powerful than I am."

I suppressed a sigh, when from the corner of my eyes I saw Keith take off up the stairs to explore for more people.

Please let Rita *not* be there. I held my hands out to him. "Just what is it that you want?"

Holmes let out a soft chuckle and then stepped over to me. "I told you I want immortality, child." He gave a sharp nod. "No, that's not exactly right. I intend to break the bonds of time and space. Imagine Keira, if you were able to go back in time, or even forward. To experience first-hand, great events in history. To sail with Columbus and be the first person to step onto the shores of the new world."

"Not the first person. Remember the natives? They were there first before they were almost wiped out." I tried distracting him with words as I struggled to erect a brick wall in my mind. Hiding behind it I scrambled for some kind of plan.

I looked over to Zara a question in my eyes. *He doesn't know who you are?* She nodded. He didn't realize his child was lying on the floor at his feet.

I egged Holmes on. "Where else in history besides starting a genocide with Native Americans do you want to travel to? What else is on your top ten list? Auschwitz? Rwanda?"

He put a hand to his cheek and had a faraway look in his eyes as he rocked back and forth on his heels. "Being on the battlefield, riding next to Napoleon, knowing you could never die, no matter what! Standing beside Caesar as he conquered the world! Landing on D-day! No! *Parachuting* on D-day!"

Guy sure likes his war. I needed to keep his mind off the Abby. He could probably sense the girls in an instant if he put his mind to it; I needed to really get under his skin. "How about seeing Pamela fall hopelessly in love with Lawrence, her *butler* of all people. How would you like to be a fly on *their* bedroom wall?" I took a chance saying that, hoping to throw him off his game somehow.

And it worked. His chin rose and his face flushed a brick red. Through gritted teeth he said, "Pamela was a fool. She threw her life away with that... that glorified *waiter*. How stupid of her. She could have worked with me... and we'd have become gods! The whole world would bow down before us!" His voice rose to a thundering bellow and he held his arms out. His aura flared all around him, a sickening green with yellow flashes running through it like lightning bolts inside a storm cloud. He let out a sigh and his face lightened. Dropping his arms he sneered at me. "Instead I get *you*, a pale imitation of what could have been. But with guidance, you have real potential."

When Keith's feet pounded back down the stairs, coming back down, I glanced up and then felt my knees go weak with relief. He was alone.

"No one up there, but I counted seven beds besides the ones for this lot."

"Ah...Keira and the seven dwarves." Holmes stepped closer, looking down his gnarly nose at me. "Think I don't know about the Indigo children? Think again. I've known of them for quite some time." He eyed me with glee. "And thanks to your little astral visit to me last night I've finally found them!" He crossed his arms and scanned the area. "I wonder which ones should I take along with us? Any suggestions, Keira?"

Before I could reply Zara leapt up and lunged at Holmes! "You bastard!" Before he could react her fingers were claws raking his face. He staggered back, his cheeks bloody. Before she could tear at him again, Keith was on top of her. He grabbed her by the waist, threw her to the floor and dove on top of her. His fist rose high and smashed into her face. I rushed over, leaping onto the thick back of the thug, only to be swatted away like a gnat. I hit the floor and my breath was knocked out in a painful whoosh. The flurry of feet rushing by me barely registered. Lilli and Shaniqua descended on Keith, pounding him with fists and knees.

A roar blasted the air and a fierce wind rose all at once. A heavy chair was swept high and ricocheted off the wall. Framed pictures whirled in the cyclone sweeping through the foyer. In the center, Holmes stood, his chin pressed down against his chest while his eyes flared red. A thin trail of spittle hung from his lips as his arms rose to the ceiling, his hands spread open.

He looked like a satanic marionette. Oh God! The demon was in full control of him. It was doing this!

Lilli and Shaniqua were lifted high and flung against the wall to land in a crumpled heap. Zara's eyes were white rimmed as she slid across the floor head first towards the stone fireplace.

Lunging, I gripped her hand, holding on for dear life in the cacophony of the storm that filled the room. A surge of rage swept up from the pit of my stomach. Every muscle in my body was a tight wire, tingling and then sizzling with power.

An otherworldly howl exploded from my throat. "LEAVE THIS PLACE, DEMON! GO BACK TO HELL!" I rose to my feet, somehow pulling Zara along with me to face the thing that claimed Holmes.

I could see it now, superimposed over Holmes like a double exposed photo. It's sickly green maw and bright red eyes gazed at me like a cobra about to strike. A sly grin twisted its lips as Holmes' hands lowered to point at me. A hard jolt of energy shot out from them hammering into my chest stopping me cold.

A wall of ice cold hammered into my chest and I gasped. I couldn't breathe! I pushed back with my own energy but it wasn't enough. Stars flitted across my line of vision and the edges began to darken. I felt myself slipping away.

And then it stopped.

I gulped air, watching the objects swirling through the air thud against the floor. Shaniqua and Lilli moaned as they lay sprawled in a heap next to the door, slowly trying to sit up. Keith floundered to his feet, staring wide eyed at Holmes. This was a new experience for him too.

If not for the debris littering the floor, the punctures in the wall where objects had hit, you would hardly have believed that it had happened. Even Holmes looked almost normal again, his jacket hanging off-kilter and blinking slowly as if waking from a stupor, but otherwise himself.

"Have you had enough? Must I kill these women before you'll stop, Keira? Or will I start with the children I know are hiding in the back room? I can easily take the ones I want and do away with the rest."

I was still gasping, my heart pounding like a racehorse in my chest. "Whatever you want I'll do. Just leave these women and children alone."

His eyes narrowed to slits while his fingers tightened to fists. "Yes...we'll see about that. And speaking of Pamela..." He turned in a small circle, lifting his eyes towards heaven.

I gulped air staring at him. He was lost in his own delusions, still thinking of my grandmother. The line separating love and hate was razor thin.

I spat the words at him, wanting to hurt him as much as he'd hurt these innocent women. "Pamela is gone. You can't reach her, thank God."

He pivoted as lightly as a dancer, back to me. "Ah, but *you* can. And who better to come back through The Veil than the woman who was so pivotal in maintaining it through her lifetime. There's a certain poetic justice in it. Having *you* be the one to summon her is just the icing on the cake." He turned to Keith, "Get the Ouija board." He turned back to me. "Pamela will come if *you* summon her." He clapped his hands together. "What a brilliant idea!"

Oh shit. I hated that blasted board, just as much as Nana had. It was a powerful tool to communicate with the other side, and he was going to use it to summon Nana!

Keith threw a hard look at me before shoving by Lilli and going out the front door. In the blink of an eye she pounced, shooting the deadbolt lock into place. At the same time, Shaniqua was up on her feet. She flew at Holmes, grappling with him, her knee punching into his thigh.

"Come on!" Zara cried as she joined Shaniqua, her fingers curled, reaching for Holmes's eyes.

I leapt into the fray, kicking at his leg. But we could

knock him down, the transformation began again. His arms stretched high, flinging the two women from him. His rage was palpable; flowing from him in a stench of hate. I managed to get the tourmaline stone from my neck and my hand shot forward to press it against his cheek. A searing spot formed around it and his head swivelled to face me, eyes blazing red.

"DIE BITCH!"

He shoved me, his voice a roar and the stone slipped out of my grasp. A blinding pain shot through my chest; it was like being squeezed by a Boa constrictor. He stood above me, holding his hand out. As he clenched his fingers, the force on my chest became a steel vise. I started to black out again.

Zara had gotten to her feet and she rushed into Holmes like a football linebacker. Her arms wrapped around his waist and they both careened onto the floor. I could breathe again. I struggled to sit up.

Just then a series of crashes sounded at the door. I sat dazed on the floor watching it as it erupted open, cracked splinters flying and Keith leapt in wild eyed. And his gun out.

Zara had gotten to her feet and was kicking at Holmes' head.

"Shoot her you fool!" he cried, whipping his head away from her flying foot.

Keith dropped into a crouch, holding his pistol out with both hands and shot twice. The first bullet took Zara in the shoulder and spun her around facing us. The second went through her chest and she folded down to her knees. She clutched at her chest, the blood pouring out. She looked down at her hands, puzzled and back up to me. Her eyes were surprised. She opened her mouth, but before she could say anything, she flopped forward onto her face.

I knew Zara was dead. For a split second the room was entirely still.

A piercing keen broke the silence; a high squealing pitch.

I spun around. Rita stood at the bottom of the stairs. Her narrow eyes were focused on Holmes.

I felt Rita's fingers, small and warm curl over my other hand and then the blast of power took hold, thundering fast within me. We stepped forward together, our voices and hands joined as one, "IN THE NAME OF ALL THAT'S GOOD AND HOLY, LEAVE THIS PLACE!"

Holmes swayed on his feet and staggered back. His hand rose while his eyes focused on me and Rita.

That horrific entity appeared all at once. A sickly blue green apparition of a skull, with burning red orbs where its eyes would be materialized out of Holmes' figure and came towards the two of us. Its presence filled the room.

It opened its black oozing mouth and a guttural shriek of pure hatred spilled forth. The women covered their ears and dove to the floor in terror, but I knew better. This thing thrived on fear; that was its greatest weapon. I gripped Rita's hand firmly. Instead of shrinking back, I hoped I wouldn't pee myself and stepped towards the Beast. I began to recite from memory the Litany Against Fear:

> *"I will not be afraid*
> *Fear is the soul destroyer*
> *And will consume me should I*
> *allow it*
> *I rebuke fear*
> *To its face of many masks I stare*
> *unafraid*
> *One by one, I will watch those*
> *masks fall away*
> *Crumble to ash*
> *And drift away*
> *In the breeze of my love*
> *And I will still stand*
> *Alone and unafraid."*

Its mouth opened wide and it towered over us, roaring

again. My entire vision was filled with the sight of its bottomless maw—an oozing cesspool of dark dripping misery. I could hear the room being spun into another vortex as chairs, picture frames, and anything else not nailed down spun around us in a maelstrom.

My head shot back. Oh shit! Before anything else happened, Rita took my hand in both of hers. "I will not be afraid!" she said in a small voice, almost crying. "I'm not afraid!" I felt something hard slip into our joined hands. Rita had picked up the tourmaline stone and inserted it into our clasped hands. '...and a child shall lead them...' popped into my head.

The power of the two of us together was jacked up even greater. I could feel it course through us both as we faced the beast. I looked up into that gnashing mouth. "I will not be afraid!" I cried out. "I will not be afraid!"

"We're not scared of you!" Rita called out, her voice hitching though tears of absolute terror. She took a step towards it. "We're not afraid of youuuuu!"

It roared at us again, but the force didn't feel as overwhelming. I took the stone from our clasped hands and held it up to the apparition. It shook from side to side, bellowing at me. I stepped forward again, pulling Rita with me.

It retreated.

And shrank.

"GO BACK TO HELL!" My voice took on that mysterious, otherworldly timbre. It didn't come out of my chest and throat as much as exploded from my soul. "I REBUKE YOU DEMON! GO BACK TO HELL!"

It retreated from us now, a bluish green mist folding onto itself. It oozed through the other side of Holmes towards the front wall of the room. He stood still as a statue, his head hanging down and arms still outstretched. We eased past him pursuing the demon.

"Evil spawn! Leave this house!" It had diminished down to the size of a wastepaper basket; and I could see through it now. As we continued our advance, it wafted apart like steam from a kettle.

And was gone. I looked back at Holmes, his arms had dropped and he wobbled on his feet shaking his head.

Again, the room was in shocked and stunned silence, but only for a moment.

"Oh noooo…!" wailed from Shaniqua. She flew to the prostrate form of Zara.

"That's it! Let's get out of here, boss!" Keith yelled. Holmes blinked and slowly turned to him. Keith was still holding his gun, panning the room with it.

Not for long.

I took a breath. "No," was all I said and with a wave of my hand Keith flew up in the air and smashed into the wall. The gun fired once, into the ceiling before he dropped it. I threw him to the floor. Lilly scampered over and picked up his pistol. With the same two handed stance, she stood above him.

"I'm very good with a gun, Mister," she said. "Don't move." She called out. "Someone phone the police!"

Holmes started towards the door, but his body jerked back, like he'd hit a wall.

Rita's hand with fingers splayed wide pointed at him. She'd done that! Somehow she had kept her focus on him and stopped him! Thank God.

Shaniqua's wail echoed in the foyer, her tears falling onto Zara's lifeless face. I broke off from Rita and raced to her side. "Nooooooo! Zara! Oh God!"

The blood pooled under her body and flowed out beside her. She was bleeding to death in front of us. Her eyes were open, a soft expression on her parted lips. Tears welled and streamed down my cheeks at the senselessness of it all. My aunt *dead* because of that maniac.

I spun around, holding onto Zara's still hand. "YOU! You killed her!"

"No. No I didn't. It was because of you, you stupid girl." Holmes shook his head, pointing his hand at me.

"Do you even *know* who she was?" Ignoring the tears, I screamed at him. "She was your *daughter,* asshole! You killed your DAUGHTER!" My voice broke and I looked down for a moment.

He continued shaking his head like some kind of dazed, animal, the walrus moustache twitching. "No. She was nothing to me. You're lying!"

I got to my feet and staggered over. "You had another daughter besides Mom. A young Indonesian woman, you had an affair with. This is her daughter and *yours.*" Snot drooled from my nose but I didn't care. For a moment he looked shaken, looking back in his mind.

"No. It can't be. Some flower...her name..." He stumbled and caught himself before he fell.

"Dahlia, you fool! Her name was *Dahlia!*" My fingers curled and I wanted to punch the disbelief from his face.

Before I could take another step, his eyes went super wide, and rolled up inside his head. He wobbled for a second before pitching backwards. He hit the floor with a thud. White foam trickled from his mouth like shaving cream, and his body arced before a series of tremors claimed it. Oh my God! From the sickly putrid yellow of his aura, he was in serious trouble.

Rita stepped forward, her voice flat, "I made something inside his head go pop." She stared at Holmes' trembling form and her eyes grew wide. Her hand went to her mouth as she watched him flounder on the floor. "I just wanted him to stop!" Holmes' body stilled and she turned to me. "I just wanted him to stop being bad!" She began to scream. "I killed him! I killed him! Oh no! I'm evil to! I'm EVILLL!"

I grabbed her close to me, "No. You're not evil. He was. I don't think he's dead. You didn't kill him Rita."

She yanked herself away from me. Wild eyed she looked over to Zara's body and screamed again. "EVIL IS HERE! EVIL!" She staggered over to where Shaniqua lay, her feet in the woman's blood and slumped to the floor wailing.

Twenty Four

I whipped my head at the sound of another gunshot by the front door. Keith scrambled back to the floor, staring at Lilli who had the pistol in her grip, a swirl of smoke wafting from its barrel.

"Make any more moves and the next bullet won't be a warning. You'll get it right between your legs, Mister." Lilli held the gun in her two hands like a cop in the movies as if she'd done this a million times. Maybe she had. "Last warning—stay down."

His hands and legs spread on the cold tile, his cheek pressing it under a wide, fear filled eye.

"Oh God, she's gone!" Shaniqua's tear stained face turned to me. "Zara! I can't feel her presence! There's nothing!" She lifted Zara's head onto her lap, rocking back and forth, her voice in a high keen of grief. "Oh Zara! Why? Why did this have to happen to you?"

Rita rose again, walking slowly over to Holmes, wiping the tears from her cheeks and sniffing loudly. She glared down at him, her words a low hiss. "You're poison! I'm glad I killed you!" She jerked upright, her hand flying to her mouth again and spun around. She raced down the hall, her sobbing words trailing over her shoulder, "Oh god, I'm evil too!"

I ran after her, grabbing her shoulder and pulling her into me. "No. No Rita. You aren't evil, he is. He's still alive!" I held her still, subduing her hands that beat against my thighs. The poor kid, facing Holmes and his goon. If she hadn't shown up when she did I don't know what else would have happened; how many more of us would have died in that room?

The door to the classroom opened and Astrid stood there, her face slack with shock. "Rita, come here." No sooner had she spoken than the poor child pulled away from me and ran to her.

"I'm sorry." The tears rolled from my eyes as I looked at Astrid. "It's over, but Zara...was shot."

"Stay here!" Astrid cast a hard look at the girls, before sprinting down the hallway. After a moment her anguished cry echoed back, piercing through me like a knife.

I took a deep breath and scooped the cell phone from my pocket. Sean answered on the second ring.

"Keira! Are you all right?" I could picture his icy blue eyes, intense with concern as he gripped the phone.

"Yes. It's over. Holmes..." I looked over at his trembling figure. "I think he had a stroke. But...but—"

"What is it? Where are you?"

My throat was so tight I could hardly get the next words out. "Lynda Abby. Bring Inspector Kreely. Holmes killed my aunt."

His voice was muffled, "Lynda Abby. Do you know where that is?" Followed by the Inspector's voice, "We'll find it. Don't worry."

"Keira! We'll be there as soon as we can. You're sure you're okay? Did he hurt you?" The worry in his voice only made me feel worse, that I'd tricked him and...

"Just get here, Sean. This place is a sanctuary for gifted children. If the Inspector can tone down the investigation and leave them out of it, I'd really appreciate it. I'll see you soon." I clicked the phone off and then slumped down on the floor, giving in to tears.

Oh God. Zara. My heart broke while I hugged my knees. I was as much responsible for her death as Holmes. If not for my arrogance, thinking I could do this on my own, she would still be alive.

"Yes, she would be." Esther's narrow gaze pierced through me. "It's all your fault she's dead. You should never have come here."

I could only stare up at her. It didn't matter that Zara had intercepted me at the airport. If Sean had been with me, if I'd listened to him, things would have turned out differently. Even Gwen and my parents had warned me about tackling Holmes again.

"You've ruined everything. You had to do this on your own, even though people...people far smarter than you, told you not to. Zara was kind. She was trying to pull you out of the fire, you idiot."

I slumped lower, while sobs wracked through my shoulders. She was right. What could I say? Because of me, Zara was dead.

"And let's not forget Rita while we're on the subject! She's convinced she's a murderer, downright evil for hurting your psycho grandfather. He was possessed and he had a henchman as well. Why in God's name would you ever think you could defeat him on your own? Because you're arrogant and stupid, that's why!"

Astrid walked down the hall and stopped watching both of us. "Esther, go back in the classroom. The police just pulled up out front." She turned to me, "Come on. Remember, these girls had nothing to do with this. They were with me in the classroom."

I got to my feet just as Sean raced down the hall. Concern warred with anger on his face when he jerked to a stop. He stood over me, his hands on his waist. "Are you hurt?"

If I expected him to scoop me up into his arms, that hope was quickly dashed.

"I told you this was too much. You should have waited

for me." His face was hard, spitting the words out like bullets.

"I'm sorry, Sean." Tears once more seeped from my eyes. "My aunt is dead because of me."

"Keira." He sighed. "I took a bullet rescuing you the last time you tried doing this on your own…and now your aunt has been killed." He looked past me to the classroom of girls, all silent and wide eyed. He shook his head slowly. "Gwen was traumatized, and god knows what these kids are going through. I told you, *I damn well told you* that you had no idea how bad it could get, but you wouldn't listen."

What could I say? I slouched even lower, trying to sink through the floor. I was never the one hurt, just those around me who cared about me.

Just like Esther, Sean was right, even if his tone was more controlled. "I'm not cut out for this Sean. It's too dangerous. I can't do it anymore, not when so many people around me are hurt or…" I succumbed to a fresh set of sobs, my hands covering my face.

"I've been trying to tell you that for the last six months. This is beyond your power. You're in over your head." He shook his head and then stalked away.

Inspector Kreely brushed by Sean, and stood over me. Even his voice was chilly. "The ambulances are taking Holmes away. He's had a massive stroke." He took a breath. "And your aunt as well. We'll need your statement as to what transpired here. The two women are in the library with one of our people questioning them. I wanted to hear your statement myself."

He was in full 'official cop' mode. Sean must have given him an earful while they drove around searching for me. An earful that was proven completely correct when they walked into the shambles of The Abby. I took a deep breath and led the way into the kitchen to talk to him. I was glad Sean wasn't there. Soon, this would all be over, for good.

Twenty Five

When I finished with Inspector Kreely, he left and returned with Astrid so he could get her statement. "You can leave us now, Keira."

I wandered past the library to where Sean was standing in the foyer. It ached to see him so distant and angry. But who could blame him? "Sean?"

His eyes met mine, yet he made no move to step closer, even take my hand or give me a hug. "Look, I'm sorry about your aunt. This whole affair was a tragedy. And for it to happen here of all places...well, I don't understand Zara's reasoning on that."

I moved closer, reaching for his hand. "I'm sorry."

The muscle in his jaw twitched and he shook his head. "That's always the way, isn't it? You're sorry?"

"It will never happen again." Every muscle in my body felt heavy as lead. I'd said this before, hadn't I?

"Damned right! I'm through here. You've deceived me, lied to me when I asked you about Holmes back in Kingston. I can't trust you, Keira. And I care too much to go through that again." He pulled away and his hands rose to dry scrub his face, "I just can't do this."

He'd sounded so final. "You won't have to. I'm going away. Maybe to Antarctica. Who knows? I need to be alone for a while. Leave all this paranormal craziness to someone who knows what they're doing. So more people won't be hurt."

Sean huffed a sigh. "Why am I not surprised? Again, it's all about you, isn't it? What about your parents? Even Gwen? No goodbye, just I'm out of here."

"No you're not." I turned at Shaniqua's voice. I hadn't even heard her come in. "You're not going anywhere, Keira. You're staying here." She came over and her hand lifted to my shoulder. "The world needs you Keira, needs what you are capable of, but..."

I shook my head. This was the last place I wanted to be. Memories of Zara and then Esther hating me so much. "I can't."

"Yes, you can! Zara wanted you here. She thought you would be able to battle Holmes. But she was wrong. There is *much* you have to learn. And I'm not referring to just psychic ability. We need you here as well, but not as much as you need to be here."

"You have got to be out of your mind!" Sean said. Thanks. Thanks a lot Sean.

Shaniqua took me in her arms. "You poor child. You spent what, a month with Pamela before she left? Of course you have much to learn." She shot a look at Sean. "Instead of constantly being put down, you needed to be lifted up." I lifted my head watching her eyes hold Sean in a steady gaze. "Others could have worked with you, they could have *inspired* you to see a better way, but they too failed you, darlin'. Perhaps their own pride kept them from being a true helpmate to you."

Sean dropped his eyes and looked at the floor in stony silence, his face red.

"Like all the children here Keira, you need *sanctuary* too.

She pulled me closer and the pain she felt at Zara's death flooded through me. Yet despite that, she was concerned with me? My stomach sunk even lower than before. How could she be so strong and kind to me? She patted my back. "An' there are girls here that *need* you to be here, child. You have good work to do right under this roof."

I pulled back, "Maybe for a few days. I don't think Astrid and Esther are going to like this." Yeah. A few days and then I'd light out of there and disappear.

For the first time, Sean's voice became reasonable. "She's right, Keira. You need to grow up, start thinking of others, not yourself. And it sure beats Antarctica."

Shaniqua's hand shot up like a traffic cop. "You hush yourself, boy. You got nothing to say here anymore. If you had been more true to Keira...this probably never would have happened!" She waved her hand at his shocked expression. "There's plenty of blame to go around for what's happened here, Sean; and you ain't taking responsibility for *your* part in all this!"

Shaniqua's dark eyes filled with tears when she took my face in her hands. "Zara is gone from us, child; you're all I have left of her... But more important Keira, you're an Indigo child...every bit as much as the kids who live here already. You need to be sheltered while you grow. If your grandmother made any mistakes it was in thrusting you into this world too soon." She stepped away. "I need to talk to Astrid and then I'm going to my room. I'll see you tomorrow."

I gazed at Sean. "Will you explain to my parents? To Gwen?" I gripped his hand and squeezed it, feeling that jolt of clear energy surge through me. I'd miss that. Just when there'd been a chance that our relationship had some promise, I'd blown it. He was still smarting from Shaniqua's dressing down; but that energy pulse said a lot too, right?

"As for your parents and Gwen...they'll understand. You'll be safe here. That's what they'll want to hear even if they do miss you."

I smiled, "It's not a prison. They can meet me in Dublin anytime for a visit." The smile fell from my lips and I had to fight the urge to hug him. "That goes for you as well."

"I need time as well, Keira. I'm not sure I'll ever get past this." He looked down at his feet, avoiding my gaze.

Inspector Kreely stepped out of the library ahead of the young officer who had been taking statements. "We're done here. Do you two need a ride back into the city?"

"It'll just be me, Dan. Keira is going to stay on here for a bit."

His eyes darted from Sean to me. "Fine. As long as I know where to find you if we need any more information. Do you want to know about Holmes' condition if I hear anything?"

I shook my head. "The man killed his daughter. How could anyone expect anymore from me?" He could die right where he was and I couldn't give a shit. That bastard could have just as easily killed *my* parents.

He sighed. "Odd isn't it? He's a prisoner in his own body now." Kreely grimaced and then headed for the door.

For the first time, Sean managed a tight smile. "Good luck Keira." With that he followed the two policemen out the door.

That was that. When I went to the stairs, about to go up and lay down for a while, Astrid and the girls were coming from the classroom. Her arm draped over Rita's shoulder, protectively. "Would you mind taking Rita upstairs and sitting with her? I've got to see Lilli for a few minutes."

The rest of the girls walked slowly by me, their eyes downcast hiding the tear streaked faces—all but Esther. As she passed by she held my eyes with hot hatred.

Twenty Six

Rita looked up at me. Seeing me, it came back to her, the confrontation with Holmes and Zara being hit by the bullet. She shook her head, turning to Astrid, "Can Sophia and Noor stay with me, instead?" Her eyes were pleading behind her thick glasses.

Who could blame her? I stepped up the stairs, following Irina and Esther.

When a small hand curled around mine, I looked down. It was Mary-Jane. Her eyes were red rimmed and her nose needed a good blow.

"Can you sit with me for a while? My stomach hurts." Her words were barely above a whisper. She'd been involved with all this as well, crying out the warning before all that had happened and she was only five. It was bound to be taking its toll on her as well.

"Sure. Do you need anything to settle your tummy? Ginger-ale or medicine?" She shook her head and continued up the wide set of stairs.

Just my luck the room she led me to was the bedroom

she shared with Esther. Great.

"What's *she* doing here?" Esther's question might have been directed at Mary-Jane but her glare was set firmly on me. Her eyes closed and she made a show of sighing loudly, "Oh no. You're staying on at the Abby, aren't you?"

I didn't have the energy to fight with her. "Yes. For a little while. Shaniqua asked me to live here for a bit." I sunk down onto the bed where Mary-Jane was sitting.

Esther got up and flounced across the room, "Brilliant! Just don't get too comfortable." The door slammed behind her.

Mary-Jane looked up at me. "Don't mind her. The only one who will share a room with Esther is me. She's kind of mean to everyone. She's fine with me though."

Well at least she had *that* going for her. It would be hard to think of doing or saying anything mean to this waif with the large brown eyes and hair that resisted any sort of combing or style.

I held her hand and my thumb drifted softly over her small knuckles. "How did you know that my grandfather was on his way? Is this your gift?"

She nodded and looked down, "All morning in class I had a bad feeling. I didn't know why or how but I knew something was going to happen. It wasn't till after lunch that I saw the picture of your grandfather in my mind and knew he was coming for you. He's a bad man."

"But Zara...you didn't have any idea that she was..." My eyes closed for a moment and I fought the tightness in my throat, "...that she was going to be killed?"

"No. I just knew that when he got here, it would be really scary." Tears flooded her eyes, "If only I'd known about Zara, maybe—"

"It's not your fault. You know that, right? Thanks to you, we had time to keep you girls out of it." But even as I said it, a picture of Rita standing next to me, doing whatever she did to immobilize Holmes flashed in my mind. The girl's power had meant the difference in ending him.

"How's your stomach now?" I squeezed her hand, trying to get her mind onto something else.

"It still hurts but not as much." Her smile was tentative and she glanced up at me before once more lowering her gaze. "I hope you stay here a long, long time. You're like my older sister, Hannah. She always stuck up for me and was nice."

"I'll be here for a while yet. I like you too, Mary-Jane." I spotted a book on the bedside table and picked it up. 'The Paper Bag Princess'. "This used to be one of my favourite books when I was your age."

"Mine too! They've read it to me it about a hundred times. Would you read it to me?" Her eyes lit up and there was a broad smile to accompany.

"Let's make it one hundred and one then." I picked up the book and snuggled in next to her so she could see the pictures as I read. If I had to stay at the Abby for a while, Mary-Jane was definitely a high point. For the next little while, I forgot about everything else as I read a story to the poor child.

Twenty Seven

Dinner, consisting of sandwiches and cups of soup, was late. Astrid helped Lilli serve and then took a tray up to Shaniqua, while the girls and I settled in the dining room.

Zara's empty chair and place setting at the head of the table was a somber presence that cast a long shadow. What food we ate, we ate in silence.

When it was just about over, Astrid and Lilli came into the room and took their seats. Everyone, including me watched them, waiting.

Astrid cleared her throat and began, "It was horrible and tragic what happened earlier today. We will miss Zara's gentle leadership and her wisdom. We'll honor her wishes that her remains be cremated and ashes scattered here at the Abby. To that end there will be a farewell ceremony two days from now. You may attend if you'd like."

Her words were punctuated by a loud honk of Lilli blowing her nose. She looked around with red rimmed eyes and then turned her gaze back to the uneaten sandwich. She wasn't the only one with tears welling.

All but Astrid, when she continued in a flat, officious voice. "Classes of course will be cancelled until after the ceremony. Hopefully a replacement director will arrive soon and we can get back to our normal routine."

It was hard to keep quiet, listening to her. Her manner and voice were cold when these girls needed comfort, rather than 'getting back to a routine'. I'd only known Zara a short time and I was busted up. I couldn't imagine how these girls felt. She'd been like a mother to many of them.

"Shaniqua has requested that Keira stay on with us." She turned to me and her face gave no clue as to how she felt about it. Considering she hadn't wanted me there in the first place, it wouldn't be a stretch to think she was less than thrilled about the prospect of me lingering any longer.

"Why? It's her fault—"

Astrid stretched a hand to Esther, palm up, cutting off the girl's words. "We will be *kind* to Keira. Zara was her aunt. It is Shaniqua's request and she is acting director until Zara's replacement arrives. "

"Great." Esther was barely audible but the roll of her eyes made clear her feelings.

Lilli banged the table with the palm of her hand. "Girls! This is hard for all of you, I know. It's hard for Astrid, Shaniqua and me as well. We need to pull together as a team to get through this."

Astrid nodded in agreement. "Yes. Lilli is right. We work together and we'll survive. There is a chance as well that the Mother House of the Illuminata will decide to move us to another location. This place has been a sanctuary and I'm afraid our security has been breached. But *they* will be the best judge of that." Her glance at me this time showed annoyance. "You are free to do as you like for the rest of the evening. Sophia and Irina, you will continue the schedule and help Lilli with clean-up in the kitchen. I know movie night is usually Saturday but in light of all that's happened if you'd like to do that, take your mind off things for a while, it would be fine. That will be all. You're excused."

I was about to get up when Astrid's voice stopped me, "Keira. Lilli and I need to talk to you."

"Yes?" I sat still, watching her.

"Your position in the house is kind of a hybrid one. You aren't a student but you're not staff either. Until Shaniqua is herself, or a new director arrives, perhaps it would be best if you divided your time between helping with the girls —not as a teacher of course— but rather as...well, as kind of a companion. If you would assist in general housekeeping and cleaning, you'll find it easier to fit in around here."

Lilli leaned closer and her eyes were soft, "Is there anything you do? Cooking, cleaning or some kind of art or craft that you're good at, that the girls would enjoy?"

That was a good question. But I didn't have a good answer. "Not really. I've dabbled in photography. I never really had to do much and now well...Aside from my psychic abilities and considering who these girls are, I don't think I can teach them much that they don't already know."

Astrid huffed, "I was wrong. You're probably going to be more of a student than I would have guessed. We'll need to teach you a few things about living in a house and contributing." She bit into her sandwich and glanced at Lilli.

I could feel my jaw tighten at her dismissal. "I could *hire* someone to help with housecleaning. I've got tons of money. How's that for contributing?" There! She'd made me sound like I was totally useless. I could contribute.

She grabbed her throat swallowing hard when the chuckle erupted, "You think *money's* a problem for the *Illuminata*? Oh my God! We could hire an army of cleaners and cooks! She nodded sharply. "No Keira, you'll pull your own weight around here."

I felt my cheeks flame and I looked across at Lilli, only to find her smiling while she ladled soup to her mouth. I really didn't know too much about this organization. I wasn't a hybrid. I was a fish totally out of water.

***

Later, I stepped inside the room that had been given to me by Zara. It was small but at least it was private unlike the girls' rooms. I took my cell phone from where I'd left it earlier to recharge.

There were no phone messages or texts to greet me. Funny. I had shot off a text to Mom before going down to dinner telling her I was fine and that Holmes was finished. I hadn't mentioned that she had a half sister and that her sister was now dead. It really wasn't appropriate information to be relayed in a text. I slumped down onto the bed. Maybe she hadn't got my earlier message.

I dialed her number and waited a few rings before she answered.

"Keira? I'm so glad you're all right!"

She sounded sincere but it still didn't explain why she hadn't replied to my earlier message. "I'm fine. It's finally over, Mom. Holmes is in the hospital with a massive stroke. But there's one thing—"

"I know about Zara. Sean called me and told me all about it. It doesn't surprise me with my father's record that he'd have other children. But still, I'm sorry she died."

It was hard to keep my voice steady, with the tears welling in my eyes, thinking of Zara. And talking to Mom like this, after such a horrendous experience made me feel like I was five again. "Me too. You would have liked her. She reminded me of you in many ways. She was kind."

"Oh Keira." The sad sigh came through right after. "From what Sean says, you're staying on there. It's a good place for you to be for a while."

My head jerked back. I'd been expecting some kind of argument, her insisting I come home! What the hell had he said to her? "Well, it won't be for long. I'll stay and see that everything gets sorted out and back to normal and then I'll be home. When are you going back to New York?"

"In a few days, I think. Keira...don't rush back. We've got everything under control. Gwen is happy to look after the house. Devon's gone home, now that Sean is on his way. You look after *yourself*, Keira. We're fine."

In one way her words were reassuring but on another

level, it made me feel empty. Didn't she want to see me? Especially after the encounter with Holmes? I had to find out what Sean had said. "Okay, I will. Say hi to Dad. Actually, is he there? I'd like to speak to him?" Maybe I'd get something from him. Mom wasn't saying too much and I didn't feel like giving her the third degree.

"No. He's up to his elbows stuffing a chicken. He says to say hi. He'll call you later."

Huh. I'd just about been killed and he couldn't take his hands out of the freaking bird to speak to me on the phone? Weird.

"Okay. I'll call you tomorrow. Bye." With that the line went dead.

I wasted no time hitting the button to talk to Sean. Maybe he wasn't on the plane yet. It rang twice and then went to voice mail. "Hey Sean. What did you tell my Mom about me staying here? She was really distant on the phone with me." My breath hitched in my throat; no, Mom *and* Dad were *cold*. What the hell did Sean discuss with them for them to be like this? "I can't believe she wants me to stay here and not come home. Call me when you land."

Sitting there on the bed, with only the murmur of the movie playing downstairs, was lonely.

Gwen. I dialed her number but once more got voice mail. The sound of her voice was good to hear though. A friend's voice. "Hey Gwen. It's Keira. First off, I'm sorry for giving everyone the slip. I did it to protect you but once more...well it ended really badly. I'm staying here for a while. Call or text me, will you?"

I peeled off my clothes and tossed them on the chair in the corner. I'd probably end up throwing them away in the morning. I couldn't see myself wearing them without thinking of Zara and all that had happened.

As I scrambled into my bathrobe, I felt alone...so alone. Not even Mom had helped me feel better. I sighed and left the room to go take a shower and then go to bed.

Twenty Eight

When I went down for breakfast the next morning, Shaniqua was seated in Zara's spot at the head of the table. Her face showed the streaks of a night of crying and her usual smile was missing as she spoke to the girls. But considering all that had happened she was doing well to be down there, resuming some semblance of normal.

"Good morning," I took in all the girls, even Esther with a glance and took my usual seat next to Mary-Jane.

"Good morning, Keira. You look like you didn't get a good night's sleep either. It was a rough night and the thunderstorm certainly didn't help." Shaniqua took a sip of coffee and looked over at me.

"It rained? I guess I slept better than I thought. I didn't hear a thing." I reached for the coffee pot and poured a cup. The girls were certainly quiet this morning, even Esther. I glanced across to Rita, who only picked at her breakfast, avoiding my eyes. I'd try to talk to her later to gauge how she was doing.

Astrid came into the room carrying platters of croissants and sausages. She nodded to me, "Would you mind taking the girls for a hike for an hour this morning? There's a footpath that leads to a small lake about twenty minutes away. The fresh air and exercise would be good for them."

I glanced at Shaniqua and she nodded. It was clear they had planned this together. It wasn't that I minded going but it rankled that Astrid had assumed some sort of *authority* over me. She was barely older than I was. "Sure. That sounds good." I tried to ignore Esther's sigh and theatrical eye roll.

Irina glanced over before helping herself to a croissant. "I'll show you where it starts and lead the way if you'd like. Maybe we can pick some raspberries. I know a spot where there's tons of bushes."

"I know a spot where there's *tons of poison ivy*. Maybe we can pick some of that." Esther mimicked the younger girl, even down to the slight, Russian accent.

A few of the girls, Rita included, smiled and then looked down at their plates. Her imitation had been perfect but still...

Irina's pale cheeks flushed, "Maybe I'll push you in the *lake*, Esther."

"Like to see you try." Esther's smile was challenging looking down her nose. "If I go in, so do you and you can't even swim. So there."

"Enough girls. Now is not the time to be squabbling. If the raspberries are ripe, we can ask Lilli to make a trifle or something." Astrid took a seat next to Shaniqua, having finished with pouring orange juice for them all.

I was still thinking of the poison ivy. I'd been raised in the Big Apple; what did I know about noxious weeds? Heck, I wasn't even all that keen on hiking. It was too much like exercise.

Sophia was sitting at my left side. She nudged my arm, "Don't worry. I'll see that you steer clear of anything poisonous. Don't mind them."

Astrid looked down the table to me. "The girls will be ready at nine-thirty. Enough time to make their beds and tidy up a bit. Would you mind cleaning the bathrooms? The cleaning woman who does the floors and bathroom called in sick today."

Clean the bathrooms? I'd hardly ever done that in my own apartment when I was going to school. And that was just cleaning up after myself, not ten other people! I felt nine sets of eyes looking at me. If I said no, they'd think I was lazy or too good for the job. Yet, still... "It can't wait a day till she's back?"

"No. Esther will help you."

"Oh maaaan!" Esther plopped her napkin onto her plate and threw a scowl at me.

My sentiments exactly. It wasn't bad enough that now I was stuck with *her* helping! And Shaniqua wasn't on my side in this. She looked down the table at me and nodded. Was this why she'd wanted me to stay? To be the new scullery maid? I wasn't seeing the upside here.

***

Twenty minutes later I was back in my room. I plucked my phone from my pocket and sighed seeing the blank screen. I hadn't heard it go off but still there was always the chance that I'd missed it. But nothing. Nothing from my Mom, Dad, Sean or Gwen. But it was earlier in Canada. Maybe they weren't even up yet.

"Well? Are you ready? I'm not doing this by myself." Esther stood in the open doorway, yellow gloves covering her hands that held a bucket with cloths, paper towels and more gloves. Her hair was secured back in a pony tail that swished over her shoulder when she turned.

I pocketed the phone and followed. We started at the main bathroom, where two shower stalls and two toilets and sinks awaited cleaning. When she set the bucket down I leaned over, getting the gloves on and grabbing the cleanser. "You do half and I'll do the other half. Fair enough?" I

157

started with the sink, dousing a thick layer of cleaning powder over the basin.

"Hey! You're not making a cake! You don't need nearly that much!" She ran the water over her cloth and scraped a layer of cleaner from the mound in my sink. Her eyes were narrow when she peered at me, "Your ignorance is showing, Princess. Watch and learn." She swiped the cloth over the other sink and then rinsed it till it sparkled.

My cloth was caked in powder as I swabbed. It took much longer to rinse the soap away till it shone like hers. How was I supposed to know that? We'd always had a cleaning lady and I'd never needed to learn this crap. Big deal. So she was better at this than me. There were tons of things I knew and had that she never would. Unlike this beeyotch, *I* had friends! Well, one friend anyway, Gwen.

By the time I was halfway through cleaning the shower stall, she had finished her side of the room.

"Seriously? You're less than *useless*." She leaned her scrawny ass back against the counter and sighed.

As I passed by her on my way for the piece de resistance — the freaking toilet!— I picked up on something she forgot to hide from me, her guard down for just a moment. Sadness. A memory of a worn middle-aged woman cleaning in a big mansion. From the looks of her, she wasn't the owner. It hit me like a train. It was her mother. Esther had only this woman to call family and even that was now gone with her having to live here for her safety.

She must have sensed my invasion into her thoughts because her head snapped up, peering at me with hard eyes. "Hurry up, will you? There's still two baths to do." With that she picked up the bucket and walked out of the room.

She kept her distance cleaning the other rooms and held the protective wall in her mind tight. The silence between us was a sheet of ice. We finished the rest of the chores in silence.

I pulled my phone from my pocket and my stomach dipped lower. Still nothing from my parents or Sean or

Gwen. When Esther stepped by me, going into her room, I wondered if she ever heard from home.

***

Later that morning, all seven girls and I stepped out of the house and into the bright sunshine of the day. It was good to be in the fresh air, escaping just for a little while, the pall that hung in the rooms of the Abby. Zara was gone and that hole in the fabric of life there, affected all of us.

Mary-Jane walked beside me, while Irina and the other girls stayed a good pace ahead. As we rounded the low outbuilding, some kind of garden shed or barn, I saw the last of them, Noor, the dark braid flying high as she raced into the forest. When we crossed the yard, there was an opening and well trod dirt path, snaking between the tall trees and underbrush.

When I had gone a few paces, Rita jumped out from behind a tree, startling the hell out of me. I let out a yelp. Seeing her grin at my reaction I had to laugh too. "Hey! I'm not really an outdoorsy person! I thought you were a bear or something!"

Her hands rose and she mimed claws, growling and showing her teeth. Then she smiled and stepped closer. "I wanted to talk to you, alone."

I looked down at Mary-Jane. "Can you run ahead for just a few minutes? I'll be right behind you, okay?" She nodded and then the next thing I saw was the bottom of her sneakers as she raced along the path.

I folded my arms over my chest and looked into her eyes past her glasses. She was a plain looking girl with mousy brown hair and a sallow complexion, but she was anything but ordinary. I'd seen that for myself. She was not only brave, she was probably the most gifted of all the people in the Abby. "How are you doing?"

"I don't know. Astrid and Sophia tried to make me feel better about what happened but I still feel horrid. Actually, scared might be a better word." She gazed at the toe of her sneaker as it dug a small hole in the dirt path. "I became another person, angry and ready to kill both those men. It happened so fast and I couldn't control it. That scares me."

I focused until I could see into her, see her aura. Her words were a serious understatement of what was going on inside. "You think that whatever evil was in Holmes entered you? Is that it?"

"Yeah. Do you think that happened? You were there. Shaniqua was with Zara so she wouldn't know. You see spirits...and demons."

"Didn't you see it too?"

"No... I saw everything flying around...and I heard something loud, like a roar..." Her eyes widened behind her glasses. "You saw it? For real?"

"Yeah..." I looked away. "It was really horrible looking."

"And now it's in me, right?"

I scoffed. "No silly." I turned back and looked her straight in the eye. "I tried to kill it, but I couldn't. It...well, it ran away. It went through the front wall of the Abby and was gone."

"Really?" She stepped back and her eyes got funny as she continued to look at me. Her voice went flat. "You're speaking the truth." She brightened, and in her normal voice she said, clapping her hands, "It really isn't inside me then!"

I nodded. "That's right." I decided to let it slide about how she got kind of odd for a moment there. Maybe I'd ask about it later.

Rita's face fell again though. "So I did that to Holmes all by myself then..."

"You were very angry, Rita."

"I never want that to happen to me again. I'm thinking of leaving the Abby. I don't have to stay here, you know."

My hands rose to rest on her shoulders and I bent lower. She was deeply shaken by this but was trying her best to conceal it. For Shaniqua and Astrid and everyone else's benefit. There was enough grief and worry without her adding to the heap. It all went through me, her pouring her feelings into me like a faucet. And for her, I was the only one with her level of power, who could possibly understand what she was experiencing.

"I don't think that's a good idea. I know you feel overwhelmed here right now, but listen—all the girls are like you kind of, right?" When she nodded, I said, "Back home it wasn't like that. Also Rita, here you're safe. As far as being possessed like Holmes was...that's not what happened. You were defending your home and friends." I was silent for a few minutes, thinking hard. "How old are you?"

"Twelve."

I huffed a sigh. "I took you for ten, sorry."

"Thanks a lot. Everyone thinks I'm littler than I am."

I snorted. "Don't worry, one day will come when you'll be happy to hear that people think you look younger than you are. But twelve, huh?" I thought for a moment. "Maybe the rage is part of your growth, you know, becoming a teenager."

Her lips pursed into a small bow. "You mean puberty, don't you?"

I nodded. "Nothing like this has ever happened before though, right?"

She shook her head.

"Well, I'm no expert but I think what happened was all you. Provoked by an evil situation and fighting back. You aren't a bad person if that's what you're thinking. It was a nightmare situation and you did what you had to do. Don't be so hard on yourself."

"That's easier said than done." She started down the path again, "I'll think about staying here, but maybe I just need to get away for a while, do normal things like shop or go to the movies with friends. But that's not likely to happen. I never really had a normal life. That's just in the movies."

It made me think of what it had been like for me growing up. On the surface things had seemed 'normal' with friends, going out and doing stuff. But they never had really been my friends—not people you'd trust with your darkest secrets. The exception had been Gwen. And now that bond was weak. She hadn't even tried to get in touch with me or answer a text.

But still, my life was probably better than Rita's. "How long have you lived at the Abby?" We started walking down the path.

"Five years. Zara was the one who got me to come here. I was doing terrible in school and my parents were at their wits end. The other kids were afraid of me, and the teachers thought I was..." she glanced up at me in silence.

"Odd," I said. It was what the teachers called me more than once.

"Yeah... you too, huh?" When I nodded in reply she continued. "It was either here or some kind of institution for special needs kids. But then out of the blue, Zara came to our house to talk to my parents. I liked her right from the start. She understood me."

The weight of her words fell onto me like a stone. Zara might be alive if not for me. And this poor girl was beside herself wondering if she had caught Holmes's possession like it was some kind of disease. So much pain and suffering. If only I'd listened to Sean and my parents. And here I was giving Rita advice, trying to help her, expecting her to listen, when I never did.

The path widened and the blue of the lake shimmered through the foliage ahead. She dropped back to walk beside me. "This Sean guy you keep thinking about...he's your boyfriend? Or would have been if..." Her words trailed off and she turned her gaze to me.

"Maybe he would have been, but I lied to him. He was hurt really badly the first time when we dealt with Holmes. I tried to avoid that this time. But he's really angry. He thinks I'm stupid, that I never knew what I was up against."

She took a deep breath and let it out slowly. There was

no need for words. Her thoughts on this were clear. I had been in over my head and I should have listened. If not for her, well...

At the sharp scream and splash, I gaped at her and rushed forward. When I got to the rocky shoreline, a blond haired girl sputtered to the surface of the lake a few feet out. Thank God, it wasn't Irina, unable to swim and floundering. The girls on the shoreline giggled, watching Esther streak through the water to shore. Hair plastered to her cheeks and she looked mad as a scalded cat.

It was hard to keep a straight face. "Are you all right?"

"What do you care, bitch?" Esther grabbed the edge of a rock and pulled herself upright, her hair hanging in strings around her narrow face.

The rock slid forward and Esther, arms like a windmill flew backwards, doing a flop into the water once more. Mary-Jane bounced on her toes, and looked over at me with a sly grin.

The little devil had done that! She'd used telekinesis on that rock to dunk Esther once more. When Esther's head popped up again, her gaze from one girl to the next showed she had no idea who'd done that. They must have all been in on it, guarding their thoughts.

I wasn't about to tell her.

Twenty Nine

The next day, through a steady rain, I trailed the flock of girls towards the garden area. I clutched the handle of the umbrella tight, peering ahead to see how much farther we had to go in this mess. Shaniqua and Astrid were dark shapes standing at the edge of the flower bed, waiting for us all to gather around.

The rain streaked Shaniqua's curly hair and rolled down her cheeks. She looked around and then lifted the top from the silver urn of ashes.

"Zara was created of stardust, as are we. Her time here, though short, touched us all. Her kindness and strength were a beacon that drew us and nurtured us here. She loved us and loved the Abby. She will always remain in our hearts and also in the very earth the Abby stands on." She gazed around at each member of the group. "She will be with us always." She took a deep breath and in a single motion swished the urn through the air scattering the ashes in a cloud before us. They spread skyward for a moment before falling with the rain to the soil.

Tears ran from my eyes even though I felt drained; I'd cried so much in the last day, as had the others around me. Beside me, Lilli's shoulders wracked while her hand covered her eyes. Mary-Jane snuggled in close to my thigh, while my hand caressed her head. My only aunt was gone; a woman who'd mothered and cared for these special girls.

I watched as Astrid's arm curled over Shaniqua's shoulder and they led the way from the grave. The young black woman held the silver urn close, almost as if Zara was still there. In a way, she probably was and Shaniqua would keep it safe and close to her always.

It was a subdued and damp gathering in the back room of the Abby, removing rubber boots, and raincoats. I jerked when I felt the vibration in my pocket, letting me know I had a text message. It was about time that someone thought about returning my calls!

I stepped off to the side, taking my phone out and letting everyone else get by. Gwen's name and small pic showed on the face of the phone.

SORRY FOR TAKING SO LONG TO GET BACK TO YOU KEIRA! ROY HAD A FEW DAYS OFF (HE WENT BACK TO FLYING WITH NORTHWING) AND WE WENT AWAY CAMPING!

WOULDN'T YOU KNOW IT, THERE WAS NO CELL SERVICE IN THE REMOTE SITE—AN ISLAND IN THE MIDDLE OF THE NATIONAL PARK!

IT WAS HEAVENLY WATCHING THE STARS. I'M VERY SORRY ABOUT YOUR AUNT, BUT GLAD TO HEAR THAT YOU ARE OKAY. STAY AS LONG AS YOU LIKE THERE. SEAN SAID IT'S A RETREAT OF SOME KIND. I'M SURE YOU'LL ENJOY A

SHELLEY DOREY

MUCH NEEDED BREAK.

TTYL GWEN

What the hell? No talk of missing me, wanting me home to carry on with our work together? No. She was too taken up with her new boyfriend and *CAMPING*? Yuck. My idea of roughing it was staying in a hotel with no room service.

At the gentle tap on my arm, I looked up into Astrid's icy blue eyes.

"Would you mind helping Lilli in the kitchen? It's not cooking, just serving the lasagne she made earlier today. Esther will help too." There was no room for saying no when she walked away so abruptly.

And speaking of the devil...Esther walked over to where I stood huddled over my phone. "Bad news I hope." She let out a dramatic sigh. "It looks like we're teamed up for chores. Again. What'd I ever do to deserve this?" She spun on her heel and stomped down the hallway, disappearing into the kitchen.

My fingers itched to shoot off a quick reply to Gwen, something snarky to make her feel guilty for not missing me. But looking down the hallway, I noticed Shaniqua walking away with her arm around Rita. She was comforting and counseling the young girl even though her heart was torn in two from what we had just done.

'Enough people in the world are hurting right now.' I thought to myself as I pocketed the phone and trudged off towards the kitchen. Helping out wasn't that big a deal, not at a time like this. In the kitchen, Lilli was taking a huge tray of lasagne from the oven, while Esther was tossing a giant green salad with wooden spoons.

I looked at Lilli. Her eyes were red rimmed and a little bloodshot from crying but she managed a smile. "What can I do to help?"

"Go back to Canada? That'd be a good start, I'd say." Esther's smart ass comment was barely audible, unlike the snicker that followed.

'Or maybe you could just shut up. That'd be a better start.' I blasted the thought at her and turned when Lilli spoke.

"Can you get the rolls from the rack and set them on a tray? And then get the pitchers of milk and juice from the fridge." She proceeded to slice the tray of cheesy pasta into squares.

I placed the warm rolls in a wicker basket and was taking them through to the dining room when something cold and wet hit the back of my arm. I jumped and spun around, only to find Esther trying to hide the grin as she looked down into the salad greens. "Have a nice trip," she said under her breath. I stepped over the puddle of salad dressing smeared across the floor.

"Listen you little witch! I've had about all I can take of you!"

"Girls!" Lilli had the tray of lasagna in her hands, glaring at us as she shoved past me towards the dining room. "OH!" Her foot skidded on the dressing and kicked up into the air like a Rockette as she tumbled backwards onto the floor! The tray of lasagna flipped in the air dumping a steaming pile of pasta, sauce and cheese. She landed, her arm twisted behind her and screamed as I heard a thunking crack.

I flew to her side and tried to help her up as she writhed on the floor. Her arm was bent wrong.

"Eeeee!" She batted at me with her other hand. "Oh God, it's broken!"

Shaniqua stood in the open doorway. "Lilli!" She bent over, brushing the hot food off the cook.

"My Arm! Ow!" Lilli's face had gone white and her eyes were squeezed shut, sucking air through clenched teeth.

Astrid scampered to Lilli's side and bent lower, her fingers tentatively touching the woman's arm. "Yes. We've got to get you to the hospital. We'll secure your arm and I'm going to help you to your feet." She looked up at me, "Don't just stand there! Help me!"

I stepped over to her side, squatting down and putting

my hands under Lilli's other shoulder. Astrid tenderly moved Lilli's arm to rest on the older woman's chest, holding it there.

"On the count of three, One...Two...Three!"

I pulled on Lilli's shoulder but it was as if she floated up and then stood there. On the other side of me, Astrid's eyes went wide and she looked over at Esther. The young girl's chin was almost on her chest, staring at Lilli with a steady gaze. She'd done that! Used levitation to help Lilli to her feet. And Lilli hadn't cried out in pain despite the jostle of her arm.

Shaniqua stepped over, grabbing a dishtowel , draping it over her arm and then securing it on the other side of her waist. "There. It's going to hurt, but we have to get you out of here and have that set properly."

Astrid and she walked the poor woman down the hall, while I trotted ahead, calling over my shoulder to the other women."Where's the keys to the van?"

"Here!" Astrid flung the set of keys in the air and I caught them in one hand.

The van was parked at the side of the Abby. I got in and drove it to the front door, just as they were stepping through.

"You stay here with the girls, Keira! I'll drive." Astrid helped Lilli into the back seat next to Shaniqua. I knew that they were both projecting every bit of calming and healing thought and energy into the suffering Lilli. It was in the air around me as I stepped out of the van to let Astrid in.

I watched the van kick up gravel as it sped down the laneway and then turned to the girls. They were all there...all but Esther, the one who had caused this.

Rita looked over at me. "It was her, wasn't it? Esther did this? I can see it in your mind."

"What?" Uh oh. This was going to be bad, if I didn't do something about it.

"Esther!" Irina stormed into the house. There was no love lost between them before and now it was coming to a head.

I raced after her. "Wait! Let me talk to her."

"Why? She hates you. She won't listen to you! She needs to be taught a lesson!" Sophia chimed in, sprinting forward after Irina.

Oh my God. They were set to tar and feather Esther if I didn't do something fast! Forget tar and feathering! What these girls could do would be so much worse! I stared at them, willing them to stop, at the same time, my voice thundered in the air of the foyer. "STOP!"

Whether it was surprise or I had actually done some psychic feat to get them to pause, they stopped in their tracks and turned to look at me.

"*I* will talk to Esther. Then you can come in but not to punish her, okay? This isn't the Wild West and you aren't a posse." They looked at each other, puzzlement in their eyes at my words. Of course. They'd never been raised in America with all the Westerns I'd seen.

When I stepped into the kitchen, Esther, with a roll of paper towels, was mopping up the last remnants of the destroyed lasagna to put in the trash. The floor where Lilli had skidded was already clean. Tears rolled down her cheeks and she actually blubbered. "I'm so sorry. Poor Lilli. I didn't mean—"

"But you did! You were so focused on annoying me that Lilli got hurt."

My mouth snapped shut when it dawned on me. Oh my God. This was a mirror image of what I'd done with Holmes. I'd been so intent on my own plans that I'd never considered the down side of them. I did just what I wanted to do, and as a result, Zara was dead.

"I know! Please don't tell on me! How can I ever face them again?" Esther crumpled to the floor, her back to a wall and wailed. "I don't want to go home! There's nothing there for me anymore!"

I stepped over to her and placed a hand on her shoulder. "I'm not going to say a word to Shaniqua or Astrid."

"But the others will! They hate me!" Again a fresh set of sobs and loud sniff close to my ear.

"We'll talk to them. But you've got to stop being so mean, Esther. Maybe if you promise them—"

"No! The only one who likes me is Mary-Jane."

Before I could guard my thoughts it popped into my head. Mary-Jane had been the one who dunked her in the lake the second time.

Esther pulled back, "What? *She* did that?"

Shit. There were no secrets in this place, not with this crew. I pulled her in again and rubbed her back softly. "They'll like you if you let them." I pulled back, "Let's finish cleaning up and then we'll go talk to them. It's not the end of the world. You'll get through it."

"No. Lilli breaking her arm is terrible. And it's all my fault." She sniffed and then grabbed the paper towel to give her nose a good blow.

I sighed. "No. It was mine too. I shouldn't have teased you back. It was my place to be the adult. You're just a kid."

She snorted, "Who you calling a kid? You're not that much older than me." But she grabbed a fresh towel and began to help with the clean-up.

"Am too!" I nudged her to the side and snorted. A small smile started on her face and stayed there. The icy wall between us shattered in that moment. I looked at her and saw a miniature of myself—headstrong, and alone. But not anymore...for either of us.

***

I stuck my head out the kitchen door and saw them all, lined up in the hallway, trying to hear what we were saying in the kitchen. Immediately, one by one their gazes dropped to their suddenly fascinating shoes.

"Come on in and help! That's the only way you're going to get any lunch." I watched Irina in particular as she stormed by me. Mary-Jane was the last, looking up at me with wide eyes.

Esther stood with her back to the counter, the perpetual sneer in her eyes, replaced with wariness. They returned her gaze but there was no fondness there. They'd each been the focus of her snarkiness at some point or another.

I took a deep breath, "This is as much my fault as Esther's. The thing between us got out of hand and Lilli paid the price, I'm afraid."

"She'll be all right, though. It was a clean break." It was Noor who spoke. Whatever her gift was, she obviously knew more about it than me.

"You can tell Astrid and Shaniqua all about this, who's at fault. That's your decision. And God knows, we'd deserve it." I glanced over and my heart ached seeing Esther's sigh, looking down at the floor.

"Or...you could take the high road on this. The high road isn't all that crowded, y'know. I know you have no great love for Esther, but it's up to her to talk to Shaniqua and Astrid and apologize to Lilli. If she doesn't it will weigh her down like a stone. Her choice." I turned to Esther, "Do you have anything to say to these girls?"

Her head rose and then dropped again, "I'm sorry." The words were barely a whisper.

I stepped over to her and put my arm around her shoulder. "I don't think they heard you."

She took a deep breath and her eyes welled with tears, "I'm sorry for all the times I was mean to you. I promise, I won't do it again."

"Yeah, right." Irina folded her arms over her chest, scowling at Esther. "You're just saying that so we won't tell Astrid."

"No, I'm not. I'm going to tell her myself, as soon as they get back. You'll see." She stood taller and pushed away from the counter.

"She's telling the truth." It was Rita who stepped forward. If anyone could back up Esther, it would be Rita. Everyone knew about Rita's gifts. And more importantly, that there was no love lost between her and Esther.

"I will speak to them as well. This isn't all Esther's fault." I looked around at them and saw doubt fade from their eyes. "Who's up for PB and J sandwiches?"

"What kind of sandwich?" Noor looked at me like I had two heads.

"Peanut butter and jelly, of course."

This time it was Rita who corrected me, "In England, we call it peanut butter and jam."

"Whatever!" I laughed and opened the cupboard getting the jar of peanut butter down.

It was a truce and time would tell if it lasted.

Thirty

It was well after dinner that the van rolled into the yard again. "They're back!" I yelled to the girls who were finishing the clean-up in the kitchen.

When the door opened and Astrid stepped through, we were lined up in the foyer waiting. She looked from me to the others, and her eyebrows rose high.

Lilli was next in, sporting a thick plaster cast on her arm. Her gaze went from Esther to me and she frowned looking away. Well, *she* knew at least who the culprits were.

Shaniqua swept in and then closed the door. "Well *that* was an adventure!" She looked over at me, "How is everything here? Have they eaten?"

"Yes. Nothing special, but food at least." I looked over at Lilli, "I'm sorry Lilli. It was my fault. I should have cleaned the floor before you got there."

Her eyes were narrow when she nodded. She stepped closer and glared down at Esther for a moment.

"I'm sorry, Lilli. It was my fault, not Keira's. I threw the salad dressing at her. I promise never to do that ever again."

She stood with her hands clutched before her tummy, looking up with wide eyes.

Astrid strode over to Esther, "I'm afraid that was the last straw for you. You can't get along and now it's gone so far that Lilli was hurt. She could have broken her neck!" She shook her head slowly. "After what we've already been through... We can't have this...not at the Abby."

My gut tightened watching the coldness in Astrid's eyes, her back ramrod straight. "No. She means it, Astrid. It was my fault as well. We'll do all the cooking...with Lilli telling us what to do, of course! Please, let her stay!" Did Astrid have any heart at all? Surely, she must know that Esther's mother was dead and that she couldn't really go home.

"You're sticking up for her? Well that's rich!" Astrid glared at me. If she had her way, Esther wouldn't be the only one leaving.

"Wait. We're not expelling anyone. Let's all just take a breath and look at this tomorrow. It's been a day." Shaniqua sighed and then looked over at Lilli. "Would you like something to eat or some tea, dear?"

"Hang on. Let me make it!" Esther tore off across the foyer and into the kitchen.

Astrid and Shaniqua exchanged a puzzled look. When Irina chimed in, offering to help Esther, their eyes flashed wider.

I winked at Rita and then turned to the other girls still waiting there, "How about we go to the common room? We can do crafts or play a board game before we go upstairs for the night?"

As we left the room, Lilli muttered, "It's an ill wind that doesn't blow some good somewhere."

Thirty One

The next two months were the happiest I had in a long, long time. Oh what the hell—no slag on my parents, but it *was* the happiest time in my life.

Something happened between Esther and I after that disaster in the kitchen. She became the kid sister I never had, and I became the big sister she had always longed for. Rita was a little envious at first, but then she took on a mentor role to little Mary-Anne; to the point where she could recite *The Paper Bag Princess* by heart.

Yes, Esther became special to me; I know how my Nana must have felt during that single month I spent with her when I first learned about The Veil and my role in the world. But all of those girls, every single one of them had filled a place in my heart that I didn't even know had been empty.

Astrid and I became... well, not close friends, but strong colleagues. We didn't have a lot of affection for each other maybe, but what we had in common was our love for those girls.

So yeah, too good to be true, right?

One afternoon as I was cleaning up from lunch Astrid came into the kitchen.

"Shaniqua would like to have a talk with you in the library," she said, standing at the door. "Come along now." I hung my apron behind the kitchen door and glanced over at Esther who was stirring a batter for a chocolate cake. Even Lilli looked up when Astrid stood waiting.

My heart speeded up a bit as I followed her down the hallway. Things had been going so well...I hadn't done anything wrong...not that I knew of. Well...I'd been practicing levitation with the girls in the afternoon free time, but there were no rules against that. It wasn't something Astrid and Shaniqua encouraged but neither did they forbid it. For Indigo kids, it was as natural as going for a hike or artwork. It was bound to happen.

I took a seat on the chair across from where Shaniqua sat on the leather sofa and watched as Astrid lowered to join her. This must be serious if Astrid was there.

Shaniqua cleared her throat and sat forward, "Keira, I think it's time for you to move on with your life."

A glance at Astrid showed she agreed, nodding her head slowly. It wasn't a matter of her disliking me anymore, since we'd become... well, whatever we were.

"You mean leave the Abby?" Even though their body language and thoughts broadcasted the message, I still couldn't quite believe it. I'd gotten into the swing of things there. The girls liked me and I liked being part of the group! I actually belonged somewhere!

"Yes." Shaniqua looked down at her lap for a moment before continuing. "Don't get me wrong, we like having you here, but..."

I sighed, there was always a 'but' wasn't there?

"...you are needed elsewhere. Your work—"

"Hold on! I've been here almost a month and the sky hasn't fallen. There's other people doing the transitioning work! As Zara said, it's not all on me to save the universe!"

Just when I finally found a place where I fit in, I was being dumped! But more than that...well the thought of leaving the Abby made my gut clench tight.

This time it was Astrid who spoke, "We didn't get on well at first, you and I, but since you've been here, I've come to like you. You've become part of our family. But this isn't who you are, Keira. You needed us but now you don't."

"But that's just it. I still need you. The girls need me! Who will help in the kitchen? I've helped with the girl's lessons and even do most of the clean-up now. You're still waiting on a new Director! Just a few more weeks and—"

"No. A new Director is arriving tomorrow. We think that's a good time for you to leave." Shaniqua took a deep breath, composing herself. Her eyes had welled up and tears threatened to spill over.

Astrid sat forward, perched on the edge of the sofa. "I know it sounds like it's all very convenient with a new staff member arriving but believe me, even if we were short staffed, we'd still think this way. We'd be selfish to keep you here any longer. You don't need us anymore."

I slumped deeper into the chair. I'd been kicked out of three schools, been fired from the only real job I ever had at the dry cleaners, been dumped by Sean, and abandoned by Gwen who was 'in-love' with Roy more than ever now. Even my parents didn't seem to mind me being out of their life while I lived here. And now this?

They were wrong. I did need them. My eyes welled with tears.

Shaniqua got up and squatted down in front of me, her hand on my knee, "We'll miss you too. You can come back and visit, you know. And there's one more thing..." She took a deep breath but before she could get the words out, Astrid jumped in.

"Esther. You've been the only one who ever got through to her. She's been here years and she was always an outsider, even with us. We think that she should stay with you...at least for a while. She is free to come back whenever she or you would like but, for her sake—"

"And yours!" Shaniqua interrupted.

"...she'll flourish under your guidance. You'll both benefit being together."

I could see why she was on the edge of her seat, laying *that* bombshell on me! I took a breath, picturing how it could be, living with her. We'd become close. Esther was my little sister now. If she agreed to come, then it would be practically official. Hell! We kind of looked liked sisters! It would be rewarding to care for her and see her grow.

Yeah, I was just as surprised by how I felt, don't worry. But it was true.

"She doesn't know any of this, does she?" But I already knew the answer from the blank, 'deer in the headlights' stare in both of their eyes.

Shaniqua reached for my hand and squeezed it. "We thought it would mean more coming from you. You've turned her around—"

"Not to mention that you've done a one-eighty as well!" Astrid laughed. It wasn't as strange as it might once have been, hearing her laugh. In the past couple of weeks she'd mellowed a lot towards me.

"Was I that bad?" I snorted before the grin took charge of my face. Of course, I'd been that bad. A rich girl who never took orders and definitely didn't clean toilets!

"Well you make a mean soufflé now! So yes, I'd say you've improved. Although you still can't play soccer to save your soul." Astrid was really getting a chuckle out of herself.

Shaniqua got up and her hand was on my shoulder, "We'll always have a place for you here at the Abby. For both of you. You needed shelter, and guidance and we did that. But, we can't help you grow anymore. You need to do that yourself."

It was hard hearing this. Scary to think about leaving, and not just for me but for Esther too. But deep down, I knew they were right. It was time to get on with my life...with our lives. "Okay. I'll speak to her."

**

After dinner that night, when we were finishing up the clean-up, I nudged Esther. "Hey. I need to talk to you about something. Let's take a walk."

She wiped her hands after draining the sink and shot me a puzzled look. "Must be serious."

I could feel her prying in my mind but I kept my guard up. There was no way I wanted any interruptions with the girls popping in. "It is." I hung up the apron and then led the way through the kitchen and to the back door. The evenings were a little shorter and there was an autumn nip to the air even now. I grabbed my hoodie and slipped it on.

When we were outside, she looked at me. "You're leaving aren't you? Going back to Canada or the States."

I nodded. "Yes. Astrid and Shaniqua think it's time."

"No! You can't! Why did they—"

"Hang on!" I put my arm around her shoulder, walking to the playground area at the back of the property. "Before I came here, I was involved with paranormal work. To be specific, I helped spirits transition to a higher plane. I need to get back to doing that. I'll explain all about The Veil and all that later, *but...*" I couldn't help smiling because this time the 'but' was good news.

She sighed and I felt her body slump. The 'but' was something that hadn't ever been good for her either.

"I'd like you to come with me."

She stopped dead in her tracks and I turned to her. Her jaw was open so wide she could have caught flies in there. "Seriously? You want me to come with you?"

"Are you kidding? I'd LOVE for you to come with me!" I gave her shoulders a gentle shake. "Please say you will or at least think about it, okay."

"But...but...what about school? And my friends here! I'll miss them!" But her brown eyes were tap dancing their way to a yes!

"We'll get a tutor, don't worry. As for the Abby, we can come back and visit anytime we like! Stay for a long visit, if we want. We'll travel all over the world. I can't wait for you to meet my parents, Gwen and..." My stomach did a flip flop, "Sean." Damn, he still had that effect on me. I hadn't heard one word from him—the jerk! It was probably over before it even had a chance to begin. But I couldn't think about that now.

"And if you decide you miss this place too much or you get sick of me, you can come back, I promise." I almost fell over backwards when she jumped forward and hugged me hard. I guess that was my answer.

"When? When are we leaving?" She pulled back, peering up at me with a wide grin.

"That's the thing...we're leaving tomorrow."

Her face fell for a moment. I knew she was picturing Mary-Jane, Rita, Irena, Noor, Sophia and Kirsten. It broke my heart to be leaving them behind as well...especially Mary-Jane.

It was hard to get the words past the lump in my throat "We'll see them again, don't worry." But it wouldn't be the same. I knew it and so did Esther. Our paths might meet again but we would have seen different sights. They'd have changed as would we. But that was life.

Thirty Two

Later that night, alone and nestled in my bed for the last time, I looked around at the sparse but comfortable room. I'd miss the routine, being part of the household but most of all I'd miss the people I'd come to know and love—even Astrid. It had been hard to believe at first that I was leaving, but I respected Shaniqua and her judgment that it was time to get on with my life.

I *loved* them. Each and every one of them now owned a piece of my heart that was theirs forever and ever.

It was a stupid kind of thing—my eyes filled with tears and they ran down the side of my face. Half of my tears were from missing all of them already...but the other half was from that swelling in my heart that I actually, genuinely loved them all. And from loving them, I loved my parents more. From loving them, I loved Gwen more. From loving them I—never mind.

My fingers closed around the tourmaline stone and for the first time in a while, I thought of Nana. Which led to the painful memory of Zara and...I sighed, Holmes. Just as

Nana had encouraged me in that vision, Zara also wanted me to be kind, to not sink to his level. He was still alive, in a hospital with an armed guard outside his room day and night, according to what I'd heard from Dan Kreely. I could leave Ireland and never look back, never think about him ever again.

But...once more there was that dreaded 'but'. Nana's words would haunt me. I *could* stop by and see him. If nothing more, it would bug him that I was still going about the task that my grandmother had bequeathed. But, that really wasn't the point of visiting him, was it? Stopping by to lord something over him was not kind; it was vindictive. Nana told me that I needed to be loving. But for heaven's sake, how could I be expected to be kind to a monster who was responsible for his own daughter's death?

I decided that I would go and not try to hurt him. I'd refrain from being vindictive for Nana's sake; not his.

The phone on my bedside table rang and I almost jumped out of my skin. Even thinking about seeing him made me jumpy as a cat. I picked it up and smiled. Mom?

"Hi Mom."

"Keira! I hear you're going home!" She sounded happy about that!

"Yes! Who told you?" But for sure it had to be Shaniqua. How many times had they actually spoken since I'd been there? The penny dropped in that moment. Plenty of times, I'd bet. "Never mind. I'm bringing one of the kids with me. You'll like Esther. She's—"

"Shaniqua told me about Esther. Are you sure you can handle the responsibility of managing a fourteen year old?"

"Yes. I know it won't be easy but I can't imagine leaving here without her. She's become a little sister to me." We were alike in so many ways, both headstrong, masking insecurity with a smart ass attitude. If I could, I'd steer her away from the mistakes I'd made. "We're leaving tomorrow."

"Your father and I will pick you up. We just got into

Dublin an hour ago."

"What? You're here? I mean in Ireland?" I held the phone away from my ear and shook my head looking at it. This had been all set up from the jump! Shaniqua knew I'd agree to take Esther and even had my parents there for a reunion of sorts. Normally, that kind of thing would bug me, but not this time. My chest almost burst, at the thought of seeing her and Dad tomorrow!

"Did Shaniqua say it was okay for you guys to pick me up? This place is kind of secretive." How much did they know about the Abby? Probably Sean had told them. "Have you seen Sean or Gwen lately? How are they?"

"Well, we haven't *seen* them in two months since we went back to New York, but we've talked to them. They're fine! They're getting the house ready for you."

That didn't make sense. Sure Gwen, since she was living there anyway, but Sean? Maybe he'd mellowed a bit. I could hope, couldn't I? What would they think when I showed up with Esther? "Do they know about Esther?"

"No. I didn't mention that to Gwen. I thought it would be best if you talked to her."

If Mom said that, it meant she could foresee a few problems. But she was wrong. Gwen wouldn't mind. She'd love Esther! "Okay. Can you make it after lunch to pick me up? I'd like to spend the morning with the girls. I'm going to miss them."

"Sure. We'll call as we're leaving Dublin. I'm so happy you're coming home. We've missed you. Bye for now."

I hung up the phone and shook my head stifling a chuckle. To think I was out of sorts with them, thinking they didn't miss me enough to even call. They'd been kept up to date on how I was doing all along.

The Abby was a sanctuary for the Indigos but it had also been my sanctuary. Shaniqua had been right about that. I'd never lived in a home with so many people. The give and take, different personalities to adjust to and get along with. It had its challenges but the rewards outweighed them by a long shot.

***

The next morning, I looked around the room. My bag was packed but it was still hard to think I was leaving. I'd miss everyone so much. I wandered slowly down the stairs, gazing at the place I'd called home for the last while. It may have been only a matter of a couple of months, but it felt like a lifetime for me.

Sophia and Irina slipped by me, rushing down to the dining room. "Hurry, Keira! Astrid said we're having waffles and berries this morning. She said it's a special breakfast, though she didn't say why!"

Rita and Mary-Jane stepped next to me, one on each side. "We know why. We don't want you to go." Mary-Jane's hand slid into mine and there were tears in her eyes when she looked up.

I stopped for a moment, fighting the tightness in my throat, "I'll be back. And I promise to stay in touch." I made a mental note to get all their birthdays from Astrid. I'd make sure to send them each something special.

Rita nudged me with her shoulder. "It's not the same. I'd rather have you than some gift. I'm even going to miss Esther. Never thought I'd say that."

"For what it's worth, I'm going to miss all of you." I looked down at Mary-Jane, "Where *is* Esther?" My gut clenched for a moment. Had she changed her mind?

"She went down early to help in the kitchen. Her bag is all packed. " The desolation in Mary-Jane's voice broke my heart.

Shaniqua stepped out of the library and stood at the bottom of the stairs. She was wearing a skirt and sweater, unlike her normal jeans and T shirt, all spruced up for the new Director who was due to arrive soon. "I can see you already know. Cheer up! It's not like we won't see them again."

She led the way to the dining room where Esther was

serving the platter of waffles. Even Lilli had taken a seat at the table. The girls who hadn't picked up on the fact that it was a send off for Esther and I watched Shaniqua with wide eyes. They knew something was up.

She took a seat at the head of the table and began, "As you know, Keira joined us for a time but she will be leaving today. She has other responsibilities that she will be getting back to."

There was a chorus of groans and they turned to look at me. If I didn't feel so bad myself, it would have cheered me to see the sadness etched in their eyes.

"And Esther will be going with her." Shaniqua plucked her napkin from the table and spread it on her lap. "It will be beneficial for both of them, and a real opportunity for Esther."

Now they stared at Esther with wide eyed wonder.

"I'm going to miss you guys." Esther took a seat at the table and looked down, hiding her tears.

Astrid then spoke, "A new Director will be arriving later this morning. Madam Cora. So lots of changes at the Abby, girls. But that's life. There's always change. The Illuminata will make a decision after Cora has been here for a while as to whether we need to change locations."

It was funny. A few weeks ago, Astrid had strongly been in favor of that. But now, everything about her screamed for the peace and steadiness of this place. I couldn't help thinking that Zara's ashes in the garden were a part of that change of heart.

"I hope we stay here. I couldn't stand another change, especially now with Keira and Esther leaving." Sophia picked at the waffles and then set her fork down.

"We'll come back for visits. And any of you are welcome to come to visit me, if the Illuminata approve, that is." I looked over at Shaniqua, "Where is their headquarters? I could help fund a place like the Abby in Canada. You guys could do some kind of student exchange there."

Astrid shook her head. "Even we don't know that. We

know there are other sanctuaries but each cell is unknown to the others. It's another layer of protection for the Indigos." She smiled over at me. "Otherwise, an exchange could have been fun."

It was funny. The Illuminata knew about me, Nana and Zara but we knew next to nothing about them. Would our paths ever cross again?

***

Astrid and Shaniqua broke with routine for the rest of the morning, suspending the classes in order for the girls to spend the last hours with Esther and me. Although we tried to keep the conversation light, the pall of our leaving soon was a looming presence in the great room.

At the sharp rap at the front door, Astrid jumped up from her chair. She looked around at the girls and forced a nervous smile. "Please excuse us. That's probably the new Director." She and Shaniqua hurried from the room.

It was about twenty minutes later that Astrid poked her head in the door. "Lunch-time girls." She took a breath and looked down for a moment, "The new director, Cora, will be joining us."

When she left, Rita looked over at me. She'd picked up on it too, the subtle change in Astrid when she mentioned the new Director. It was more than nerves, meeting her new boss. And she wasn't the only one sensing it. The older girls had become quiet, exchanging furtive looks.

I stood up, forcing a cheerfulness I certainly didn't feel. "I don't know about you but I'm hungry. Let's try to be positive. This isn't the last supper. I'll be back and you want to make Cora feel welcome right?"

Esther came over and walked next to me when we filed out of the great room. "I think I'm getting out of here at the right time. I didn't like the look on Astrid's face."

I looked at her but held my tongue. I couldn't disagree with her, but then again, Astrid took a long time to warm up to people. It could be more of an Astrid issue than anything else. At least I hoped that was it.

When I stepped into the room, a middle aged woman in a grey business suit was sitting at the head of the table. She couldn't be less like Zara if she'd tried. Her eyes were narrow behind her glasses and it looked like a smile seldom creased her sharp features. Even her hair, streaked with grey, was secured in a tight bun, not a strand out of place to mar the white silk of her blouse. But more than that, her aura was wrong. There was a greenish hue to it, unlike Shaniqua's or Astrid's golden glow. The last time I saw a greenish hue...was Holmes.

Uh oh.

I instantly chided myself for not giving the woman the benefit of the doubt. She could just as likely be ill or something. She's some bigwig with the Illuminata for heaven's sake.

Shaniqua stood up from her spot next to the new Director. Her eyes took in all the girls, but passed quickly by me, "Girls, this is Cora Gaines, the new Director. You may address her as Miss Gaines."

"Hello girls. Miss Swanson. It's nice to finally meet you all. Of course, I've read your files but there's nothing like seeing the real person is there." Her lips twitched but the smile didn't quite reach her eyes. "After lunch I would like to meet with each of you individually, to get to know you better." She looked down the table at me, "Of course, that won't be necessary for you, Miss Swanson. The driver who brought me will take you into Dublin when we finish lunch."

I sat forward and managed to keep my tone light, "Thanks, but my parents are picking Esther and me up at two." I smiled and glanced over at Esther, throwing a wink to ease the tension that showed in her wide eyes.

"I'm afraid I can't allow that. Security at the Abby has become quite lax. Police, ambulance attendants, hoodlums and all kinds of people have been here. This is a *sanctuary*, not Grand Central Station where people come and go freely." She plucked the napkin next to her plate and spread it on her lap.

I was about to speak but Shaniqua beat me to it. "Keira's parents aren't just anybody. They know and have experienced the paranormal all of their lives. I'm sure—"

"That's just it. You aren't sure. You've never met them, have you? And as for Esther going with you, Miss Swanson, I can't allow that. I don't know why Shaniqua and Astrid ever suggested it. Esther is a minor and we are her guardians, sworn to safeguard her well being. She's special, as are all the Indigo children."

"What? I'm not going?" Esther leaned forward staring at the older woman. "You can't do that!"

"Hold on! Esther wants to come with me and it was agreed on before you stuck your nose in!" I rose from my seat, walking over to Esther and putting my hands on her shoulders. "Tell her Shaniqua! Astrid?" I stared at them. But their gazes dropped to their plates.

Oh my God. The Cora bitch outranked them and there was nothing they could do.

Cora's eyes were hard chips of glass glaring at me, "When Esther comes of age, she may go then if she likes, but not now. We have a responsibility—"

"No! I'm going! You can't stop me!" Esther jumped up from her chair and raced out of the room.

Astrid stood up, her lips a tight line staring at her new boss, before running after Esther. The rest of the girls were wide eyed, staring from Cora to me.

"I had hoped this wouldn't happen. This is what comes of having an outsider stay here. Girls, this must be upsetting. You may be excused." Cora stood up, holding her claw like fingers on the edge of the table.

Rita and Sophia cast a dirty look at her before turning to herd the younger girls from the room. Cora's chair shot forward, hitting the back of her knees, so that she stumbled and landed on her ass in it. Her teeth ground together and she glared at Sophia and Rita, before turning to me.

"It's time you were on your way, Miss Swanson. I don't appreciate the influence you've had on the girls."

"Fine! But I'll be back with my lawyer! You can't keep Esther here. Not if she wants to go!" I spun on my heels to the door but turned to throw one more shot at her, "*You're* the one who needs to go Cora. How'd you ever get this job? You certainly are no Zara!"

I went through the door, my jaw clenching when I heard her final word, "I'm also not dead, am I?"

Thirty Three

When I stepped into the bedroom, Astrid stood next to the door while Esther sat on her bed, fire in her eyes, glaring at the floor. I rushed over and sat next to her, putting my arm over her shoulder. The poor kid. She wanted to be with me as much as I wanted to be with her.

"She can't do this!" She turned and tears blurred her eyes, looking at me.

""I'm so sorry, Esther! I'll fight this. If there's a way to get you living with me, I'll find it." I fumed, glaring over at Astrid. "Why didn't you say anything? How could you suggest this without knowing she could stop you?"

She sighed and slumped lower, "Honestly, we didn't know she would do that. With the two of us agreeing it would be good for Esther, that normally would have been sufficient. She's old school, totally different than how we've been running things."

"I'm going to lodge a complaint. She shouldn't be in charge of these kids. This is a sanctuary not a prison and she's acting like some kind of warden! What the hell are her qualifications?" My heart broke when Esther's hands rose to cover her face, the tears flowing.

"She's got a degree in parapsychology. She's been with the order for about five years. This is her first house to manage. I guess the order thought we needed more regimentation and she's the perfect fit."

"I'm going to contact them and tell them how wrong she is for this place. I'm going to get Esther out of here, but I don't think the girls left will do well with Cora running things." My eyes closed for a moment thinking of Mary-Jane and Kirsten. The youngest of all of them, needing love and support, not regimentation.

"Good luck with that. Like I told you, it's a secret society. We are in contact by mail with no return address and email."

"Well she worked in the head office. She knows where it is. I'll find out if it's the last thing I do." I hugged Esther closer. "Be patient. I'll come back for you, don't worry."

She sniffed and sat straighter. "If she lasts...she doesn't want to mess with the kids here. It could be bad for her health."

Astrid strode over, "No. Don't even think of that, Esther. There are far worse places to be than living here, even if Cora is strict. You can't do anything to her. Promise me you won't."

"I'm not making any promises. You said I was leaving with Keira, but that didn't work, did it?"

Oh my God. Now it was even more important to find this Illuminata headquarters to get Cora removed. Removed before the girls turned on her completely. I wouldn't want to have any of them as an enemy.

Thirty Four

By the time I arrived in Dublin at the hotel where my parents were staying the anger had settled to a cold determination. I would find this Illuminata organization and have that woman removed, right after I got Esther out of there.

I knocked on the door to their suite and bounded into my father's arms when he opened it. "Dad!" I nuzzled his cheek, inhaling the familiar aroma of his after-shave, before planting a kiss there. The tension in my chest melted away in that moment.

My mother reached for me, nudging my father aside. "Keira." Her voice hitched as she encircled me in her arms. "We've missed you so." The happy tears filling both of our eyes said it all.

"Mom! I'm glad you guys came over here to be with me. After everything that's happened, it means a lot."

She pulled back a bit and her fingers lifted a lock of hair that had fallen onto my cheek. "It's been hard on us as well. When Sean told us about Holmes and Zara, we wanted to catch the next plane over. But he also thought you staying at the Abby, would be good for you. After talking to Shaniqua,

I had to agree. Still it was tough."

She shook her head, "And that poor child, Esther, having the rug pulled out from under her feet at the last minute."

I followed them into the living room and flopped down on the sofa. "Yes. Leaving her was hard, but what could I do? That horrible woman..." But I wasn't ready to go down that path yet. I took a deep breath and said, "Sean. He was really angry that day. And I think if I'd listened to him, it would have turned out differently. Actually, I should have listened to you as well. It ended up being more than I could handle on my own."

Mom took a seat next to me, "What an evil man, Holmes is. He killed his own daughter and he could have killed you as well. Thank God he's finished."

"Well, he won't be a threat anymore." I took a deep breath. "I think I should go to see him. I had a dream about Nana before this all came to a head. She wanted me to show kindness to him. I'm not sure I can actually be kind but seeing him would bring closure, if nothing else. He's in a hospital not far from here."

Mom's eyebrows rose and she looked over at Dad. This was probably the last thing she'd expected me to say.

Dad leaned forward in his chair. "You're sure about this? I think it will bring the pain of that day all over again."

I nodded and my mother took my hand, giving it a firm squeeze. "I see you're determined. You're not going alone though. Your father and I will be with you."

"Yes. I think that would be better." As far as I knew, Mom had never seen her father, although Holmes had seen her plenty of times. I sighed, "We'll go tomorrow and get it over with."

I turned to Dad. "What do you know about the Illuminata?" Nana had known of them, so surely Dad, being a Guardian must have some information.

He blew a mouthful of air through puffed cheeks, looking perplexed. "I know about the Illuminati but not so much about the female order. I knew they existed but not much more than that I'm afraid."

"As for them keeping Esther...she's only twelve. You might have to wait four more years, Keira. If this Illuminata are her legal guardians, then it wouldn't seem like there's much that you can do. Despite what the poor kid wants." Mom got up and went to the bar to get a drink. "Soft drink, anyone?"

I shook my head, "No thanks. But this Cora woman is horrible. She is totally unlike the other people working there. Even the furniture shows more warmth than that old crow." Just thinking of her made my blood boil.

"I may be able to make a few calls and find out more about this group. Even a secret society can't stay totally hidden. You said she *was or is* a parapsychologist. Finding out where she graduated might be a good start." Dad took the can of coke that Mom handed him.

"Cora Gaines. It's not that common a name and her accent was weird for being here. I could swear it was like she was from Boston."

He snorted. "That's one you should recognize, all right. Maybe Harvard or MIT? This Illuminata gang is all over the place it seems. But that's a start anyway." He got to his feet. "I might as well begin this now, while we're in Ireland. Chances are they've got an office here somewhere." He took his drink and was fishing his cell phone from his pocket as he left the room.

Mom took a seat next to me again. "Putting the problem of Esther and the Illuminata aside...have you thought about what you're going to do when you get back home? Will you and Gwen continue working with the transitions?"

What she wasn't saying, but was dying to know, was what would happen with Sean. "Yes. And Roy as well, if we can convince him to quit his job again." I couldn't help but chuckle, "That shouldn't be too hard, not with Gwen being part of the package. I'm actually looking forward to it, after this break." What I didn't add was that I'd hoped Esther would learn more about it and eventually help.

"Well, I guess I'm not surprised." She looked down into the glass of coke for a moment, "But Sean...I think you need to talk to him. I know he's upset but there was something between the two of you. He's a special person."

I shook my head. "I'll talk to him but I'm not holding out much hope. I crossed a line that I don't think he'll *ever* get over."

"She smiled, "Ever is a long time. When were you thinking of flying back? Your father and I haven't been away in a while. We'd planned on going to a few more places before we go back. Of course you're welcome to come with us, London, Paris and of course Tuscany. What do you think?"

"A second or maybe tenth, honeymoon? No. I think I'll stay here for another day or two and then fly back. If Dad can make some headway with the Illuminata, maybe I'll stay longer and get that settled. At any rate, I should check in with Mr. Thompson and let him know I'm ready for assignments. I've been off the grid for too long."

Even as I said it, I knew getting back to work was going to be weird. There were still loose ends to be resolved. First Esther, then Sean.

***

Sleep was a long time coming that night. Whether it was the noise of the city after getting used to the peace of the countryside Abby, or thinking of those poor girls, wondering how they were doing with the new Director, I tossed and turned for half the night. When I finally dropped off, the crazy dreams were a continuation. Except, instead of Cora, it was Sean who was the Director and he was leading a hike to the lake. He kept going too fast and the girls begged me to make him slow down. When we finally got to the lake, he grinned and pushed me off the high rock into the water. But before I splashed into it, the girls used their levitation skills and I was back at his side.

"Keira?" My eyes popped open to see Mom smiling down at me, the light from the wall of windows, a halo round her slender body. "It's almost eleven. We let you sleep in."

Considering the wacky dream, she hadn't done me any favors. I tossed the covers back and sat up, blinking slowly to focus. "Where's Dad?"

She straightened and folded her arms across her chest. "He's just outside. He's got something to tell you." Her lips twitched into a smile.

I jerked upright. "The Abby? He's found out something about the Illuminata?" This was great news!

"Before you get your hopes up, it's just a start. But I'll let him tell you." She winked at me and then wandered out of the room. She was already dressed for the day. They really had let me sleep in.

I threw my robe over the nightshirt and went out to the kitchen area to get a coffee. Dad was in the living room, perched on the sofa, with his laptop open on the coffee table before him.

"Good morning! You've got some news for me?" I took a seat next to him, cupping the mug and leaning forward to see the screen.

He turned to smile at me, "A friend of mine, Ralph Stevens, went to Harvard. I contacted Ralph and he was able to find Cora Gaines in the student archives. She graduated Cum Laude, in 2001. An Alumni periodical listed her as securing a position with Blackwatch Security."

Mom took a step closer, peering down at him. "That seems an odd career choice, considering her degree, don't you think? What would a security firm want with a woman who graduated with a parapsychology degree?"

Dad sat back and folded his arms across his chest, staring at the screen. It showed the website for the company, an animated ad of security cameras, tall office buildings and executives with shark-like grins. "I've heard this company has some classified government contracts. It doesn't jive with what I know about the Illuminata for her to ever consider working for a firm like that. It's quite a leap."

"It might explain her treating the place like a prison, so concerned with security that you guys weren't allowed on the grounds. And she couldn't get me out of there fast enough." I sipped my coffee trying to make sense of it. There'd been that nasty green aura around her. Almost as sickening as Holmes's had been. What I'd taken as some kind of latent illness, cancer or diabetes, might be far more sinister.

Mom slipped down to sit next to me. "Should we hire an investigator? We don't have the resources or talent to take this much farther. What did she do between working for the security firm and where she is now?"

"That's a good idea. If you know of any good ones, Dad, can you call them? In the meantime, I'm going to speak with Shaniqua. Surely, she'd want to know this if the Illuminata doesn't already. It could be nothing but then again, it could be important. Besides which I want to see how Esther and the rest of the girls are making out."

I got up and went to the bedroom to get my phone from the charger. When I hit the button to call Shaniqua, it went to voice mail right away. It was almost noon, a time when she'd be working in the office. "Hi Shaniqua. It's Keira. I'm just calling to see how the girls are. I wanted to talk to Esther if I can. Would you please call me back this afternoon during free time?"

There. That was all I could do for now.

My shoulders slumped when I thought of the chore facing me that afternoon. The visit to see Holmes. It was the last thing I wanted to do but I'd be glad to have it over with. I looked up at the ceiling as I wandered into the bathroom to take a shower. 'If you're listening Nana, I'm doing this. I'm trying but he'll be lucky if I don't pull the plug on his life support.'

Thirty Five

After a few phone calls on my behalf, the way was cleared for us to go to the hospital to see Holmes. The smell of cleaning solutions mingled with antiseptic drifting into my nose as the three of us walked down the hallway to his room. The uniformed officer got to his feet when he saw us pause at the door to Holmes's room.

I took a breath, straightening my shoulders. "We're here to see David Holmes. Inspector Kreely called you?"

"You're Keira Swanson?"

I nodded, "And my parents Richard and Susan Swanson. We won't be long."

"Just the same, I'll need to be in the room with you." He opened the door and held his arm out, inviting us inside. He stood near the door folding his arms across his chest.

When I stepped closer, I could hardly recognize Holmes. A thin tube crossed his upper lip, while another was attached to his wrist. But his face was a pasty pallor, holding barely more color than his white beard and moustache. The sickly green aura clung to his wasted body. His eyes flew open and I jerked back.

My heart thundered in my chest and it was hard to

breathe. I counted to ten, focusing on my breathing, getting control once more. He was no threat to me now. His eyes were hard as iron but he couldn't do anything to hurt us.

Now that I was here, I didn't know what to say. My mother's fingers closed over my hand while Holmes's gaze flitted over all of us. I edged closer, "I'm only here because of Nana."

"GET OUT!"

Again I jerked back. The thought he'd projected blasted into my brain. The soft beeping of the machine behind him sped up. If he wasn't careful, he'd blow a gasket again.

My eyes narrowed, glaring at him. "Stop it. You lost. It's over now." I thought of Zara, what she'd said about Holmes. "If there's a shred of decency left in you, you should be sorry, not angry. There's nothing left here for you. You destroyed your daughter and tried to kill me as well."

Dad stepped closer and tugged on my sleeve. "Come on. You've seen him and that's enough. He's still the horrible monster he always was. He's incapable of remorse."

Mom turned and stepped away from the bed, while I continued to stare down at the husk of his body. I knew Dad was right on this. But maybe given enough time, wasting away, he'd feel some shame. Had that been Nana's hope?

"You caused so much pain, but look at you now. You're more to be pitied than anything else. Goodbye Grandfather."

I turned away. *'Keira.'* For just a second when the faint whispered plea of his mind, entered my head, I paused.

I fought the tear that threatened to spill from my eye, thinking of Nana. I'd tried but this was as good as I could manage. I'd seen him and it was over. Over for him and over for me.

***

When I got back to the hotel, I took my cell phone out of my purse. There was nothing from Shaniqua but I had to try again. It was the free time period at the school and there was a good chance that I could get her this time. But once more, the call went straight through to voice mail.

My parents looked across from their spot on the sofa. Mom sighed and then took Dad's hand. "Still nothing?"

It didn't make sense. Unless the new director had really changed things up. I shook my head, trying to shake the feeling that something was wrong. But my gut was a tight knot, refusing to get the memo to be patient.

"Maybe we should go out and explore the city. Leave all this behind and have a nice lunch somewhere." Dad got to his feet, pulling Mom along with him. He was trying his best to take our minds off it and off the horrible visit with Holmes. When he saw that I was still worried, he added, "I've placed a call to a private investigation firm. They've got the preliminary information. We need to be patient and wait to hear from them. There's no sense moping around here."

"You guys go ahead. I think I might lay down for a bit. I didn't sleep all that well last night." I managed a smile and then got to my feet, stretching my arms high.

"We'll bring something back for you. You rest and things will look brighter when you get up." Mom followed Dad to the door and looked back, a warm smile on her lips, "Try not to worry, Keira. Your father's right."

He nodded and then held the door open for them to leave.

It hadn't been a total lie to them. I *was* going to lay down but there was more than one way to skin a cat. I'd try astral travelling again. I hadn't done it since the time with Shaniqua. Being at the Abby, not wanting any kind of exposure for the girls had stopped me, even though it was a neat thing to do. But now, I'd have to try it again, to see what was going on there.

I lay down on the bed and went through the breathing exercises, getting myself to the level of consciousness just shy of sleep. Considering how tired I was and drained from the visit to the hospital, it took less time than I would have thought possible. A sizzling vibration rose from my chest, extending out to my fingers and toes before the welcome pop zapped between my ears.

I was free, drifting slowly to the ceiling and glancing down at my body. No sooner had I thought of Esther, than I was there at the Abby! The older girls were all in the great room, sitting in a big circle while Cora and Astrid stood to the side watching them. I hovered next to Esther's shoulder, sensing the tension in her body, her eyes narrowed and focused on a book that was the centre of the circle.

"Go on Esther. It's okay. This is just a measurement Cora wants to add to your file." Astrid stepped closer, a clipboard in her hand. "I've seen you do this before so I know you're capable."

Esther sighed and then took a deep breath, sitting higher. The book, the size of a thick dictionary or encyclopedia began to vibrate, creating a soft hiss on the wooden floor. It lifted higher and the sound fell off, so that silence filled the room. Higher and higher it rose, gaining velocity. It was almost at the ceiling when suddenly it crashed to the floor, startling everyone with the sharp thud.

"Good. I think that's the last of them now. We'll take a break before the next exercise." Cora looked positively glowing, she was so happy, clapping her hands together.

But she was the only one. The girls looked like they were ready to kill her, staring down at the book. Rita's head turned and she looked right at me. Oh my God, her mouth fell open. She knew I was there. I might have known that she would be the one to intuit that I was there, if not actually see me. My finger rose to cross over my lips, signaling for her to stay quiet.

Sophia was the first to rise. "Can we see Mary-Jane and Kirsten now? I'm not doing any more of your stupid tests until I see them."

Irina flashed a smile that even I could see was forced. "We're not going to do anything *bad* to you. Have we ever hurt Astrid or Shaniqua? No. We know it's wrong to hurt other people."

"Well, until I know I can trust you, it's best to keep the little ones safe from you." Cora's chin rose high, dismissing Irina with a sniff.

Esther's voice was barely above a whisper. "Keep *you* safe, you mean." She stood up and scowled at Astrid. "Why do we have to do these tests? Zara never made us. Why the sudden interest in our psychic abilities? You're treating us like lab rats."

Astrid glanced at Cora before turning to Esther. "It's something that Headquarters wants. They're doing some kind of study. It's only for a little while and then we'll be back to our normal routine."

Rita cleared her throat, catching my eyes. She shook her head and then joined the others in leaving the room for a break.

My mind went to Mary-Jane and I was there. She and Kirsten were in the bedroom that Esther and she shared. Mary-Jane had the book she loved open, reading it to Kirsten. I heard the lock of the door click and then it opened. Shaniqua stood in the opening. "I'm sorry girls. This will just be for another couple of days and then I promise, we'll get back to classes."

Wow! Even Shaniqua was buying into this?

Cora. An instant later I was in the library where she sat behind the desk. Her claw like fingers gripped the cell phone to her ear. "Yes. It went well. Telepathy is next. I'll send the results later today in an email." There was a hard glint in her eyes.

She could be talking to the home office and this was legitimate or maybe...

That security firm where she worked! In the next instant I was back in the hotel room, rejoining my physical body. My spidey-sense tingled along with my fingers. We needed to find out more about this Cora Gaines.

Thirty Six

That evening, I was doing my own bit of research, the laptop sitting on the bed before me, when a message icon popped up on the computer screen—would I accept a Skype call from Gwen?

My eyebrows rose and I quickly clicked on the icon. I had to grin seeing her sitting at the kitchen table, a bottle of beer next to her hand. "Hey Gwen! How're you doing?"

"Keira! I thought you'd be home by now. Don't you miss us?" She laughed and took a long swallow of beer. Roy wandered by behind her and waved to me before disappearing from the screen.

"Absolutely! But Mom and Dad are here and I wanted to spend a few days with them. They're leaving day after tomorrow for London and a mini vacation." It really hit me seeing her face and the familiar surroundings of my kitchen, how much I missed her and being home.

"So, you're flying back then? We'll pick you up at the airport. Just let us know the flight." Her gaze drifted to the side and she smiled. Roy must have settled at the table next to her.

"I'm hoping to. You know, when I was at the Abby, there was a young girl there, Esther, who I thought would be coming home with me. She's a great kid and we became pretty close. I was going to—"

"Wait! You're adopting her or something? How's that going to work out with the transitioning? We go all over the world. How old is she?" Gwen's face was a puzzled knot.

It was funny. Usually, it was HER family commitments that we had to work around when we were working. The shoe was on the other foot now. But unlike Devon, Esther would go with us, so it wouldn't have been a problem. But Gwen didn't know that.

"She's fourteen. And gifted." I sighed and leaned closer to the screen. "But that's not going to happen now...at least, not right away. There's a new director—"

Her mouth pulled to the side and she looked down for a moment. "Shit! I forgot to tell you how sorry I was to hear about your aunt! I kind of got wrapped up with actually talking to you. It's been a while!"

"Thanks. Yeah, it was pretty horrible. I wished I'd listened to you guys. It was a total nightmare that day. Zara was such a sweet person. You would have liked her." It was still pretty painful when the image passed through my mind of that horrible, horrible day.

I took a breath and continued, "At any rate, this new director, Cora Gaines, is a total jerk. She practically kicked me out and then she said Esther had to remain in their care."

"That's rough. It must have been hard on the kid too." Her head dipped to the side and she shrugged. "But what can you do? She's a minor and if they have custody..."

"How much did Sean tell you about the Abby?" Without waiting for a reply, I continued, "It's a sanctuary for Indigo children. They're gifted with all kinds of psychic ability. The Abby and the organization that runs it, the Illuminata, protect them. Otherwise, they could be exploited by men like Holmes or some other nasty outfit."

"Wow. I've never heard the term, Indigo. Sean mentioned that it's some kind of secret organization but not much else about it." I could see her fingers plucking at the label on the bottle of beer she cupped between her hands.

"The kids got the name because there's a blue aura surrounding their bodies. At any rate, I'm trying to find out more about this director. I don't trust her. Get this. She graduated from Harvard with a degree in parapsychology yet she worked for some security firm. Blackwatch. Does that make sense to you?"

"Blackwatch. I've heard the name before but I can't remember the details." Gwen's eyebrows knitted together and her eyes were narrow.

"Dad says they were involved with the government with some classified contracts." From what I'd read on their website, they had their fingers into a lot of different pies.

Roy's face filled the screen, "That's it! There was a piece in the news a while ago about them. They've got a mercenary division. They were in Iraq and Afghanistan as I recall."

Gwen nudged him aside, "So that totally doesn't make sense for her to work for them."

"That's what we thought too. Dad has hired a private investigation firm to look into her background and find out whatever he can about the Illuminata."

"You mean, Illuminati, don't you?"

"No. This is the women's equivalent to that organization. But they work for peace, not money and power. I want to wait till the last minute to leave here. I've got the feeling that their main office, or at least the office where Cora came from, is here in Ireland. If she's secretly still working for that security outfit, she's the last person who should be around the Indigos."

Gwen was silent for a few moments. She glanced over at Roy and then blurted, "I can go over and help you with this. If you hear from the investigation firm, tell me. I don't want you going off half-cocked against this Illuminata or Blackwatch or some other crazy outfit."

Roy again appeared, standing behind her with his hands cupping her shoulders. "If that's the case, I'm going too! It's been pretty quiet around here without you, Keira." He chuckled.

I had to laugh too. Hail, hail, the gang's all here. Well not quite. "I promise that I won't do something on my own. I think I learned my lesson. And when Mom and Dad leave for their vacation, I might need you. That's if I hear something tomorrow. If not, I'll be home and have to continue this investigation long distance."

My stomach did a flip flop, but I had to ask. "How is Sean doing? Did he go back to his old job in Toronto?"

Gwen sighed and her voice became softer, "No. He's still living with Dad, doing some projects around the house to keep busy. He was here for dinner last night."

I bit my tongue to keep from asking if he was still angry...if he'd even mentioned my name. I could tell from the way she spoke that nothing had changed in his feelings towards me. I'd blown any chance of a relationship with him.

Roy once more edged into half the screen. "I'll see what I can find out from my old military buddies on this Blackwatch outfit. In the meantime, keep us in the loop with whatever you find out."

"For sure. Give my best to your dad when you see him..." A weak smile flitted across my face, "...and Sean too. We'll talk later."

Gwen shook her head and laughed. "I can't believe I might be going back to Ireland after how it went the last time!"

"If you come here, I promise it'll be waaay better." I wasn't going to get into the visit to the hospital. I wanted to put that well behind me.

"Okay. We'll talk later. Take care." Gwen smiled and then the screen changed, back to the Blackwatch website.

But it was a few minutes until I could focus on that. At least things with Gwen were okay again. It might be awkward though working with her when Sean was living back in Kingston. I'd have to deal with that when it came up. There was no sense adding *that* worry to my plate.

Thirty Seven

My eyes felt like they were ready to fall out from reading and researching about Blackwatch, and I was just dozing off, when my cell phone beeped. I turned the bedside light on and picked it from the table. The small screen showed...Shaniqua?

"Hello?"

"Hi Keira. Sorry I'm so late calling you." Her voice was hurried and very low, barely above a whisper.

I sat up quickly, the adrenaline surging in my chest. Something was up and it wasn't good, not from her hushed voice. "How is Esther?"

"She's angry, and sad, but otherwise okay. The girls are doing fine, all things considered. But—"

"It's Cora isn't it? I was there today. You know, the astral travelling thing. I saw her assessing the girls. What's up with that? In all the time I was there, you and Astrid never did that. The girls played around with telekinesis and telepathy but you never went out of your way encouraging or discouraging it." Somehow, I couldn't imagine that this was something sanctioned by the Illuminata. I just needed her confirmation. "Let alone *testing* it, Shaniqua."

"No. It was something the girls would do on their own. You don't force art but rather you provide the tools and an atmosphere for it to grow. The girls are special. They understand that." Her voice became louder, "Zara never wanted them to feel like circus freaks or trained seals. God knows they got enough of that before they came here."

The scene that day in the library had been like that, seeing what the girls were capable of. I took a deep breath to calm the anger that was rising in my chest, "How much do you know about Cora? The Illuminata sent her but did you know she worked for a private security company before she joined your group?"

"What? That can't be true. The Order screens candidates. You have to be squeaky clean to get in."

"Well, this one slipped by. She graduated from Harvard and then went to work for Blackwatch. Have you ever heard of them? They're *mercenaries,* Shaniqua.

"Blackwatch? You're kidding! Yes, I've heard of them."

"You've got to let the order know. Actually, let *me* tell them. How do I get hold of them?"

There was a banging noise that came through the phone and her words were hurried, "I've got to go." Followed by the click of the connection ending.

I held the phone to my chest, while my heart and mind were going ninety miles a minute. Something was terribly wrong about this whole situation. The phone call was secretive and ended too abruptly, like Shaniqua had been caught doing something wrong. It was a private school for God's sake, not the CIA!

I could only pray she'd be able to alert the order and something would be done. Tomorrow. Maybe I'd hear something from that investigative firm that Dad hired. The heck with patience. I'd call them in the afternoon. Time was running out.

Thirty Eight

The next morning, when I came out of the bedroom ready for the day, Dad was on his cell phone, pacing across the living room. He motioned for me to come closer and mouthed, 'Investigator'. Sometimes he forgot that I could read what he was thinking.

Well, when I needed to. Like right then.

He clicked off the phone and turned to me. "They've found where this Cora Gaines was living before she went to the Abby. She's been in Galway, for the past few years, in a one bedroom apartment on Aetna Green."

Mom came over and handed me a mug of coffee. "I'd say you're pretty close to finding the office where she worked. It's got to be in Galway." She went over to take a seat on the sofa. "It's funny. This Illuminati outfit has a website but there's nothing for the Illuminata. This would be so much easier if there was."

Dad looked over at me before taking a seat next to Mom, "So, does this change your plans to fly home?"

"Yeah, I think it has to. It'd be silly to fly home when we're getting close to this. Plus I'm still hoping to convince them that Esther would be better off with me." I wandered over to the window and gazed out at the cityscape, barely registering the view as my mind raced. "I spoke with

Shaniqua late last night. She called me. It was as if she was sneaking her call to me the way she sounded on the phone and then ended it pretty abruptly."

"That doesn't sound good."

I turned to face my parents, "She had no idea of Cora's background. She was shocked when I told her. This Cora is doing tests on the girls to assess their psychic power. She thought that was odd for the Illuminata to suddenly want that data."

Dad sat forward, "If you're staying you'll need the contact information on the investigation. I've been dealing with a guy named Harry Bennett. He figures that he's going to be able to track down the location of the offices in Galway she worked at. When we get that info, you can contact the Illuminata directly."

I frowned, "No. I think I need to see them face to face. How else will I make a case for Esther leaving with me? They'll need to meet me. If it was just Cora...well, I wouldn't even bother staying. That should be cut and dry."

I walked across the room to sit in the chair facing them. The looks on their faces, the quick glance at each other showed they weren't too crazy about that idea.

Dad edged forward and put his hand on my knee, "Keira. If she's working for a big security firm and is up to no good with the Indigos, then you'll need to be careful. Tackle one thing at a time. Contact the Illuminata and let them deal with their problem. Then make your case once it's dealt with."

Mom nodded, "Yes. It was fine with Shaniqua so once this Cora is gone, it's safe to assume that the original plan will stand." She glanced over at Dad, "You father is right. Call them, but keep your distance. I don't like the sounds of this Blackwatch outfit."

I sat for a few minutes thinking of what they'd said. They were concerned for my safety and there was no way they'd leave for their vacation if they thought I was going to push the point. That wouldn't be fair to do that to them. And they'd been right about David Holmes that I shouldn't tackle him on my own. Plus there was the feeling in my gut, my intuition that this could get very bad for the Indigos.

"I'll tell you what. I'll take your advice and just call them when I have a contact number or email addy. I know you're worried about me and I don't have the greatest track record for taking advice. But, I promise you I will this time." I smiled before playing the trump card to ease their concerns, "In fact Gwen and Roy said they'll fly in tomorrow to keep an eye on things and help out."

My father sat back and blew out a long sigh. He smiled at Mom, "Is this our daughter or did some alien take over Keira?"

"Very funny!" But the corners of my mouth curled up.

Mom grinned, "Just Gwen and Roy? I thought Sean was going to work with you? Maybe I should call him."

"Don't you dare! He's really angry Mom. I don't think he'll ever speak to me so don't even go there!" But she was teasing and I knew it. Still my cheeks burned and I had to look away to hide the flush.

She grinned and then turned to Dad, "Well, I guess we're a go for London then. No need to cancel the tickets." Turning to me again, "I'm glad that you're handling it this way. I may not have your psychic abilities but common sense counts for something, I'd say. I don't want you mixed up in any way with that Blackwatch crew."

"Believe me, neither do I! Holmes and his shady thugs taught me my lesson." I rose to my feet, "I'd better let Gwen know. I'll send off an email since she's probably still in bed."

She took my empty mug and brought it to the small kitchenette. As I was about to go into my bedroom she called, "After you email, let's go out for brunch and some shopping?"

Some things would never change and for that I had to smile.

Thirty Nine

When the taxi door closed the next day, my parents and their luggage safely tucked away inside, going to the airport, I gazed down the busy street. It was six hours at least until Gwen and Roy would arrive. I was jumpy as a cat, and the thought of going back into the hotel to wait had no appeal.

Even though I'd spoken to Harry Bennett the investigator, to make the initial contact, my hopes that he'd have something for me were dashed. He said he had a couple of leads but this organization obviously operated under a cover name. And nothing from Shaniqua, which wasn't a surprise.

I started walking. Anything to keep busy and ease the jitters from my skin. Halfway down the block, I paused gazing into a shop window of Irish linens and wool sweaters. Should I go back and try the astral travelling, see what was going on at the Abby? But what if this time, Rita saw me and blurted it out? That wouldn't be good. Besides which in the state I was in, it was doubtful that I could settle my nerves enough to do it.

I closed my eyes and sighed. No. I'd kill some time sightseeing, trying to enjoy the clear sky and fresh air. When I'd gone halfway down the next block, the hair on the back of my neck tingled and I sensed eyes watching me. I stopped at another shop window, and glanced up the sidewalk where I'd just been. Two men in business suits chatted, while three teenage girls in jeans and T shirts ambled behind them. I opened my mind and picked up on their thoughts as they came closer. Nothing to worry about with office gossip and movie critiques.

Just as I was about to carry on, a reflection in the glass caught my eye. A tall man, dark hair under the cap of Irish tweed, a beard and sunglasses stepped out of a coffee shop. He wore a navy vest over a white shirt and jeans, casually walking along carrying a plastic shopping bag. There was nothing striking about him but still, my gut clenched when I turned and continued.

I took a deep breath and shook my head. This was silly. I was just being paranoid. I hadn't made any calls, nothing to draw the attention of Cora or that security outfit. As far as anyone knew—well anyone except Harry Bennett the investigator—I was a tourist taking in the sights. I knew no one. And if Holmes had somehow made some kind of miraculous recovery, Inspector Kreely would have called.

Still, I couldn't shake the feeling I was being followed. And considering my abilities, it would be foolish to dismiss them outright. I paused at the corner and strode over to a bus bench, sliding in next to an elderly woman in a flowered dress. I took my phone from my pocket and hit the button to call Shaniqua, all the while watching the progress of the man in the vest and cap.

He paused at the corner but considering the light change to red, that wasn't out of line. A voice sounded in the phone, "No service for this number. Please try again." I sat straighter, looking at the phone. Shaniqua's service was down or...cancelled. She'd ended the call the other night so fast, maybe Cora had taken her phone.

"Do you have the time?"

I turned at the old woman's voice and after glancing at my phone, I told her, "Ten minutes after twelve."

"Thank you dear. That bus is late as usual. I'm supposed to be home for my grandchildren, to give them lunch. That daughter-in-law will be giving me what for, the little snip. I'll be lucky if I get to see the bairns again!" She sniffed and shook her head.

I pulled a sad face and then, "Excuse me. I have to..." When I turned there was no sign of the tall man in the cap. Not walking across the street or even going back the way he'd come.

Well, that was probably a good thing. At least I hoped it was.

I got up and hustled to catch the light, crossing the wide street. It looked like there was a small park about halfway down the next block. I'd wander around it and then think about grabbing something for lunch. But still that sense of someone watching clung to me. I glanced behind and my eyes gaped wider before turning and hurrying my step. He was back! About twenty steps behind me now!

A whiff of vinegar and the smell of french fries wafted from a small restaurant to my right. There was no way I was taking a chance alone in a park if I was being followed. Besides which, my stomach let me know with a growl I hadn't had much to eat that day. I ducked inside and spotting an empty table near the window, I grabbed it. My eyes were peeled to the outside, watching for the guy but again, there was no sign of him.

A middle-aged waitress, with her hair in a prim bun stopped at the table and handed me a menu. "Just yourself?" She smiled and grabbed the place setting across from me with a sweep of her hand.

"Yes. I don't think I need a menu. An order of fish and fries with a coffee, thanks." I gave her a quick smile and then turned peering once more out the window. Groups of working people on their lunch, mingled amidst the shopping crowd. But no sign of Mr. Cap.

"You're American?" She chuckled. "It's not just the accent, we call it fish 'n chips. And it would be tea rather than coffee. I hope you're enjoying your stay in Dublin."

"Thanks! I am." I pulled my chair closer to the table and smiled up at her. 'Good tipping Yanks' was in her eyes and her brain as she left the table.

***

When I stepped outside after the best fish and fries in my life, I paused, gazing both ways before heading back to the hotel. It wouldn't be any fun playing tourist, not if I kept looking over my shoulder. As I was turning to go back, from the corner of my eye I spotted him again. This time he was across the street, standing near a brick wall, pretending to read something on his cell phone. I eyed him more closely, his height, lean but muscular body and the dark hair and swarthy complexion. He must have noticed me watching him, because he turned slightly and his profile showed.

Oh my God! There couldn't be two of him! It was SEAN! What the hell was he doing, spying on me? I huffed a fast breath. Mom! Had she called him despite telling me she wouldn't? But I would have known that. Even without my mind reading talent, she was a terrible liar. But I still didn't know why he'd be there, not when he was so pissed with me!

Hmph! This could be fun, playing along with this, leading him on a wild goose chase. There was a large department store halfway up the block. I ducked in there and took a spot behind a rack of ladies dresses. I held one up before me, as if I was considering it but all the while my gaze was zeroed in on the revolving door entrance. In no time at all, he appeared, his hand pulling the dark sunglasses away from his eyes that peered around the airy space.

When he walked down the center aisle, I couldn't resist.

The mouse was now stalking the cat. I snuck up behind him and tugged on the bottom of his vest.

He spun around and then jerked back, his eyes wide, staring at me.

"Doing some shopping, Sean?" The flush of his cheeks above his beard was a welcome sight. "It's a little out of the way for you isn't it? Shouldn't you be in Kingston?"

He huffed a long sigh. "This isn't what it looks like. C'mon, let's get out of here." He grabbed my arm and almost dragged me through the revolving doors to the sidewalk outside. "I know about the Indigos. Someone bad is after them. It may have looked like I was tailing you but actually, I was checking that you weren't being followed. You're like a magnet for this kind of shit."

I could only blink at him, trying to make sense of this. It wasn't my Mom who had told him all this...

I gasped. Nana? It was all there, pouring from his mind, the dream he'd had, her insistence that he help me. "She sent you because of the Indigos. It's worse than I feared. I just knew that new Director was bad news." The fact that he'd come to Ireland despite his anger at me underscored the urgency of the situation.

When he nodded, I added, "Do Gwen and Roy know you're here? They're on their way as well." My mouth was going a mile a minute. It was better than the cold silence of the last time I'd seen him at the Abby. But maybe things were a bit better between us now. They say time heals...and he'd come here to help me. That had to count for something.

"Great." He rolled his eyes while a flash of Gwen being held hostage by David Holmes flitted through his mind. "One more person I have to worry about."

I had to bite my tongue to keep from lashing out at him. Sometimes he could be so insufferable with his superiority complex. "I didn't twist her arm, you know. She and Roy want to help me with this. My Dad hired a private investigator to get more information on this Cora Gaines, the new Director at the Abby. We found out that she worked for a security corporation, Blackwatch, before working for the Illuminata."

I started walking down the sidewalk towards the hotel and he fell into step beside me. "Have you eaten yet?"

He shook his head. "Blackwatch. I've heard the name. That does sound like a leap to go from working there to working with gifted children. I'd hate to think how an outfit like that could use someone with telekinesis or telepathy. Especially if it was a child who they could nurture and mould. Just think what they could do with a kid like Rita. Scary."

"My thoughts exactly." I stopped at the entrance to the hotel. "We're here. I'll order room service for you while I figure out our next move. Who knows, maybe Shaniqua was able to contact the main office of the Illuminata to tell them about Cora and her background."

He looked down at me as I swept through the door he held open. "It may be too late. If Cora has contacted Blackwatch..."

He didn't finish the sentence. He didn't have to. A picture of some mercenary types with the Indigos flared in his mind, a vivid snapshot that I could see as well. It wouldn't be good.

And we thought Holmes was bad.

Forty

Sean entered the hotel room ahead of me. I watched him stride from room to room, even checking the closets. He turned to me, "I didn't get the sense that there was anyone here but you can't be too careful. Your grandmother was pretty insistent that you were in danger."

"Danger? What sort of danger?" Shit, hasn't there been enough of this crap? Isn't transitioning souls hazardous enough without this shit?

He shook his head slowly. "I don't know what kind of danger, Keira. But it's got to be bad to get Pamela's soul in a knot."

I sank down onto the sofa. "You think they know that I'm onto them? Maybe Cora heard the telephone conversation I had with Shaniqua and she alerted them. Blackwatch has offices all over the world." It hit me then that he'd been right to shadow me to see if I was being watched. But also, it made me shiver thinking of the poor girls being near Cora. It was killing me not knowing what was going on.

"How about you try phoning Shaniqua again or even that investigator? I'm going to take you up on the offer of room service. I'm starving." He stepped to the desk and picked up the menu.

I took the cell phone from my pocket and hit the button to try Shaniqua, even though it was probably a waste of effort. Just like before, the message played that her number was not in service. I ended the call and thought for a moment. If the investigator had turned up something, he would have called, wouldn't he? Even so, I tried his number with no luck either.

It was time for more drastic steps. I'd have to do the astral travelling and I didn't feel like arguing with Sean about that. The girls' safety was the most important thing.

"Again, no reception and I just got voice mail from the investigator. Look, I'm going to try to get a nap in before Gwen and Roy get here. I didn't sleep well last night and it's really hitting me now." It took every ounce of concentration to shield my real intentions from him. "You have lunch and I'll see you in an hour."

He stared at me and I could feel him trying to probe deeper. He wasn't buying my song and dance about a nap, but there was nothing else he could say. "Okay. Give me your laptop. I might as well see what else I can come up with on this Blackwatch outfit while I'm sitting here."

***

It took longer than any other time to get to the state where I could leave my body. Sean sitting in the next room probably had a lot to do with that. Before I left for the Abby, I popped into the living room to see what he was up to. He was perched on the edge of the sofa, the laptop on the table in front of him while he munched on a sandwich.

The golden aura surrounding him did nothing to hide the strong set of his jaw and the intensity of his eyes staring at the screen. Just like the first time I'd seen him, I melted a little at how gorgeous he was. I never thought beards were attractive; but his scruff (which of course he grew so he could help *me* right?) looked pretty good.

In the next second I was in the Abby, hovering above the foyer before flitting to the back room where they would usually be at classes. But there was nothing. No sign of them even when I went upstairs and checked their rooms. It was then that I noticed the empty closet, the door hanging ajar in Esther's room. The silence was eerie and even impressions of their energy was missing in the air. They were gone and had been for a while.

I checked the office, even the kitchen. Everything was in order but no sign of even Lilli. When I looked in the living room the furniture was covered in white sheets. Oh my God. I was too late. But what was really puzzling was the void. I couldn't sense Esther or Rita or anyone. And why wasn't I able to be with them wherever they were with just a thought?

The next moment I was back in the hotel room, back inside my body again. It took a little while until I felt centered again, the energy building. Why hadn't I travelled to Esther or any of the girls this time? They'd left the Abby but still I should have been able to go to them? I didn't want to think what it could mean, the absence of any energy. Surely, that company needed the girls alive? They wouldn't hurt them... I raced out the bedroom door, my heart beating fast. "Sean!"

Startled, he jumped to his feet. "What's wrong, Keira?"

It registered briefly that he was actually really concerned for me, before I blurted, "They're gone! I went to the Abby and it's vacant!"

His eyes widened and he gripped my shoulders. "Oh man... did you astral travel?"

"Of course I did!" I set my chin. Just let him say *one word* against me doing that...

He didn't. He paused for a second, and then nodded. "Good idea." He ducked his head and looked at me closely. "Did you get any sense of them at all?"

An ice pick of terror shot through me. "No! Nothing! That bitch took them somewhere or...or..."

"Don't think that! But this is bad...bad for the kids. We've got to find them! The more time that goes by, the less likely that we'll be able to. I think we need to call Inspector Kreely. Maybe he can help."

"Sean..." I couldn't finish, my chin quivered and the rest of the words stuck in my throat. He *told* me time and again that I didn't know how bad bad could be! Gwen's nightmare hadn't been enough! Zara being shot to death was my wake up call, yes! But...*the girls?* I couldn't help myself even if I wanted to; I burst into tears.

He looked into my eyes and his gaze softened, before he pulled me into his arms. "It's gonna be okay. We'll find them and stop this."

I felt his hand rubbing my back softly, as I clung to him. If only he was right. I wanted desperately to believe he was. "There's a girl there...Esther. She's fourteen. She was going to leave the Abby to live with me. And poor little Mary-Jane. She's only five for God's sake!"

He pulled back and his eyes met mine. I brushed the tears from my cheeks and sniffed, waiting for his reaction. Whatever he said couldn't hurt me more than how I felt right then with Esther and the other kids in so much danger. I should have fought harder when Cora said she had to stay. At least one of them would have escaped.

"You were going to adopt this girl?"

Shit, I never thought about adoption! I'm only ten years older than her! But still...I nodded. "If that's what it takes, yes."

"You're serious." His eyes searched mine, and I opened my mind to his probe. "Shit. You *are* serious."

"Yes. Yes I am. I love her dearly Sean." I said it out loud for the first time, and it felt right. "She's the sister I never had. I'm a better person because of her."

"Oh my God. I can hardly believe it. You must really have connected with her to want to do that." There was surprise in his eyes and he blinked as if seeing me for the first time. Right then, his thoughts and feelings were an open book to me. He was still a little angry with me but it was anger borne from concern unlike the time when Gwen had been threatened. But there was also genuine affection for me and a new level of...respect? I held myself back a little. Was I reading too much into his reaction? He put his tongue into the side of his cheek for a second. "She must be something else for you to feel this way."

I had to laugh. "At first we were ready to kill each other, but it's only because she's so much like me."

"Don't tell me. A 'mini-me' version of you? I don't think I could handle two Keira's! I can hardly handle one." He grinned and it was a blast of sunshine. He didn't smile nearly enough.

Even so, I gave him a swat on his arm, "You should be so lucky to have two of us around. You'd like Esther."

He huffed a long sigh but I knew he was teasing. His hands rose to cup my cheek. "We'd better call the Inspector. We've even more reason to help them...to help this girl."

"Esther. Her name's Esther." I gave him a sharp look. "Not 'this girl'."

"Right. Let's find Esther then." And like that, it was okay.

We walked over to the sofa and took a seat close to each other. I watched him take his cell phone from his pocket and punch in Dan Kreely's number. At least it was late in the afternoon, unlike all the times I'd called him and got him out of bed.

When the Inspector answered he put the phone on speaker. For the next fifteen minutes or so, we brought the policeman up to date on our suspicions...because even though I knew in my bones that the girls were in trouble, there was no proof at this time.

"Cora Gaines. Shaniqua Chibuzo and Astrid Hagen. If they've used a credit card in their travels I might be able to track them down. Technically, it's not following procedure."

"What do you mean? They're gone!"

"Take it easy, Keira. Procedure requires a family member to file such a report in a situation like this. Those children are legal wards of that place. The people in charge—"

"That Cora bitch!"

"The people responsible for them could have just decided to go on a trip or something. My point is that there aren't any official grounds to do any inquires." He huffed out a gust of air that I almost felt over the phone. "But where you two are concerned nothing is normal. If you're suspicious, then that's all I need to know. Let me make some calls and I'll get back to you when I have something." I heard a buzz of background noise. "I'll have to conduct this quietly, but I'm at work at the moment, so the resources I need are close at hand."

"Thanks Dan! If the investigator finds something, I'll let you know." It felt better already, having him helping us.

"I'm just glad that Sean is with you this time."

"Don't forget Gwen and Roy. They'll be here in a couple hours." I looked at Sean and saw him roll his eyes. It wasn't that he didn't want to see them but it might complicate things and he'd have more to worry over.

The Inspector rang off and then I sighed, taking Sean's hand in mine. The surge of energy between us was still there, tingling through my body. If he was reading my thoughts he'd know how much this meant to me, to move past the anger and hurt between us. It might not last, that was usually the way between us, but for that moment, it was good.

He turned and nuzzled into my neck; his breath was hot in my ear. "Couple of hours, huh? And here we are... finally alone...in a swanky hotel room at that!"

Just the touch of his lips on my skin and I felt myself melting into his embrace. It would be so wonderful to just stay there forever like that, but the kernel of worry in my gut tugged me away from his embrace. "We can't." My eyes closed and my breath was ragged before I spoke, "It wouldn't be right. Not with the girls in danger and us trying to find them."

He puffed a long sigh through his mouth and sat back. "Yeah...you're right. But you can't blame a guy for trying." His eyes were longing when he gazed at me; and I won't deny seeing that felt good. He took my hand. "I was so mad at you before. I know you're headstrong and you mean well, but you have to start listening to me. I've got more experience in all of this."

"Oh really? Lots of paranormal work shuffling papers at a desk in an office, huh?"

He shrugged. "Just take my word for it, for now. I *do* have experience dealing with this good versus evil paradigm, okay?" He looked at the ceiling, shaking his head. "Feels like that battle's been going on forever, sometimes." He dropped his head and gave my hand a squeeze. "And you're pretty new at it..."

Before he could say another word I cut him off. "Please. Don't start." I sat straighter and looked into his eyes. "I know you want to protect me and Gwen and everyone you care about and I admire you for that. But I've seen some bad shit too. So I'm not entirely naive when it comes to good versus evil. I faced the demon in Holmes, saw a little girl destroy it and my grandfather. My aunt was killed because of it." I really didn't want to fight with Sean, but he had to start treating me as an equal. I'd come too far in all of this to be treated as an amateur.

"Just don't ditch me again to go off fighting these things on your own. You're strong but not invincible. You need me." He started stroking my hand. A smile flashed on his lips, "Maybe I need you too. Ever think of that?"

I pulled back and looked at him, really looked at him. This stubborn and arrogant guy was admitting to needing me? I wasn't the only one who had grown up a little in the past couple of months. "I never thought I'd hear you say that. You've always been so confident and assured." My polite way of saying arrogant. I wasn't about to shatter the moment by pointing out the truth.

He grinned, "I read minds too, Keira. I'll forgive you for thinking me arrogant. I'm not perfect, I know that."

'Pretty close to it but not quite there yet.' The last thought flashed in my mind and I shook my head smiling. Yeah, it was still Sean, all right.

My cell phone buzzed interrupting the moment. I plucked it from my pocket and smiled. My parents...who else? "Hello?"

"Keira? I just thought I'd check in with you. Everything okay?" Mom's voice blared through the phone.

Sean leaned over and his lips were close to the phone when he spoke, "Hi Mrs. Swanson! Susan, I mean."

"Sean? He's there?" It was so loud I had to hold the phone away before my eardrum was punctured.

"Yeah, Mom. He got here before Gwen and Roy. He was worried about me." I couldn't help the smile when he rolled his eyes and then rose to his feet. He mimicked taking a drink, questioning me with his eyes. I nodded and he wandered over to the bar fridge.

"Thank goodness!" Her voice was muffled as she gave Dad the piece of news. "Now we can go to dinner and not worry about you. Have you heard from the private investigator?"

"Not yet. But Mom...the kids are gone from the Abby. She took them somewhere. At least that's what I'm praying, that they're still alive."

Ignoring her 'oh no!' I continued, "We've asked Inspector Kreely to help us locate them. He might have more luck than the P.I." It was a waiting game, something I was definitely not good at. The frustration came through loud and clear.

"Just stay put, Keira. Let the police and the investigator handle this." My Mom knew me too well.

"We have to wait. There's really no choice. Other than knowing where Cora lived before coming to the Abby, we don't have anything more to go on." I took the glass of coke that Sean handed out to me.

"Do you need us to come back?"

"No. There's nothing that you can do more than what we've already done. I'll call you as soon as we hear anything." I looked into Sean's eyes when he sat next to me. At least he was here to help me with this. Mom had been right about that.

"Okay..." It was clear she wasn't convinced that she wasn't needed. "Stay in touch. And be careful."

There was nothing to do but just wait. I hung up the phone and the waiting continued.

Forty One

It was almost three hours later when there was a knock at the door. "Sean? What are you doing here?" Gwen pushed into the room, her eyes like golf balls staring at her brother. Roy was right on her tail also doing a double take seeing Sean.

"I had to come and make sure you guys didn't do something crazy, didn't I?" He gave her a quick hug and then it was my turn to greet her.

Just the sight of her and Roy brought tears to my eyes. I've been pretty damn weepy lately, that's for sure. "Gwen. I can't believe how great it is to see you." I hugged her tight before brushing the wetness from my eyes. "And Roy. I've missed you guys!"

"Another Irish adventure...who could resist that?" Gwen's smile faded, "Have you heard anything? Are the kids okay?" She slipped her light jacket off and handed it to Sean.

"What's this I hear about you adopting one of them?" Roy's face showed concern under the look of disbelief.

I took his arm, leading him into the living room. "Esther. Yes I was. But the bad news is, they're gone. I have no idea where and there's been no word from our investigator."

"Or Inspector Kreely." Sean turned from hanging Gwen's coat up and joined us.

"But how do you know they're gone? Did you go out there? Surely there was some clue." Gwen took a seat on the arm of the chair where Roy sat.

"Umm..." I hesitated. I wasn't sure if I ought to disclose how I did this. Things have been weird enough. I glanced at Sean, watching him roll his eyes. He shook his head before gesturing me to go on. I turned to Gwen, "I've learned a new skill, Gwen; astral travelling. I can leave my body and with just a thought be anywhere I choose to be, able to see people and things."

Roy snorted. "What? That's crazy!"

"Crazy or not, Roy, I'm telling the truth."

"It wasn't a dream or something? I mean, Keira, okay...I get the ghosts and stuff. But you sound like you're going over the deep end." He turned his head. "Right, Sean?"

"Oh...she's definitely in the deep end, bud." He held his hands out palms up. "But she's telling the truth."

Silence hung. "No shit?" Roy said.

"Nope."

Roy took a breath. "Oh boy." He looked over to Gwen. "Keira's found a new level of weird, babe." He gave his head a small shake and laughed weakly. "Good thing more people don't do that, the airlines would go broke and I'd be out of a job." He got up, "Anyone care for a drink? Something tells me I'm going to need one."

Gwen slipped into the seat he'd vacated. "Wait. You really did this, Keira? I've read about it. Carlos Castaneda wrote a few books where he'd tried it, but I never knew people really could do it. That's wild...and awesome!"

Sean's hand rose like a traffic cop's, "Hold on! I know you Gwen...I know that glint in your eye. You're not doing it. I don't even like Keira doing it!"

Roy came back and handed a beer to each of us. "What's so bad about it, Sean? It sounds kind of cool." It was now his turn to perch on the arm of the chair.

Sean shook his head, "Just think about it for a minute. You're floating around in another realm, a place you've never been. You don't know the entities that are out there. There're good ones but there's also nasty beings; things that would like nothing better than to destroy you. It's too dangerous."

I'd had enough of his paranoia. I'd done this a few times and never encountered anything bad. I'd only ever saw people I knew. And Shaniqua was wise about these things. Even Zara had wanted it. She wouldn't have helped me learn it if there'd been danger. "How do you know, Sean? You said yourself, that it's something you've always avoided." I sensed the wall shoot up guarding his mind. What was he hiding?

His jaw muscle twitched when he looked over at me. "Just trust me on this, will you?"

Gwen turned to me, totally ignoring her older brother, "How can you be sure you'll be able to get back to your body? That's one thing I have to agree with Sean about...the danger. You could become lost in this...this 'other realm'...forever."

I closed my eyes and huffed a sigh. "You still maintain a connection, like a lifeline that will bring you back to earth. I mean your physical body. Usually, with just a thought, I can be with whoever I think about. But not the last time. It was different somehow...which really makes me nervous about the kids."

Roy cleared his throat and glanced at Sean, "This outfit, Blackwatch, they could use the Indigos' talents, couldn't they? And this Cora is mixed up with them? I don't like this."

Sean shook his head and shrugged, "What can we do? The police and a private eye are looking for them? We'll probably hear something tomorrow. Inspector Kreely is good."

"I don't agree." Gwen was picking at the label on the bottle staring down. She took a deep breath and fixed her gaze on me, "Maybe I can help you, Keira. You know how it is with us. When we join forces...we're really strong."

Sean set the beer bottle down with a thud on the table. "But not invincible! You're not doing this, Gwen! I may not be able to control Keira but I'm your brother for God's sake. You have to listen to me on this!"

Gwen sat forward, her eyes hard chips of steel, "You can't tell me what to do, Sean. Keira is right on this. And if it will help us find those kids, I'm in."

Roy sat quietly for a few moments, shifting on the seat as the tension built. Even I kept quiet, waiting for Sean or Gwen to explode.

She set the beer on the table and rose to her feet. "Let's do this." She gazed around, and her face was puzzled. "Where? How? Let's get this over with."

I couldn't help smiling up at her. Gwen was a warrior woman, ready to take on the world...even her brother who was seriously ticked off. "Let's go in the bedroom. We have to have quiet and be restful in order to do this."

Sean leapt up from the sofa, "No! This is dangerous. We need to--"

"C'mon, Keira." Gwen led the way across the room, ignoring Sean.

I glanced back at the two guys before following her into the bedroom. Sean was furious.

Roy's forehead was lined when his eyes met mine. "You're sure it's safe for Gwen?"

Sean's anger had spooked Roy and now I had two of them worrying. "Yes." I ignored Sean's exasperated sigh and followed Gwen, closing the door behind me. As I settled on the bed beside her, my stomach sank lower. The truce with Sean hadn't lasted very long. Would we ever manage to get along enough to work together?

Forty Two

O kay. So how does this go?" Gwen lifted her head from the pillow, looking over at me.

I'd astral travelled with Shaniqua but she had been experienced in it. I had no idea if the energy surge when Gwen and I connected holding hands would give me the boost to find Esther and the kids. But we had to give it a try. I'd never forgive myself if I didn't.

I reached for her hand and held it. At first it was just a calming warmth flooding up my arm, and into my chest. So far so good. "We need to reach a state of deep restfulness, just bordering sleep. You're awake but your body is very relaxed. For me—and I'm pretty sure this is the usual thing—I feel a vibration start in my core that extends outward. Don't fight it or be frightened. Just flow with it. You'll feel kind of a pop in your head just as your spirit leaves your body."

"Kind of like deep meditation? How will I know I've left?" She settled her head on the bed and took a deep breath.

"Believe me, you'll know. You'll see your body below you. I'll wait for you if I reach that state before you. And if it doesn't work for you, we'll try again, later. Don't feel pressure with any of this." I settled myself deeper into the bed, beginning the deep even breathing exercise that was second nature to me now.

Whether it was our combined power or the fact that I'd done this before, it didn't take as long for me to reach the state where I left my body. I could see Gwen below me, her face reflecting the peacefulness of her mind. I knew she was close to the state where she'd be free of her physical body. I focused on her ethereal being, willing her to join me as I hovered high, the ceiling just inches away from me.

The release, the sizzling pop in her head went through me as well. I smiled seeing her form, the misty entity that was Gwen rise to join me. Her eyes were wide with wonder when she looked over at me, a grin blossoming on her face. My hand closed over hers and once more the energy flowing between us filled me with its warmth. Her chin rose and her mouth fell open as it claimed her too.

Esther. At the thought we were no longer in the hotel room. A cloud enveloped us, grey billowing mist that blurred my sight. Where was Esther? Once more my attempt to find her was...was blocked? Where had that thought come from? Yet, I knew it was true. Somehow, I knew she was alive but on the other side of this mist, impossible to see.

Mary-Jane, Rita, Astrid...Past images of the three people flitted through my essence, yet still the grey mist surrounded me. No sign of them at all.

Gwen's eyes were round when she gazed at me, her fingers now threaded with mine. This wasn't the way this astral travelling worked and she was aware of that as my consciousness merged with hers.

Was it only the people at the Abby who I was prevented from seeing? Sean's name coursed through me and instantly I was above him, watching him stare out the window in the hotel room overlooking the city. He turned and his flinty eyes met mine. I jerked back at the anger in his aura. My hand slipped from Gwen's and I fell, spiralling down to my physical body. The last impression was the silken thread connecting Gwen's spirit to her body.

I gasped and felt the heaviness sink into my being--my spiritual self now submerged in ponderous flesh. After a few breaths, my eyes opened and I turned to see Gwen. She was deathly still, her breath shallow and faint.

My gaze shifted slightly to take in her aura. The bluish haze that was uniquely Gwen was gone, leaving only a shimmering silvery glow. Oh my God. She wasn't back yet. When my hand had slipped from hers, she'd been somehow left behind!

With a gentle squeeze of her hand, I tried to summon her. *Gwen*! My mind screamed her name. The silken thread would lead her back! It had to. My heart pounded fast in my chest as I watched her still form. This had never happened to me before! What was I to do? There was no way I'd be able to get to the physical state where I'd be able to travel again...not for a while anyway.

But this was her first time doing this. Maybe, just maybe, she was prolonging the experience on purpose. That had to be it. I'd just have to give her some more time. But when she came back, I was going to give her hell for worrying me.

I sat up, holding her hand and watching her. Gwen! Enough with the exploring. Time to come home! My own breaths were short and fast while my heart pounded hard.

I couldn't sense her at all.

Something was wrong.

Forty Three

I prayed, begged, promised to never do this again if only she would return. Tears ran down my cheeks as I watched her comatose body. It had been an hour that I'd been sitting with her, but still there was nothing. She was gone. Well, the essence of Gwen was gone. Her body was still as a statue, just barely breathing.

When a hand landed softly on my shoulder, I almost jumped out of my skin! I turned to see the horror in Sean's eyes watching his sister.

"Gwen?" He started to lean over, his hand about to shake her but I stopped him.

It didn't seem right to jar her so suddenly. "No. Leave her be." I didn't say it and I had to guard my thoughts from him. What if somehow the connection of her spirit could be broken? Would she die? I couldn't take that chance.

"Why isn't she awake? Was she able to do...this astral travelling?" Sean's voice was just above a whisper.

Roy walked to the other side of the bed, gazing down at her a moment before turning to me. "Is this normal? You're awake. Why isn't Gwen?"

"She's still out there." The words sliced through my guts. I gazed at Gwen feeling the heat of Sean and Roy's anger with me.

"I don't like this." Roy's fingers brushed Gwen's cheek. "C'mon Gwen. Wake up." He looked over at Sean and I, "She's a light sleeper normally. Why isn't she waking?"

Sean turned to me, "I *knew* you shouldn't have done this! Did something go wrong? Did you see anything when you were in that state? Anything unusual?" His forehead was a map of worry lines.

"We were together. But there was a cloud around us. I couldn't see any of the girls. Yet, when I thought of you, I was in the suite immediately. You were watching the cityscape and then you turned and..."

"I knew it! I knew you were there. I felt your presence and I turned to see you and then you were gone. There was nothing I picked up of Gwen's presence though." He sighed and looked up at the ceiling. "I should never have let you do this."

"Let us do this? What? You think you can order us around? You're my self-appointed boss or something?" The words were out before I even knew it. Why did he always have to act so superior?

"Grow up! You never listen to anyone, even when they might...just might, know what the hell they're talking about!" His eyes were narrowed and his words a hiss.

"Will you two give it a rest! Gwen's not waking up and all you can do is argue! Can you do something Keira to get her to wake? I thought you knew how to do this." Roy's voice was razor sharp.

"She doesn't know half of what she thinks she does." Sean grumbled as he looked down at Gwen, "She's barely even breathing."

Roy glanced over at him, "Maybe we should get her to a doctor or the hospital. They can give her a shot of adrenaline or something to get her to wake up."

"No! That's the last thing she needs. She has to come back naturally. I don't know how I know this but I do. Moving or jolting her awake will be too much of a shock to her body." My thumb rubbed the back of her hand while I said a silent prayer for her to wake. C'mon Gwen!

A glance at the clock showed that she'd been out well over an hour after I'd come back to myself. I had to do something to help her. I hated to think that Sean might be right about dangerous entities out there but this wasn't looking good at all.

"I'm going to try this again. I need you two to leave so I can get to this state. I'll find her and bring her back." I wasn't entirely sure this would work but what option did I have? I was responsible for her doing this in the first place.

Sean's mouth fell open gawking at me. "Are you totally nuts? You actually think you can find her and then bring her back? What if the same thing she's going through happens to you? No more of this astral traveling. If she doesn't come to in another hour, we get her to the hospital."

Roy looked over at us and he sighed. "Look if we're going to wait an hour, why not let Keira try this? She's done it before and she was able to get back. I don't know how she'll find her...but I say it's worth a shot."

"This is ridiculous!"

"No! It's not." I turned to Sean, "The last thing I saw before I returned to my body was the silken thread holding Gwen's spirit to her body. I'll follow that thread. I'll find her!"

He shook his head and then spun on his heels, storming out of the room. I looked over at Roy, noticing the tears welling in his eyes.

"I don't understand any of this, Keira, but Gwen trusted you and I know you'll try your best. Bring her back to me." He slumped out of the room and closed the door softly.

I settled in next to Gwen and took her hand once more. Only an hour to do this and my heart was still thundering hard in my chest. Nana, if you're out there, I could sure use some help with this. How was I ever going to relax enough to reach the state needed? And the clock was ticking—a fact that didn't help either.

Forty Four

I laid there quietly doing the measured breathing for what felt like an eternity. My heart had resumed its normal rhythm but horrible thoughts and worry buzzed in my mind. Oh God. I had to let the fear go if I was ever going to be able to do this. One eye creaked open and I saw the clock sitting on the bedside table. Forty six minutes had passed and I was still nowhere near the state I needed to be in.

I closed my eyes and focused on my breaths.

At the twitch of Gwen's hand in mine, I looked over at her. Oh my God! The blue aura was once more cloaking her body! She was back! I sat up and gazed at her, noticing her eyelids flicker and her breathing become deeper.

Her eyes popped open! I had to fight the tears that welled in my eyes. Gwen! She was back!

"Keira! That was fantastic!" She tried to sit up but I settled my hand on her shoulder, keeping her still.

"You need to be quiet for a few minutes. Get your blood circulating again until you're really yourself again." I sighed and shook my head before brushing the tear that rolled from the corner of my eye. "You scared the hell out of me, Gwen!"

She smiled and took a deep breath. "That's a first. Me scaring you!" She smirked and looked away. "Feels pretty good though."

"Jerk!" I tapped her arm. "What did you see? Can you remember?"

The door burst open and Roy rushed over, Sean immediately on his heels.

"Gwen!" He sat on the edge of the bed and his hand cupped her cheek. "We thought we'd lost you. We were going to take you to the hospital."

Sean pushed in beside me, relief warring with anger in his face. "Never again, Gwen! That was dangerous. You barely made it back here." He stared at me, "No more of this, do you hear?"

There was a whole lot more blasting in his mind that his tongue censored, but it came through loud and clear to me. There was a fleeting glimpse of an evil entity, gnashing sharp teeth and many arms clutching Gwen. He really believed what we'd done was dangerous. It hadn't been some kind of macho power play, but rather deep dread.

Gwen sat up. She brought Roy's hand to her lips and kissed it, the love flowing from her eyes to his. But that quickly transformed into an angry determined look when she turned to Sean. "I don't know why I didn't return with Keira. But what I found out while I was in that ethereal state has convinced me of something."

She turned to look at me, "You're the one, Keira! You've got power and goodness inside that even you don't know you have. You're needed here. The world needs you. The Veil and right now, the Indigo kids especially need you!"

The one? What the hell is that supposed to mean? "What happened, Gwen? I don't understand." Rather than visiting the kids in astral travel something more profound had happened to her.

Her eyebrows drew tight together and she looked puzzled. "It's fading so fast!" The rest of her words came out in a rush. "It was your grandmother. Well not her exactly...but a presence that I knew was her. She gave me a glimpse of The Veil, and the dark forces threatening it. I saw you, but you were expanded, your energy field so much larger than I would ever have thought possible. You stood between The Veil and those dark forces. You were beating them back!"

As I listened my jaw fell open. There was no doubt she'd seen this. Every fibre of her being was tingling with excitement and...awe? It was a far cry from how I felt right then. I'd come damned close to losing her, and then to find out she'd had this vision alongside my grandmother? My head was swimming. And for sure, I didn't deserve to be on any pedestal. 'The one?' Yeah, as if.

Sean leaned in, "Gwen. I don't know what you think you saw..."

She turned on him, "No! I saw it!" She held her hand up pointing at me while her eyes took in the two men. "Keira is the main protector now. There are others, of course, but she's the focal point, the tip of the spear." She lowered her hand and turned to Roy, "You believe me, right?"

He looked down at the comforter and cleared his throat, "I don't know what to believe, Gwen. I know that I almost lost you. And that Keira was the one who put you in that position."

"Argh!" Gwen shook her head and then reached for my hand. "The important thing is I know now! And if I hadn't done that astral traveling thing, I might never have known. You'll always have me at your side Keira! I'm going to be a part of this, supporting you however I can."

I felt the energy in her body jolt through my hand and up my arm. For just a few seconds I saw what she had experienced, felt the love of my grandmother and...respect too. Nana had been powerful but if Gwen was right, I was even more so. My face grew warm. To be held in such high regard was foreign, like wearing some kind of crown that was too big for my head.

I dropped my head and stared at the comforter. I had always wanted to 'be somebody', you know? Like the Kardashians, maybe. Or a movie star. I wanted to *be important* or something like that. But all my life I screwed up time and time again. I couldn't even hold down a job at a dry cleaners, and now I'm 'the one' or something? No, no, no no...that's silly.

I raised my eyes to Gwen's. She held my gaze with an intensity of certitude that was almost scary. "Yeah, Keira, you are," she said aloud. "You're the guy, kiddo."

"But...but..." She put her fingers on my lips shushing me. It was all well and good running around haunted houses and helping spirits. But the immensity of what she was saying really hit me just then.

Nana had told me during our short time together that The Veil was super important for keeping the world on an even keel or something. Sure, I kind of believed her. But Gwen's bearing witness right now...about *me* and my role... It was too much to take. I took her hand from my lips and shivered. "I'm not ready for this," I said.

"Nobody is," she replied. "But it's the truth and you know it."

I gripped her fingers tightly and felt that buzz between us. I took a deep breath. "We'll figure out what the hell you mean later. What about the children? Did you see anything when you were in that realm to tell us where they are? Are they even alive?"

A loud buzzing of a cell phone broke the silence. Sean yanked his out of his pocket. "It's Dan Kreely." He held it to his ear. "Hello?"

There was silence and his eyes grew wider, listening to the Inspector. "Ennis?" He held the phone away from his mouth for a moment turning to me, "Astrid used her credit card at a restaurant and gas station in Ennis. He talked to the owner of the gas bar. They were headed west. The only place they could have been going was some place called Loop Head."

Sean tapped his screen to put the phone on speaker. "When? When were they there?" My heart was beating fast. There was hope yet.

Kreely replied right away. "Yesterday. It's a peninsula on the west coast about three hours out of Dublin. I've contacted the police in the area to be on the lookout for a dark blue van with seven children in it. Most of the area is a forest reserve."

"Three hours drive?" Sean looked over at Roy who nodded and pulled his own phone from his pocket. "We could be there tonight."

"I'm on my way as well. I'll contact you when I'm there and we can meet up." With that the Inspector disconnected the call.

"We're going there? Now?" Gwen rose from the bed and glanced over at Roy who was peering at his phone, scrolling through sites with the brush of his finger.

Sean slipped his phone back into his pocket and rose to his feet. "Much as I hate Keira doing this astral travelling, I have to admit it's confirmed what we feared. Something is very wrong. She wasn't able to see any of the girls. And this Cora Baines being with that Blackwatch outfit is bad news on all fronts."

"Finally, you believe me." I rose from the bed and gave him a weak smile. But my gut was a tight knot thinking of the girls. At least we knew the location, but what if we were too late? Was this a Blackwatch facility? Were the girls already in their clutches, about to be spirited away to be used by that horrid company?

The next three hours would be hard to get through.

Roy had turned talking on his phone all the while. He smiled and slipped the phone in his pocket. "The rental car will be here in ten minutes."

My head jerked back and I stared at him. "Wow. That was fast."

He grinned, "It helped that I offered to pay double the fee. The company credit card of course."

I couldn't help smiling back. I would have paid a thousand times the amount.

Forty Five

It was close to midnight when we pulled into the gas station where we were supposed to meet the Inspector. There was a dark car parked to the side. The dome light that flashed when the door opened revealed the tall figure of Dan Kreely.

He nodded before walking over to where we were parked, stopping next to the driver's side, where Sean was seated. He leaned into the open window and his eyebrows rose high, "I see the gang's all here."

I slid over closer to Sean and peered at Dan. "Have you found them?"

He shook his head. "The local police have been patrolling the area but there's no sign of the van. It's weird. It's as if they've vanished. But the attendant here, working yesterday swore he saw the vehicle going out towards the lighthouse point."

Roy eased forward, "Could a boat have picked them up? They couldn't just disappear."

Once more, Dan shook his head, "But that wouldn't

explain the van disappearing as well. And if you've ever seen the point, it's nothing but sheer high cliffs along there. There's no way a boat could dock or anyone be able to get down to it if it were."

Sean turned to look at me. He was thinking the same thing that I was. *The Indigo kids are nearby'* echoed in my mind. I gasped. I grabbed his hand and closed my mind, reaching out.

Yes! I *felt* them! I couldn't sense any of the girls individually, but I could feel their presence; like hearing a familiar voice in a crowd, I felt them. I couldn't pin it down any better, though. There was something blocking any clearer impression; it was the same energy that prevented me from finding them in my astral travel. But they were nearby!

I looked over at the Inspector. "I need to go out there. It's not that I don't trust that the police did everything they could to find them, but these kids and the people watching them are special. Maybe the company has property there that's off the beaten path."

The Inspector sighed. "Alright. But I'm going as well. There's nothing there but the lighthouse and the forest. I've been out on that point and I'm somewhat familiar with the lay of the land. Plus, I've got a local man with me. We've already checked the area but since there are children involved here, we'll do it again...with you." He raised his hand and pointed down the road. "You see that light in the distance? That's the lighthouse. The clerk here saw their van turn into the parking area. That's where we're heading. Just follow us." With that he turned and strode back to his vehicle. It was only then that I noticed the other dark shape in the car with him, the local constable.

As we made the short drive up the road, stomach roiled and it became harder and harder to breathe. I rolled the window down, letting in the damp cool air of the coast.

Sean looked over at me, "Are you all right?"

"I don't know. There's something about this place. It's like when I astral travelled and tried to see the girls and I was surrounded by clouds. It's the same feeling, but worse." I took a deep breath. "The air is heavy and suffocating." I looked around to each of them. "Don't you guys feel it?" They all shook their heads; nope, just little ol' me.

"We'll find them, Keira. I know we're close. I just know it."

The policeman pulled off into the lighthouse's parking area, his car facing the tower that was about five stories tall. A beam of light shot from out from its peak to the ocean. On either side of the parking lot were dense woods that stretched away.

As soon as we pulled in, the nausea I'd been feeling earlier, claimed my gut. I reached for Sean's arm, "Stop the car!" I barely got the door open, stumbling out to the pavement when my stomach heaved. I gasped, my eyes tearing up as another deep retch took hold of my body.

I hunched over, dry heaving now. If I hadn't felt like death warmed over, it might have been embarrassing to be seen hurling my stomach up, my arm extended grasping at nothing.

It was getting harder and harder to catch my breath, but I still was retching as they surrounded me. I was still bent at the waist when Sean put his hand on my back, rubbing it gently.

Sean's touch was helping. I could feel my stomach calm down and I was able to catch my breath. I took two deep breaths and straightened up.

Sean kept his hand where it was. He leaned in closer to me, "This is not normal, Keira. There's a barrier here. Someone or something has cast a protective shield to keep people away. I can see it. It's like a grey shroud that begins at the edge of the parking lot." He pointed to the left. "It goes out into those woods. That's what is making you sick."

I stared at him, and then looked off to the side where he said the barrier was. I unfocused my eyes like I would do to see a person's aura and there it was, plain as day. It was a dense grey wall. Just looking at it made my gut roll once more.

"I don't see anything." Gwen stepped closer to the edge of the parking lot.

The Inspector and the other policeman got out of the car, "What's going on?" Dan walked closer to Sean. "What's wrong with Keira?"

Sean blew out a fast sigh before answering, "I know how this is gonna sound but it's Cora Gaines. She's put some kind of protection barrier up to shield their location. The fact that Keira is sick...It's affecting her on a physical level."

The other policeman, a young red haired guy in his late twenties, snorted. "A protection barrier? I don't see anything."

Sean pointed at the dense forest. "Right there." He turned to the two cops. "Did you check out that forest?"

Dan shook his head. "No, not at all. That's the Bain Taragh. It's been a wild unclaimed forest for as long as anyone can remember." He glanced to where Sean was pointing and looked away. "Nobody ever goes in there."

"Why not?" I said. "It sounds like a perfect hiding spot." I started across the parking lot. "And it's shielded. We need to check it out. Come on Sean."

Kreely and his sidekick held up their hands. "Nooo..." they said in unison. "There's naught to be seen there."

Sean shouldered past the younger cop. "I'll be the judge of that. C'mon guys."

Roy and Gwen didn't move. "Nooo..." said Gwen. "There's nothing there, Keira..." Roy's face was just blank as he stood next to her.

"Sean!" I called out and he spun around. "Whatever it is, it's gotten to them!"

He stood still assessing the others. They were all stock still. He nodded. "Yeah, I figured as much." He looked at me. "But you're not weirding out like them."

"I just puked up my guts!"

"Yeah...but...you're not..." he gestured at the others, "all zombie like. C'mon."

"I'm not leaving Gwen and Roy!"

"Don't worry." He dropped his head and let out a sigh. "They'll be fine in just a moment," he said quietly. I watched as his face grew angry. "Damn it! Awww maaaan!"

"What's the matter?" I went to him and put my hand on his chest. As soon as I touched him a sensation blossomed in me. A light diaphanous sensation, like I was being lifted up amongst clouds, a blue sky and a golden sunset in the distance overwhelmed me. I didn't *see* it...I felt it though. It was the most beautiful thing I ever experienced.

"Oh my..." I said.

Sean snorted. "You ain't seen nothing yet, Keira." He lifted his face to me and I gasped. He was more beautiful than ever. He was totally hot, but there was something else. Something *more*. He flashed a smile and it was gone. He turned back towards the forest. "Let's shut this stupid barrier down, what do you say?"

I stumbled after him, the oppressiveness of the barrier slowing me. I took a deep breath with every step.

Sean, on the other hand marched right up to the edge of that grey presence. He stood before it and put his hands on his waist as he looked it up and down and side to side. "Nice job, Cora," he said out loud in a sardonic voice.

I came up next to him, my hand on my chest. "I don't know how much further I can go, Sean," I gasped.

"No sweat. It's just a draping. Once you tear it open, it all falls apart."

"A draping? Like a veil?"

"No, this isn't The Veil. This is a barrier. The Veil's an opening." He held up his hand, his index finger extended. "And if you cut it, it falls apart." He winked at me. "Get a load of this!"

His hand rose high and then fell sharply.

I gasped watching him. Sparks of light followed his fingers! His dark silhouette was highlighted by sizzling light that followed his hand, like a power saw cutting through nails in wood. Before I could even grasp what was happening, a breath of fresh air blew against my cheeks, filling my lungs with the salty scent of the ocean and the tangy smell of pine and cedar. Immediately my stomach settled, and I stood taller. Whatever he'd done had made it easier to breathe and made me feel lighter.

But how? How had he done it? He was gifted like me but instead of feeling sick, he'd been able to break through whatever barrier had been erected. When he turned to face me, there was a glow in his eyes above a jaw set tight and determined.

"Come on!" He beckoned to all of us before disappearing into the forest bordering the lot. I looked over my shoulder to see Gwen and the others trotting up to us as if nothing had happened.

Gwen stepped over to me and took my hand, while Roy sprinted after Sean. She held her cell phone before us, lighting the way, revealing an old footpath that lead through the trees. I was still reeling from what I'd just seen and followed her silently. Behind us I could hear the Inspector and the other policeman scrambling to keep up.

Sean had seen that wall. He'd known what it was and then sliced through it like a hot knife slicing butter. I hadn't seen it until he pointed it out. Neither Gwen nor Roy had seen it either. But more importantly, he'd broken it! How was that possible? I'd known he was gifted but this was on another plane altogether.

"Gwen? I can't believe that Sean did that. Did I imagine it?" I tugged at her hand, stopping her for a moment.

"No... it was all hazy to me until he did that thing with his finger... I don't know how he did it but he did! I think he's got some explaining to do." She grinned and pulled me along again. "Hurry! He seems to know what he's doing and we've got to get to those kids."

Her words yanked my thoughts back to the problem at hand. We'd broken through a barrier put up to keep us out. That could only mean a more serious threat to Esther and the rest of the kids. I hurried to keep up, trying to avoid roots and pine cones littering the path.

The sudden staccato of a machine gun broke the stillness of the night. It had come from up ahead where Sean was!

"Stay where you are! We've got this." Inspector Kreely shoved past me. The other policeman raced by, his hand holding a weapon.

Oh my God! Sean might have been hit...or Roy. Gwen and I flew down the path behind them.

Forty Six

I stumbled once, almost pitching forward face first. If not for Gwen's firm grip on my hand I would have. Another gunshot cracked through the air and I screamed in terror.

"Stay back!" Sean called from a few feet ahead of us. I could barely make out his body in the deep darkness surrounding him. He was hunkered behind a large tree trunk, waving at us to stay away.

Another head popped into sight and then Roy's voice hissed, "For God's sake take cover, Gwen." She ducked behind a tree and I ran to Sean. "Keira stop!"

I sprinted forward and stood next to Sean, the both of us sheltered by the tree. I risked a quick peek. The tree line stopped and for about two hundred feet it was a grassy meadow, bathed in floodlights set on its edges. At the end of the meadow was a low concrete structure, just a doorway. I peered at it. "What the hell is that place?"

"It's a bunker," Sean said.

"Hold your fire! We're police officers!" Dan Kreely's

voice came from behind us. He darted to a tree on the other side of the path, holding his gun in the air beside him.

"Go away! You're trespassing on private property!"

I gasped hearing Cora's voice. She had the girls and she was armed as well! Oh my God! The girls must be scared to death! What would she do to them next? I had to save them somehow.

Inspector Kreely yelled once more. "Put down your weapons! We just want to talk to you."

It was the distraction I needed. I darted out from behind the tree. I was fully exposed, but by god I was getting those girls! She wasn't taking them without a fight, even if it killed me!

"No! Keira!" Sean's voice was a wail.

I could see Cora's silhouette in the doorway. She had the rifle raised, but then she lowered as she peered forward. Another fair haired woman appeared behind her, gaping over the older woman's shoulder. It could only be Astrid. Still I ran towards them.

"Oh my God! It is you! How did you get through?" Cora lowered the gun to her thighs and stepped back into the doorway. "Are they with you? Did you lead them here?" Now that I was closer, I could see the horror in her eyes.

I slowed down and took tentative steps closer. "Lead who here? The police? Yes! You're going to be arrested, you creep! Let the girls go!"

Cora stepped forward. She grabbed me by my blouse and started to shake me. "What the hell are you talking about? I'm protecting the girls! Your coming here has put them in danger, you fool!" She was so angry a spray of spittle landed on my cheek.

Sean appeared at my side. "Settle down, Cora, all is well."

Cora gaped at him, her eyes wide open. Her mouth moved for a moment, but nothing came out. She let go of me and found her voice. "Oh no! What are you doing here? How are you mixed up with the likes of her?" Cora seemed to wilt under Sean's gaze.

Before he had a chance to speak Astrid raced out of the door and gripped my arms, her face lined with worry, peering at me. "Keira. This is important. Were you followed? I mean aside from the two policemen."

It was then that Dan and the other officer along with Roy and Gwen stepped up to join us. Dan was the first to speak, "We know about your association with Blackwatch. We need to see the children, to know that they're safe. Now!"

"What? *Blackwatch*? Me?" Cora shook her head and slumped forward. "You bloody fools have got this all wrong. I was protecting them *from* that outfit! I know what they meant to do with them...*especially* Rita! This is a safe house, to be used as a last resort. The Illuminata ordered us here, until we can get the girls out of the country."

I probed her with my gift—she was telling the absolute truth. But my heart stopped when I saw the other thing, and pulled out from her mind.

She looked up at Sean and what I saw in her eyes drove a knife through my heart. It was clear that they knew each other. It was also clear that she was deeply and fully and completely in love with him. I glanced at Sean and saw anger mixed with concern in his eyes as he watched her. His thoughts were unguarded for a moment.

It was apparent that he still cared deeply for her as well.

Forty Seven

T he girls! I need to see them." Dan's voice was a low growl as he stepped forward through the doorway.

His words jarred through the mist that clouded my mind, the mystery of Cora and Sean. I followed him inside a small anteroom with a tiny window and a metal door shut tight stood at the other end. It opened onto a flight of steel stairs going down. I could hear their voices, Esther and Rita trying to calm the younger ones. I flew down the steps.

They were in some kind of living room, perched on the sofa and loveseat staring with wide eyes before Esther saw me come into view.

"Keira!" She bounded from the sofa and her arms were around me, clinging to my body while she cried. "I was so scared! But you're here! We're safe now, aren't we?"

My heart broke seeing fear in the girls' eyes and Esther's sobs. I held her tight, running my hand over her back. "It's okay. You're going to be fine." Rita and Mary-Jane rushed to my side, and joined in what was fast becoming a group hug. It felt so good to be with them, to see that they were safe.

"Satisfied?" Cora stepped into the room. "They're safe here...or at least they were until you showed up."

"Is this all of them?"

I ignored the Inspector's question and turned on her. "They were perfectly fine at the Abby until you appeared! We know about your work with Blackwatch, the assessments you were doing on the girls and reporting back to that company! They can't have them! Not now or ever!"

Cora's head fell back and she let out a loud exaggerated sigh. Astrid came forward and glanced over at her before turning to me. "She's not with them. She was spying on the company. Cora has been with the Illuminata since she was a teenager."

"Don't waste your breath, Astrid. She's an outsider. She'll never understand." Cora stepped out of the room, brushing by Sean and Gwen.

I watched Sean turn and follow her outside. What kind of history did the two of them share? Before I had time to go down that train of thought, Astrid derailed me when she spoke.

"She was a double agent, Keira. When your grandfather and his goon broke into the Abby, the motherhouse of the Illuminati became alarmed. How was he able to find it? More importantly, his goon is still alive and in prison. God only knows who he told about the Indigos. He saw what they're capable of. They sent Cora to clean house and get the girls to safety."

It was only then that I realized that I hadn't seen any sign of Shaniqua. "What happened to Shaniqua? She tried calling me but--"

"She's here. Actually she's outside doing a patrol of the perimeter. Neither of us were aware of Cora's mission until the very last moment. That's how guarded her identity is with the Order." Astrid bent and swept Mary-Jane up into her arms.

Dan cleared his throat, "Can all this be corroborated? I'd like to speak to someone higher up with your organization. I want to make sure that the children are safe and in good hands."

"Of course. Give me a minute and I'll place the call. The mother house will contact your superiors to verify Cora Gaines' role and why the children are here." Astrid set Mary-Jane down and walked from the room to another door leading deeper into the bunker.

Gwen stepped forward and ruffled Mary-Jane's hair with her fingers, smiling down at the child. She looked over at Esther who still held my hand while her other hand wiped the tears from her cheeks. "So this is Esther?"

I smiled, tapping each girl's head, "And Rita and Sophia and Kirsten and Irina and Noor and of course Mary-Jane. Girls, this is my best friend, Gwen and her boyfriend Roy."

"Wow! You're so tall!" Sophia grinned up at Gwen.

Esther tugged my hand, "Can I go with you now?" The look in her eyes tore my heart anew.

I pulled her in close to me and kissed the top of her head softly. "I'm going to do everything I can to make that happen. But this time, I'm going through the proper channels--the head office of the order."

"Keira!" At Shaniqua's voice, her dark eyes flashing above a broad smile as she stepped into the room, I grinned.

The fact that she was carrying a gun, dressed in green camouflage clothes was so out of character that I had to stifle the laugh. When the portly cook, Lilli appeared behind her, wearing the same outfit, I couldn't help the chuckle that burst from my mouth. It was so good to see both of them.

"You two are a sight for sore eyes, even if you look like Rambo!" I stepped away to give both of them a big hug.

When Astrid stepped back into the room it was like old home week. She nodded to Dan Kreely, "You'll be getting word any minute now. When that happens, we really must ask you to leave. It's been quite a night and the girls need to go to bed. We'll be leaving early in the morning when the order sends word."

"Oh no!" It was a chorus of wails as the girls crowded

around me. "Just a few more minutes! We want to see Keira."

When Dan's phone buzzed he scooped it from his overcoat and stepped out of the room. It had to be the call Astrid had spoke about.

Gwen and Roy took that opportunity to step outside as well, leaving me with the tearful goodbyes. I turned to Astrid, "I need to speak with your head office. I'd still like to go through with adopting Esther."

She smiled and gripped my shoulder, "I kind of guessed that would be the case. They will be calling you to set up a meeting tomorrow. There are certain terms and conditions that must be met...now with the enhanced threat from Blackwatch."

"I understand." When Esther squeezed my hand I looked down at her and smiled. No matter what, I'd make this happen. "It won't be long Esther. I'll find you and when I do we're going to celebrate. Just hold tight for a little while longer."

I gave each of them a hug and then took my leave. When I stepped outside, Cora and Sean were off to the side, the light from the small window giving faint illumination on them. For the first time in my life I felt a burning tightness in my chest staring at Sean standing so close, speaking with Cora. It was then that I realized how much I cared for Sean, even though he could get under my skin like no one had ever done before.

Cora turned and brushed by me before going inside and shutting the door. It was a cold goodbye...more like good riddance. Sean stepped forward his thoughts guarded and face set in a tight grimace.

I had to find out more about them. Sean had a lot of explaining to do. First breaking through that protective shield and then this thing with Cora.

But how the hell could they have something going on? Cora was almost my mother's age! Ewww!

Forty Eight

We were no sooner back to our car in the parking lot than a wave of nausea once more claimed me. I glanced back from where we'd come and saw the faint grey shimmer of the protective shield. She sure hadn't wasted any time getting that in place again.

But rationally, who could blame her? If not for Sean we never would have found the shield let alone break through it. When we settled into the car once more, I turned to him. He was still being very quiet and was once again, guarding his thoughts from me.

"So you and Cora know each other?" I tried to keep my tone light even though that green eyed monster in my head was squirming.

He nodded and then put the car in gear following the policemen. "It was a long time ago."

Gwen sat forward, her hand on the back of the seat next

to my shoulder, "I don't remember her Sean. Where'd you meet her? Toronto?"

He sighed, "I don't know. Maybe. It was a long time ago."

Roy spoke, coming to Sean's rescue from our interrogation. "I'm glad the children are okay. I can't believe they have this power that they can shield themselves in broad daylight. The police said they searched the area all day."

That led to my next question, "How did you break through that shield? Sparks flew from your hand."

He leaned over and tapped my thigh lightly. "I'm not just another pretty face you know. Maybe now you'll listen to me when I advise on a course of action."

He was trying to make light of it. Maybe he didn't want to say anything more in front of Roy and Gwen. But for sure, I was going to get to the bottom of it.

For now, I was happy to know that the girls were safe and that it would be just a matter of time before I could adopt Esther. Seeing her tonight had reinforced my decision to have her live with me.

But that would be another day. For now, I was happy that it had worked out and they were safe.

The End

Author's Note:

Not too long ago I was in a coffee shop. Sitting there eating my honey cruller and sipping my double double, a small girl caught my eye. She was about five or six, and was at the table beside me accompanied by her grandparents. When our eyes met, she got from her seat and approached me. She stood before me and we gazed at one another in silence.

In her eyes I saw what I can only describe as the wisdom of the ages. Her gaze was intent and somewhat curious. I wasn't being looked at; I was being *experienced* by this child. And it felt a little strange, but at the same time a sense of peace flowed over me.

That encounter was the seed of the Indigo Children in this book...

The Final Episode is now available

Keira's struggles against David Holmes only appear to be ended, and The Illuminata will stop at nothing protecting the children. As she prepares for a struggle to bring Esther into her life, Keira learns that there are even greater threats looming. Threats that dwarf her own growing powers...

It's available on Amazon right now.

Shelley Dorey

ABOUT THE AUTHOR

Michelle Dorey, writing as 'Shelley Dorey' is the author of more than twenty spine-chilling novels featuring ghosts, haunted houses and the supernatural. She has been on the Amazon best seller list many times throughout her career.

A voracious reader of the masters like Stephen King and Dean Koontz, she decided to try her hand at writing after going on a Ghost Walk in the enigmatic city of Kingston, Ontario, Canada where she lives. Her first book, Crawley House was inspired by a true tale of a family's nightmare, living in a home owned by Queen's University.

"Expect the supernatural when the bedrock of a city is limestone. Throw in the fact it is bordered on three sides by the mighty St. Lawrence River, The Rideau River and Lake Ontario and you are in for some thrills and chills of the paranormal variety--which of course is my cup of tea."

Does she love Kingston? You bet! Her husband Jim, a transplanted native New Yorker born and raised in the Bronx, agrees. Michelle and Jim like nothing better than spoiling their two pugs with treats and long walks in their neighborhood. Funny, but the slightly neurotic dogs always refuse to go for a stroll in the cemetery nearby.

OTHER WORKS

All of Michelle Dorey and Shelley Dorey books are exclusively available on Amazon

Women's Paranormal Fantasy By Shelley Dorey

The Mystical Veil Series
Hex After 40 Series
Celtic Knot Series

Ghosts And Hauntings By Michelle Dorey

The Hauntings Of Kingston Series
The Haunted Ones Series
The Haunted Cabin